CROSSCURRENTS

THE RISE OF THE PENGUINS SAGA

STEVEN HAMMOND

ROCKHOPPER BOOKS

This is a work of fiction. Any references to historical events or real locales are used fictitiously. Any other resemblances to actual events, locales, or persons, living or dead, are purely coincidental.

RISE OF THE PENGUINS

First Edition

Edited by Murphy Rae with Indie Solutions
www.murphyrae.net
Cover art by Gabriel Barbabianca
Formatting by Tanya Adams

Exclusive content at:
riseofthepenguins.net

Dedicated to

Nixie Pearl Hammond

ACKNOWLEDGMENTS

Thank you to Joshua Muster, Cathy Speiser, Tanya Adams for all of your support and help. I couldn't do this without you.

THE RISE OF THE PENGUINS SAGA

DRAMATIS PENGUINIS

Supreme Commander Liutites-Royal Emperor

General Diutes-Royal Emperor

Antaean-Royal Emperor, Overlord of the Southern Realm

Mearna-Royal Emperor

Ceocilus-Royal Emperor

Lieutenant-General Lavour-Chinstrap

Captain Mevoule-Chinstrap

Corporal Meuseaux-Chinstrap

Captain Nok-Rockhopper

General Treeg-Rockhopper

Keerka-Rockhopper

General Leepoh-Gentoo

Colonel Kimmer-King

Commander Kiley-King

T'Cuh-Ka-Magellanic

Cuh-trük-Magellanic

K'K' Ru-ki-Emperor

Kra K'K' ki-ro-Emperor

Pìn-Blue Penguin

DRAMATIS PERSONAE

Gina Rosedale-Climatologist
Randy Lee-Photographer
Vance Lyons-President/CEO of GT
Colonel Maycotte-US Military
Captain Logan-US Military
Sergeant Turnbull-US Military
Corporal Guerra-US Military
Private Jenkins-US Military
PFC Reyes-US Military
Specialist McPearsons-US Military

CROSSCURRENTS

CHAPTER 1

THE ANTARCTIC COAST, near Pack Ice Command: An elite Royal Emperor warrior approached Supreme Commander Liutites as he stood alongside General Diutes. The pair of commanders were watching a new breed of Royal Emperor arrive. The new breed was every bit as large as the Overlord was, but they lacked the grasping flippers of most Royals. They were streamlined and obviously built for speed in the water. Their coloring was distinguished by the lack thereof; they were matte black and had the appearance of a shadow more than that of a living creature. These penguins were bred for stealth.

"Supreme Commander, a report from The Falklands, sir," the newly arrived elite Royal Emperor said as he approached.

Liutites simply nodded an acknowledgment and waited for the messenger to give him the report.

"The islands were conquered within hours and there were no known human survivors."

"Excellent," Diutes interrupted. "This is going far better than we had planned."

"Yes, a surprising accomplishment for such inferior clans," Liutites said doubtfully, looking at the messenger and waiting for the rest of the story.

"There is more, sirs," the messenger informed him.

"As I expected," Liutites said as he glared at the messenger, a sick feeling in his gut.

"It appears the human's military was informed before the islands could be secured," the messenger said nervously. When Liutites didn't respond, the messenger continued. "In short, the human flying machines returned and decimated our forces—which rendered the initial victory unsustainable."

Liutites remained blank and unreadable, even as Diutes began to pace in anger and frustration. "Commander T'Cuh-ka?" he asked without elaboration.

"He ordered the retreat and has withdrawn the Magellanics from the PDA."

"Commander Boulét?"

"Dead, sir."

"Commander Kiley?"

"Joined in the retreat."

"Who is currently in command, and where did he retreat to?" Liutites asked through a tightly clenched beak, his anger simmering.

"Presumably Commander Kiley is in command, but it was overheard that General Leepoh took command temporarily. They retreated to Rockhopper Colony 23."

Liutites tried to control himself, but in spite of a great effort, his body quivered in anger. "This is not acceptable. I will not have my forces led by that crackpot Gentoo or that spineless Kiley," he said, nearly stammering through his rage. Liutites looked at Diutes and exhaled. "General Diutes, you are now in command of the assault force. Reestablish the pursuit of our objectives. Anyone not willing to comply with your orders is to be executed as a traitor. T'Cuh-ka is first on the list should you find him. His orders were to occupy the islands. Take half of the Shadow Warriors with you and go to RHC 23 to restore order."

"Yes, sir," Diutes said, pride filling his voice at being advanced to the position of Commander.

"I will meet with the Overlord at once. And, Commander, after you restore discipline, remain at RHC 23 and wait for my orders. You are being sent there as enforcement, not to take initiative." Liutites spun and left the newly appointed commander without saying another word.

Diutes stared at his brother's back. "Yes, sir, Supreme Commander," Diutes said, fuming inside. In fleeting moments, Diutes went from pride to humiliation. His pride in his brother's seeing him as more than a pawn gave way to humiliation when it became clear that his brother didn't think he was capable of truly taking command of the PDA. Resentment burned inside. *One day, Liutites—my brother—you will find yourself impaled on the tip of my beak,* Diutes thought, continuing to watch Liutites walk away.

CHAPTER 2

"How can a storm last for two weeks straight? I know this is the bottom of the world and all of that nonsense, but really . . . come on," Randy complained, watching the unceasing white blow by the window.

"It's not *one* storm. Its successive storms," Gina informed him. "And if you don't remember, we *did* have that three-hour break last week."

"Oh yeah. I thought I dreamt it because I was asleep when it happened."

The pair was becoming increasingly frustrated by their situation. With the continuous windstorms, there was little chance of a rescue flight getting into the air, let alone flying overhead. They had planned to spend the long Antarctic winter doing research, but that had become impossible. So in order to keep from going stir-crazy, Randy spent his time trying to learn penguin language and teaching Meuseaux. Gina had spent her time helping Meuseaux recover from his injury and preparing things in case the penguins came back and were not so forgiving. She also, with annoying persistence, corrected Randy on his penguin grammar lessons.

Corporal Meuseaux had healed enough to make a couple feeding runs to the coast. Each time the Chinstrap left, however, Randy fretted over the penguin's safety like a worried mother. Gina couldn't resist giving him a good ribbing about it. The Chinstrap had also made progress in learning the Blue penguin's language. Through this education he had learned that the Blues had suffered just as harshly as other penguins, if not more so, under the Overlord and Supreme Commander's rule.

"What's wrong? Don't you like spending all of this quality alone time with me?" Gina answered his testiness with playfulness.

"No—I mean yeah. I mean—what was the question again?" Randy asked, pulling off his wool cap and running his hand through his hair, letting go of his frustration. "Actually, there's nothing else I'd rather do than spend time alone with you. I'd just prefer to be doing it without the constant threat of an army of killer penguins hell bent on seeking revenge for the atrocities laid upon them by humankind. You know—someplace safe and warm."

"I know, I know," said Gina as she went to Randy, who had surrendered to the nearest chair. She sat on his lap and kissed him softly on his scruffy cheek. "Someone will find us eventually. But until that time, we'll just have to make the best of it," she said with a devilish smirk.

Randy stared into her eyes for a long moment and leaned toward her for a kiss. Meuseaux rushed into the room. "A penguin is coming," the Chinstrap announced hurriedly.

Randy popped up, nearly knocking Gina to the floor, and the two immediately reached for their weapons. "How many?" he asked.

"Just one, a King," Meuseaux answered, staring at the front door.

"How do you know?" Gina asked, not confident in the penguin's answer.

"Penguins can hear on the subsonic level and they can hear each other's calls from miles away," Randy said boastfully, never missing a chance to share his knowledge of penguins.

"Thanks for the biology lesson, Professor," Gina retorted. "How do you know there is only *one*?" she asked, clarifying her question.

"Penguins are very seldom quiet. This one is alone. I am sure of it."

The group stood in silence, including the Blue, who seemed to have understood their alarm. The humans could hear nothing but the constant howl of the wind.

"He is close," Meuseaux said.

Silence once again prevailed as Gina, Randy, and Meuseaux crept to the door. The Blue stayed noticeably away.

Meuseaux leaned in close to the door, and after a few moments, turned and shook his head at Randy and Gina, indicating he no longer heard anything.

A sudden rap on the door startled the group, nearly causing Meuseaux to fall over in surprise. The King penguin called out—first in the penguin language and then in broken English. "Human, I need help. I mean not harm to you."

Gina and Randy looked at each other and then to Meuseaux. "What did it say to you?"

"He called me by name and said he was sent by a friend," the Chinstrap answered.

"Could it be a trick? There could be a thousand others out there waiting," said Gina.

"Not trick or trap," the King, barely audible, said from the other side of the door. "I alone."

"Do you hear any others?" Gina asked Meuseaux.

"No, I am sure he is alone."

"If there were others, do you honestly think they would knock politely?" Randy rhetorically asked in answer to Gina's earlier sarcasm.

"Yeah, you're right," Gina conceded. "They probably would try to peck through the door."

"Exactly. And that Emperor said she would send a messenger to contact Meuseaux."

"Right. Okay, so how do you want to do this?"

Randy looked around while he thought and handed the gun to Gina. "Here, you take this, and I'll open the door. Meuseaux, be prepared."

Meuseaux nodded his head affirmatively, and Randy slid the makeshift barricade away from the door and jerked it open quickly.

Without ceremony, the King casually strode into the room and shook the cold from his feathers. Randy did a quick check outside and shut the door.

The King ruffled his feathers further and looked at Gina. "I am glad you survived."

Gina knew at once that this King must have been the one who had let her escape. But Meuseaux knew at once that it was Colonel Kimmer, and Meuseaux launched an attack.

"No! Meuseaux, no!" urged Gina. "This is the penguin who let me escape."

Meuseaux stopped his ineffectual attack against the much larger King, who had not bothered to fight back. "I doubt that. This is Colonel Kimmer. He is one of General Diutes's cohorts. He carries out the orders of his Royal Emperor masters and is likely responsible for the deaths of an untold number of penguins who were *sacrificed* to the Leopard Seals, as you call them. And I am sure he is responsible for the attack on Randy."

Randy retrieved the gun from Gina and leveled it at the King. "Is this true?"

Colonel Kimmer lowered his head in a gesture resembling remorse. "Yes, all of it, but I serve the Overlord no longer." Kimmer then looked at Gina. "After the human saved my life, I allowed it to escape, and that nearly cost me my life."

"I doubt he is the one who allowed you to escape. He is as ruthless as Diutes or Liutites," Meuseaux continued venomously.

After the Chinstrap's outburst, Randy and Gina looked at Kimmer, who continued to speak. "That *was* true. But when this one saved my life, I realized there may be more to the humans. I felt indebted to return the favor. I guessed, at most, that I would lose my rank, but when I returned to PIC the Supreme Commander decreed that I should be executed as a traitor and a pacifist. Soon after, however, I was aided by those who had assisted you." Throughout the conversation, Kimmer kept switching between penguin and human, which made it difficult for the humans to follow.

"Did you take part in capturing Randy?" Gina interrupted, indicating Randy with a gesture.

"Yes," Kimmer answered. "I do apologize," he said as he bowed to Randy.

"To be honest, and I feel bad for saying this. Had I known it was you who took him, I don't know that I would have stopped Davis from shooting you," Gina said.

"Then it is fortunate for all three of us that you did not know and that we took him," Kimmer said somewhat cryptically.

Gina was clearly confused by the King's reply and looked to Meuseaux for clarification, thinking something had been lost in translation.

When Meuseaux was unable to clarify the statement, Kimmer explained further. "Had we not taken your mate, neither of you would have survived."

Randy sat upright in concern and stared hard at Kimmer. "Why would we be dead?" he asked cautiously.

"Because all of the other humans are, and had you not been at Pack Ice Command, you would have suffered their fate as well."

"Wait, wait, wait—are you telling us that every other person in Antarctica is dead?" Gina asked before Randy grasped the horror of it. "There are, or were, thousands of people here."

"Yes, there were, but there are millions of penguins."

The room remained silent as the implications of what was said filtered through their minds.

"There is more," Kimmer said, turning to Meuseaux. "The Overlord's plans are to drive the humans from everywhere the penguins live. I understand they have already been successful on several islands. The PDA also had initial success in the Falkland Islands, but they were driven away by a vicious counter-attack by the humans."

"I thought the PDA was formed for the defense of penguins—not for waging war against another species," Meuseaux said with a mix of anger and fear.

"Do you know what this means for you?" Randy asked the two penguins, getting the gist of the conversation even though they continued to switch between languages. "Now that our governments know the penguins are capable of such things, they'll stop at nothing to eliminate the threat."

Kimmer and Meuseaux traded glances. Both understood full well Randy's meaning. "We have to stop the Overlord. This war could be our extinction," Meuseaux said.

"I doubt the Overlord can be swayed. I believe the extinction of some clans is what he intended," Kimmer replied, avoiding Meuseaux's eyes.

Gina and Randy stepped back in silence as they regarded Meuseaux, who stood silent with his beak agape.

Kimmer elaborated in the penguin common language. "From what I know, the Overlord has planned these events since he was a hatchling when he heard stories of past human atrocities and of a great northern paradise. He knows the humans are powerful. That is why you will rarely see a Royal Emperor in combat."

"I don't understand," said Meuseaux.

"Antaean sees all other clans as inferior, including the Emperors who raised him. By sending the PDA to battle against humans, our numbers will decline, perhaps even to complete obliteration. At that time, he will be able to lay claim to all of the feeding waters and breeding grounds left abandoned, and from there he plans to take the northern paradise as his own."

"Then we must fight back," Meuseaux demanded.

"It is much easier to say than to do, Meuseaux. There is more, the reason I was sent here."

The Chinstrap wasn't sure if he wanted to hear more. Wasn't it enough to hear that your leader was angling ways to render you extinct?

"If I don't make it to find the PDA forces, you must deliver this message." Kimmer hesitated a moment before continuing. "Antaean's and Liutites's treachery goes deeper still. Your colony was not destroyed by human retaliation."

With a sickening feeling in his stomach, Meuseaux asked what he meant.

"The Overlord and Supreme Commander knew of dissent among several Chinstraps from your colony. Liutites, under command of the Overlord, ordered Diutes to wipe out your colony and make it look as if the humans had done it."

"Just because of *dissent*?" asked Meuseaux, outraged. He thought about it for a second longer and realized it wasn't so difficult to believe. After all, he was nearly sacrificed to the Phocids simply for being in the wrong place.

"It was intended to motivate those of your colony who were not there—to inspire hatred and give them a reason to fight."

Meuseaux fumed inside. "It has inspired me," he said with loathing. "I swear to you that I will see the Overlord *and* Supreme Commander Liutites dead. Where are our brothers and sisters of the PDA now?"

"The last I heard, they were at Rockhopper Colony 23, south of the Falklands. But that was days ago, and Liutites had sent General Diutes to take command," Kimmer informed him.

Gina took advantage of a break in the conversation to ask Meuseaux what had been said. After the Chinstrap's synopsis, she looked at Kimmer. "When you said that the PDA was initially successful at the Falkland Islands, did you mean that no one survived there as well?"

"Yes," Kimmer answered plainly and without hesitation.

"What about the military? There's a strong presence there," Randy added.

"I do not know the details. I assume they were away or were responsible for the retaliation," Kimmer said to Meuseaux who continued his translator duties.

"The British Navy was probably on their way here."

"A distraction?" asked Randy.

"Probably," Gina affirmed.

"Well, for one thing, if the Overlord plans to take the arctic, which is what I'm assuming you're talking about when you mention a northern paradise, he's too late. The arctic circle is already overrun with people," Randy told the King.

"I don't believe he is that concerned about the North. There is more to the story, but that was all I was privy to," Kimmer told Meuseaux in penguin common.

A faint call from the Blue penguin as it came from its hiding place caught Kimmer's attention. "What is this?" he asked, having never seen its kind before.

"A Blue penguin. His name is Pín," Meuseaux answered, going to the little penguin's side and hoping it had not sensed Kimmer's rudeness. "He was a spy for the Overlord and Supreme Commander," he continued in penguin common for ease of conversation. "The humans captured him while we were making our escape. Randy, the male, refused to kill him, so we were obligated to take him with us."

"Why didn't he kill him?" Kimmer asked, showing he still had a small bit of Diutes's training left in him.

"He seems to *like* penguins, though after these events, I doubt he will continue."

"I have seen him kill a penguin," Kimmer reminded Meuseaux.

"An event he regrets, I assure you, but you *did* attack him," Meuseaux, in turn, reminded Kimmer.

Kimmer conceded the point as he looked at Randy. "True. These humans could prove to be great allies."

"They could also prove to be great friends," Meuseaux added.

Kimmer stood in silence. His life had changed dramatically. He had gone from being a high-ranking officer under General Diutes and leading the initial attack against the humans to being slated for execution and escaping with the help of a secret underground resistance. And now to this. He knew what needed to be done. He had to incite open rebellion against the Royal Emperors. "In two days, when storm finishes, I will be leaving," he said in human.

This proclamation caught Gina's attention. "How do you know the storm will be over in two days?"

"And where are you going?" Randy followed up, still a bit suspicious of the King's intent.

"Penguins know," Kimmer answered Gina without further explanation and turned to Meuseaux. "I am going to inform the Order of Kings of the Overlord's treachery. Then I will find the PDA. More specifically, I will find Lieutenant-General Lavour. He is key to this."

Meuseaux wasn't quite sure how to take Kimmer's assessment of Lavour and inwardly asked why a Chinstrap would play a key role in any rebellion. "When will you return?"

"On the day of night," answered Kimmer. "If I do not, then *you* must seek out Lavour and tell him what I have told you."

^^^

Two days later the storm subsided as predicted, and Colonel Kimmer departed without saying anything further on the subject of revolution. Corporal Meuseaux watched the King walk away until he disappeared over the horizon. He hoped Kimmer would return, unsure if he was up to the challenge of tracking down Lavour on his own. He talked big and threatened loudly, but he honestly doubted he could take the lives of Liutites and Antaean. He thought of Lavour and decided that if Lavour, a mere Chinstrap as well, was to play an important role in the inevitable insurrection, he might not be alone in attempting to put his world right.

CHAPTER 3

With the forces of the Penguin Defense Alliance gathered on Rockhopper Colony 23, the warrens of the Rockhopper Defense Ministry became the base of operations. The PDA fell under the joint direction of Commander Lavour, General Treeg, General Leepoh, Commander Kiley, and the recently arrived Macaroni penguin, General Natoo. Nok was put in charge of finding targets of opportunity, which were becoming rarer by the day as word of attacking penguins and the rough near-winter seas of the South Atlantic kept most fishing vessels at port. Along with his new responsibilities, Nok was promoted to Colonel, a rank he wore proudly.

It had been weeks since the failed conquest of the Falklands, and the mood was becoming tense.

"We still have heard nothing from PIC," the King, Commander Kiley, said in frustration. He was not a patient penguin and was not keen on sharing command with a Chinstrap.

"I think, for now, that's a good thing, Commander," General Treeg said in a calm manner. "The assault seems to have been a partial success after all. The humans appear to be wary of going to sea, which has had a positive effect on our food supply."

"That may be only half true, General Treeg," Natoo spoke up. "With so many penguins concentrated in this one area, it might be *us* who will be guilty of over hunting."

"That's why we need to be on our way—that and the fact that, if the humans find us here, they could kill all of us with a single attack," Kiley warned.

"If you remember, Commander, Commander Lavour suggested we send two-thirds of our forces to sea in case of such an event—an idea with which you, at the time, vehemently disagreed," Leepoh reminded him.

"It wasn't prudent at the time. It was too soon," Kiley defended himself while looking at Lavour.

Lavour looked at Leepoh, silently urging him not to rile Kiley. Even though Lavour's proposal had been a good one, he was still growing into his position of commander and wasn't used to praise in a public forum. "As things stand, I think we should wait until our messengers return from PIC and stay the course. I have no doubt we'll be hearing from somebody soon. I believe our best course of action is to attack only those humans who threaten us or our food sources. Once we know more from PIC, we'll address the issue of relocating those who have been displaced by the war."

"I agree," said Treeg. "Colonel Nok, how has your search for targets been?"

Nok sat upright immediately, eager to take part in the conversation of the commanders. "Our targets have diminished considerably. I did encounter a group of T'Cuh-ka's Magellanics. I was informed that the humans have sporadically attacked their nesting sites, and they were forced to abandon their nests. The Magellanics have taken to sea for the winter."

"Did they really expect to be able to return to a normal life after the Supreme Commander's gross miscalculation of the island campaign?" Kiley snorted in derision.

"We are, unfortunately, *in this* now. If we become divided, the humans will exterminate us," General Natoo said in a calm but firm tone.

"What should we do—continue attacking human settlements while the Overlord and Supreme Commander hide in their fortress, safe from any real danger?" Kiley asked, becoming more irritable.

Lavour wasn't quite sure how to read Kiley; at one minute he might sound loyal to the Overlord's cause, and at another he sounded nihilistic. Through it all, however, he still maintained an air of pompous self-importance and prejudice against other clans. "The purpose of the Penguin Defense Alliance was to *defend*," Lavour said calmly to Kiley. "While the PDA was *securing* the human settlements in Antarctica—my colony was destroyed . . . There was no defense," he added with more passion.

"Then what do you propose we do?" asked Leepoh with a hint of pride in his voice at seeing his friend rise to his position.

Lavour studied Leepoh and the others carefully. He felt that somehow, what he said next would be pivotal. "We do what we were supposed to do—defend. We seem to have quickly lost sight of the PDA's purpose. There are clans on the verge of extinction—the Humboldts for example. We should go to their aid. This is *our* alliance and we should use it for the benefit of all. No more of this invade and conquer mindset that we seem to have fallen into. That is a path to destruction, and we will never succeed with it. The humans are too powerful. We should be defensive and rarely offensive. We should go to the Pacific to protect and assist the Humboldts. That would be a start."

The other leaders looked on in silence, digesting Lavour's words. Even Commander Kiley had no opposing viewpoint.

"That was quite a speech," a malevolent voice hissed from the shadows of the stone warrens. "But it is not for you to decide."

The council of PDA leaders spun their heads in surprise and found General Diutes emerging from the darkness.

"General Diutes, when did you arrive?" a startled Commander Kiley asked while snapping a salute.

"Long enough ago to hear talk of treason," he said while eyeing Lavour. "And it is *Commander* Diutes to you. Supreme Commander Liutites has seen it necessary to remind you of your orders. Given what I have heard here and your failure at the Falklands, I see that he was correct."

General Treeg stepped forward, not intimidated in the least by the imposing figure of Diutes. "I assure you, *Commander*, there is no need for a reminder of our directive, and the Falklands battle was not a *failure* as you call it. Had the order to retreat not been given, the bulk of the Penguin Defense Alliance would have been slaughtered."

"Am I to understand that you were there, Rockhopper?" Diutes asked in his condescending way.

"No—were you?"

Diutes glared at Treeg in response to his insolence.

"Several of the Rockhoppers from this colony *were*, however, and—" Treeg began, but Diutes interrupted him.

"Then who are you to judge as to whether it was a failure?"

"Who are you, Diutes? I believe you were holed up at PIC or in one of your Forward Command posts."

Diutes stared daggers at the bold Rockhopper. "Your impudence will be remembered, Treeg."

"Do not come to *my* home and threaten me, Diutes," Treeg told him, becoming increasingly angry.

"Or what, General?" asked Diutes in a quiet hiss as he raised his flipper. On his mark, ten Royal Emperor Shadow Warriors emerged from the darkened crags. The large, solid black and powerfully built penguins caused an instant stir amongst the leaders, not only for their size, but also out of discomfiture for their having been able to gain entrance without being noticed.

"*What* are those?" Colonel Nok asked Lavour quietly.

"Another of the Overlord's abominations," Kiley whispered over their shoulders.

Diutes didn't trouble himself with explanations of the new warriors; he instead let them draw their own conclusions. "The Overlord agrees with your assessment of the situation, Lieutenant-General Lavour," Diutes told him after a few moments of tense silence.

Lavour shifted uncomfortably at hearing that the Overlord thought along the same lines as he did.

"He is *Commander* Lavour now," Leepoh informed Diutes defiantly, never being one to avoid stirring up turmoil.

Diutes glared at Lavour, who didn't flinch under the threatening look. "What sort of *commander* has others speak for him?"

"Liutites, for one—and the Overlord," Leepoh said immediately.

Diutes appeared as if he wanted nothing more than to drive his beak through Leepoh's heart. But, with the lesser clans already on the verge of revolt; now wasn't the time. "Perhaps you would like to offer your opinion of them directly one day."

Leepoh eyed Diutes. "Hah!" he blurted out. "Perhaps one day I shall, General."

Diutes studied Leepoh, when it seemed he was about to forego caution and strike the Gentoo down, right then, for his insolence, he backed down. The Overlord was still in need of the lesser clans. "Back to the matter before us," Diutes said through a clenched beak, trying to give an impression of civility. "*Commander* Lavour is correct. We must now concentrate our efforts in the waters of the Pacific. A contingent of our forces will remain behind to harry the humans northward from here along the Atlantic coast of the Americas, to give them reason to believe we are headed in that direction."

"There are to be no attacks as you pass through the cape, unless absolutely necessary." Diutes paused as if to make sure all attention was on him; however grudgingly he may have felt about it, it was necessary to pander to the sub-penguins. "Several human vessels are currently breaking through the ice floes—presumably to investigate the events at the homeland. We must draw their attention away. Once we pass through the straits and around the cape, a small force will break away and head toward New Zealand. The rest will continue northward and assist the Humboldts, who are being persecuted by the humans. From there, we will continue north." Diutes waited for the inevitable questions.

"Why would we continue north? The waters are far too warm once we pass the Galapagos," observed General Natoo.

"To establish a stronghold at the northern ice realm," answered Diutes, as if the revelation was insignificant.

"Are you saying the Northern Paradise is real?" Natoo followed up. "You've been there?"

"Yes, it is *real*," answered Diutes, trying to sound patient and tactful but coming across only as patronizing. At Forward Command, if anyone other than the Overlord or Supreme Commander had questioned Diutes about anything, the inquisitor would have ended up severely punished or worse, but there would be no such tactics here. Even with his Shadow Warriors close by, he was heavily outnumbered and knew that dealing punishment would cement rebellion. "I have not been there. The journey will be a test of our strength. But the survival of our kind depends on it."

"Why should we abandon our homes for this fabled *Northern Paradise*?" Treeg asked, doubtful of the Royal Emperor's intentions.

"You are not abandoning your homes. The humans are coming in greater numbers, and you will soon be driven from them. We cannot fight them forever. The Overlord knows this, and this is why we must establish colonies elsewhere, if we, as a species, are to survive," Diutes said.

"And who will establish these colonies, or should I ask, who will oversee them? How do we know the humans won't drive us from there as well?" asked Leepoh, fully intent on pushing his limits with Diutes.

Diutes clamped his beak tightly to avoid lashing out at the Gentoo. He was by no means a diplomat and resented having to pretend to be one. "All penguins will have the option to colonize the North. As far as the humans, there are no certainties. Perhaps . . . once our goals are met in the South, we will reach an accord."

"An accord," Treeg blurted out. "How and why would we reach an *accord* with those beasts?"

"I don't know. That is up to the Overlord, and I am not privy to such information," Diutes lied. "We must continue and, come morning, we will do so. Gather the forces, Commander Lavour," he said with a shiver of disgust.

"What is our destination, then?" asked Lavour while throwing a warning glance to Leepoh to go along with him. He didn't trust Diutes, but he knew that now wasn't the time to prolong the discussion; he would talk privately with the others later. It was his turn to appease—to appease the vile Antaean's puppet, Diutes.

Diutes seemed thoroughly pleased with himself at getting the others motivated so quickly. "We will move through the Strait of Magellan, as the humans call it. There is a strong human military presence there now, so we will have to travel in small groups. Each group will wait a fixed time before entering the strait. I will lead my regiment around the cape and rejoin the main force on the Pacific side. And I repeat: do not engage the humans unless it is *absolutely* necessary. Our primary goal is to aid and assist the Humboldts of Patagonia and Peru." Diutes puffed his chest as if he would be a conquering hero; the others ignored his display of self-importance.

"General Treeg," Diutes continued. "Send messengers—preferably those who will not be accompanying us—to gather the forces."

Treeg watched the Royal Emperor suspiciously before responding, "Yes, Commander, of course."

"Very good. We will leave at first light from the southern point. Commander Lavour, see to it that all are in their assigned groups by morning."

"Yes, sir," said Lavour while snapping a high beak salute. It was a tall order to get *all* the troops in ranks by morning, and Lavour wondered if Diutes had ordered it just out of cruelty.

Diutes didn't bother to return the salute and ambled out of the warrens with the Shadow Warriors trailing him. Once he was out of sight and they were sure they were alone, the commanders huddled together.

Commander Kiley spoke first. "I don't trust him. Something's wrong."

"I agree," said Lavour. "It's not in his nature to be so solicitous of other clans."

"Perhaps he is under pressure from the Supreme Commander," suggested General Natoo.

"That much is obvious, but I have a feeling there may be more to it," Leepoh said.

Natoo had nothing to say in response.

"When we leave here tomorrow, you must be on watch," Colonel Nok said to General Treeg. "From what I hear, Diutes is never one to let a penguin speak to him out of line."

"We will double our watch," said Treeg as he lowered his head. "It's a shame it has come to this. We should be able to trust our leaders. Our fight is with the humans."

"And it's no longer a fight with just any humans," Lavour added. "Regardless of the PIC's edicts, we will go after only the humans who truly are a threat or danger to our way of life. But, for now, *our* direction and PIC's coincide." He knew what he was saying was treasonous, but everything about this war was beginning to stink. None of it felt right and deep down something gnawed at him, something he couldn't place.

Lavour looked at the faces around him. "All of us here, in this place and at this moment, have a choice to make. Do we keep going along with the status quo, following the Overlord and his minions blindly into the next disaster, or do we—" he paused, choosing his next words carefully "—chart our own course and decide our own fate? This group gathered together here, we could form our own alliance, free from the control of PIC."

In the flickering torch light of the warrens, each of the commanders exchanged concerned but defiant looks. They all knew that if they went through with what Lavour had suggested, the Overlord would stop at nothing to teach them the errors of independent thought.

"I agree," Leepoh finally said rather stoically. "We should not be subjugated to the rule of tyrants."

"Tyrants?" asked Natoo. "Isn't that a bit extreme?"

"No, it's not," answered Lavour. "You have obviously never lived under the direct rule of the Royal Emperors. They reprimand with physical violence or worse. And what sort of leaders would chastise their officers for retreating after losing tens of thousands of warriors in a losing battle? I have spent a great deal of time at PIC, and I have seen their ruthlessness, even to their own kind." He paused again as something ruminated in the back of his mind, but he couldn't place it. "This talk of a Northern Paradise—it's just a motivator, like a plump squid swimming just before your beak, that you can never reach."

"That's the stuff of nightmares," Leepoh said quietly, but not quiet enough.

"For now," Lavour continued, "we should use their resources, but once our goals have been achieved, we should separate from the influence of the Royals altogether and use our new alliance to defend ourselves from all dangers, including the likes of tyranny."

Natoo looked to the others for reassurance, including Commander Kiley, who had remained quiet during Lavour's speech. "The Macaronis are with you," he said.

"Then it's settled," said Leepoh after hearing no objections. "This autonomous *Alliance of Independent Colonies* will set out to do what the PDA was intended for."

"Do we still get to kill humans?" Nok asked. Even though he had lost some of his eagerness to give the humans battle, he was sure there were some who deserved it.

"Of course," Leepoh reassured him. "Just not so indiscriminately."

CHAPTER 4

After Lavour, Leepoh, and the other commanders dispersed to inform their respective clans of the upcoming moves, General Treeg called Colonel Nok aside. "Nok, my friend," he started. "You don't have to go. We could use you here. You've become quite an impressive leader."

Usually proud and boastful, Nok took the compliment with surprising humility. "Thank you, sir. But I *have* to go. I *have* to help my friends. I . . ." Nok paused as if lost in thought. "During the battle of the Falklands I was knocked unconscious by an explosion from a human weapon, and General Leepoh stayed with me—at my side—at great risk to himself. He stayed there until he was sure I was all right. And I have no doubt that Commander Lavour would do the same."

Treeg looked at Nok for a while as he thought about the devotion Nok's new friend had shown him and the devotion he returned. Cort had thought of Nok as a brother and, in turn, Treeg thought of Nok as his son. The memory of Cort brought a fresh welling of pain for his loss; the risks of this war were becoming too high. "I don't want to lose you, Nok," Treeg said, trying not to sound too sentimental.

The love and respect he felt for Treeg shone through Nok's eyes, as well as the pain of losing Cort. "He was and always will be my brother, and you are my father as well."

Treeg lowered his head and looked away in an attempt to hide the fear of what Nok was going to say next.

"And that's why I have to go—to do my part, however small or large, to try to prevent these sorts of things from happening in the future."

Treeg eyed Nok long and thoughtfully. "Then be safe, and give the humans hell."

"I will, and don't forget—I have a commander *and* a general looking out for me," Nok said to reassure Treeg, as well as himself.

"That's good enough. Remember, I'll need someone to take my place around here—someone courageous, intelligent, and strong."

"Yes, sir. I'll be on the lookout for just such a penguin."

Treeg was surprised by Nok's wisecrack; in all of the time that Treeg had known Nok, he had always been very serious, and with what he'd been through as a fledgling, Treeg didn't blame him. But Nok's new attitude made him feel more at ease about his friends. He was beginning to feel that he was in good company. "You've been hanging around that Gentoo too much."

"Yes, sir, I believe you're correct," Nok said with a touch of mirth.

Nok saluted and began to hop away when Treeg stopped him, "And, Colonel Nok," he said.

"Yes, sir?" he asked, turning back to him.

"There's a certain female who's been inquiring about you. You know her. Her name is Keerka. It would probably be in your best interest to seek her out before you depart." Treeg took satisfaction in seeing Nok suddenly become uneasy, and he took his leave.

Nok stood in stunned silence while he watched Treeg leave. This was the *last* thing he expected to hear. He had known Keerka for a very long time, but she had had a mate until he was taken by a Sea Lion a few years ago, and the thought of a female taking interest in him sparked a rush of emotion that he had kept buried for as long as he could remember.

All that ever mattered to him, after the loss of his parents, was making sure that it never happened again, and though he had never achieved full success in preventing such things, he had never abandoned the goal. He decided he was getting ahead of himself and that she probably wanted to see him for something far more innocent.

He hopped out into the moonlight, feeling far more optimistic than he had in a long while.

CHAPTER 5

Randy woke up with a start. Gina did the same from her bunk across the room.

"Airplane!" they said in unison.

Both leapt from their beds and desperately tried to add the layers of clothing necessary to survive the freezing temperatures. They twisted and struggled to dress as the roar of the prop-driven plane grew ever closer.

"To hell with it," said Randy as he threw on his boots, wrestled the door open and began to run down the hall.

"Randy—wait," Gina called after him. "It's sixty below out there!"

He looked back at her to her give a sarcastic reply but tripped over his still-untied boots and fell to the floor. As he lay there, he heard the airplane pass over and head into the distance.

"There'll be another," Gina told him, pulling him to his feet.

Randy walked slowly to the window, sighed, and looked at the orange and blue sky. He opened his mouth to say something in reply to Gina's comment but couldn't find words anywhere near as hopeful.

It had been several days since the King penguin, Colonel Kimmer, had left in search of the PDA forces. The wind had stopped, exactly as he said it would, leaving Gina—the climatologist—awestruck at the penguin's ability to know when the weather would change. Kimmer had said he would return on the *Day of Darkness*, which Gina and Randy interpreted as the winter solstice—the day when the sun would not show a trace in Antarctica.

The days had grown very short, and the hope of being found by anyone other than penguins was growing dim. Considering the frequent windstorms, their diminishing hope was well justified.

"What if that plane reports us? What do we do if we *are* found?" Gina asked Randy as she brushed her hand along his back to ease his disappointment.

"What do you mean?" he asked, sounding confused as to why she thought it might be a bad thing.

"Well, what about Meuseaux? We can't leave him here. The others might kill him."

"Do not fear for me," Meuseaux chimed in. He had been standing in the hallway, curiously watching at Randy's actions while attempting to get dressed. Meuseaux's speech had improved dramatically over the past weeks. He no longer dragged his S's and his grasp of the language had grown by leaps and bounds.

"But I do," Gina insisted. "I owe you everything. Without you, I never would have found Randy. I probably would be dead somewhere out on the ice. Plus, you helped us escape from the guards. So, regardless of what happens," she said, looking at Randy then back to the Chinstrap, "we won't leave here unless we know you will be safe."

"Right," Randy agreed. "Not only from the other penguins but from all threats."

"You are too kind, my friends. But I remind you that you saved me as well. However, I assure you, I will be safe should you find the opportunity to leave here. Those who helped us know where I am, and Captain Mevoule will check on me soon enough."

"How do they know where we are?" Randy thought aloud.

"Kimmer found us, so I presume they know," Meuseaux answered.

"I know, and that's what worries me. If they know, there's a good chance that the Supreme Commander might find out. You did say the female who helped us was his consort."

Meuseaux seemed to mull over the possibilities. "There is always that risk. But if Liutites were to find out that she had betrayed him, she would pay with her life. For now, we must trust that he won't find out."

CHAPTER 6

"Find them!" Overlord Antaean roared as he struck Supreme Commander Liutites across the face, knocking him to the ground.

Liutites lay on the ground for more than a few seconds before pushing himself upright with his beak and glaring with hatred at the Overlord.

"Whomever you find who may be responsible for this, bring them to me immediately after questioning," the Overlord continued. "And I will kill them myself."

Liutites stared at Antaean, wanting nothing more than to strike him dead. "My lord," Liutites grumbled, barely controlling his rage. "We don't even know who they are or how they freed the prisoners."

Two Chinstrap prisoners had been held in a secured area and, once again, like many before them, had managed to find freedom. The Chinstraps had not been charged with a crime; they had been imprisoned only as an example to any who might doubt the Overlord's authority. Some in the PIC said it was a show of force. Others said it was a sign of frustration at not being able to uncover the clandestine group that was responsible for certain *atrocities,* as the Royal Emperors called it.

"That is the problem, you idiot," the Overlord said in his most insulting tone. "Perhaps Commander Diutes would be better suited for this task."

That was more than Liutites could bear. He sprang to life, rushed toward the Overlord, and dove, fully intending to pierce Antaean's heartless chest. The Overlord was caught completely off guard and braced for the life-ending stab. At the last possible moment, Liutites tucked his head under and instead of ending Antaean's life, knocked him to the ground.

Antaean quickly swatted Liutites off of him. Both scrambled and jabbed their beaks into the ice to give them the leverage they needed to stand upright. They squared off to face each other, preparing for the fight, but Liutites was met by the tips of six spears, and the scuffle ended as quickly as it had begun.

"Am I to understand by this outburst that you are challenging me for power and control of the PDA?" asked the Overlord in an amused, albeit twisted tone.

There was nothing Liutites wanted more, but now was not the time, not while the Overlord's war against the humans still raged. He was not about to inherit that bit of the Overlord's insanity. He, however, took satisfaction in knowing he could have killed Antaean. He would challenge him soon enough, and if Antaean managed to survive, Liutites would banish him to the North. Liutites was not a fool. He knew what the Northern Paradise was and why the Overlord had promised it to him. The humans were thick up there; they had already slaughtered the Great Auks and, eventually, they would do the same to the penguins. One day, the Overlord's *empire* would belong to Liutites.

"No, *my lord*," Liutites finally said. "I only wish to retain that which is mine. Diutes does not have the intelligence to advance to Supreme Commander. He is only a brute. It was an insult to suggest otherwise," Liutites explained, noticeably omitting an apology.

The Overlord glowered back at Liutites; doubt crossed over his face and disappeared as quickly as it had come. "Very well. Guards, stand down." He turned his back on Liutites, a gesture of dismissing him as a threat. "You may keep your position. However, I will not tolerate any future failures. We are at war, and we do *not* need this distraction. Find this covert group by any means necessary. Crush them and bring the survivors to me."

The Overlord turned to the guard who had stood closest to him during Liutites's attack. "You, come before me," he said, completely devoid of emotion and with his eyes fixed on the resigned guard. "Kill him," he said to the others in a low hiss, and they acted immediately and without hesitation, taking their brother's life. With the guard dead at his feet, Antaean fixed his stare on Liutites. "This guard failed in his duties. He won't fail again."

It was an example of the unquestioning allegiance Antaean's followers showed. Liutites knew that if he were to take control of PIC and the PDA, he would have to inspire that sort of absolute loyalty in the Royal Emperors under his command. *I should have killed him when I had the chance.* But Liutites didn't want merely to usurp the Overlord; he wanted the authority he wielded as well. "My lord," Liutites said, offering only a vague high beak salute as he took his leave of the Overlord.

Liutites sulked and berated himself as he walked the vast corridors of Pack Ice Command. His mind went to the one penguin he could trust to help him weed out the clandestine faction, one who had always shown more loyalty to him than to the Overlord. *Mearna.*

Liutites picked up his pace and even began to toboggan through the corridors until he reached the winding and upwardly sloping passage that led to the rookeries. As Liutites began ascending the passageway to the upper levels, Captain Mevoule rounded the curve in front of the Supreme Commander and appeared to be startled at seeing him. Mevoule, regaining his composure, snapped a high beak salute. Liutites briefly entertained the idea of slapping the Chinstrap to the ground, if for no other reason than to release some frustration. He decided to hold back. But a few questions wouldn't hurt.

"Captain Mevoule, is it?" Liutites asked even though he knew full well. "What business do you have in the rookeries?" He knew that answer as well, but after the morning he had had, he felt the need to flaunt his authority.

"Determining the cleaning roster, sir," Mevoule answered, managing to mask the nervousness in his voice.

Liutites stared down at the Chinstrap, letting the silence fill the air with a palpable tension for several moments. "Very well," he finally said. "Carry on."

"Yes, sir," Mevoule said, sagging noticeably.

"By the way, Captain Mevoule," Liutites said without looking at him. "Have you seen Mearna?"

Mevoule froze and attempted to hide his panic. "Yes, sir, I believe I saw her in rookery two not too long ago."

Liutites said nothing more and continued about his business of seeking out Mearna.

∧∧∧

Mevoule watched the supreme commander walk away. He felt sure his legs were going to give out from under him. "This is too much," he said quietly. He wondered whether, after his earlier interrogation, Liutites knew or suspected something, but Mevoule guessed he'd already be dead, or worse, if Liutites knew. Nevertheless, he decided it would be a subject to discuss at the next meeting of the Resistance Council.

Over the past several weeks, many more—including the so-called *feral* Emperors—had joined the council. The Overlord's spies, the Blue penguins, had turned against their masters after witnessing the brutal murder of one of their comrades. The council was, at first, reluctant to have the Blues join, but the Blues had since proven themselves very useful and very loyal. The size of the council was becoming a concern. The more who knew, the greater the chance of being found out.

Once Mevoule was sure he was clear, he quickly ducked down a side passage to his left, made several turns, and then shot down a seldom used and roughly hewn corridor. His path appeared completely random, but it was necessary in order to be sure he hadn't been followed. He continued until he reached the darkened corridor where the entrance lay. As he approached, it opened and he was ushered in quickly.

"Come in," one of the shadowy figures said as he stepped into the flickering light. Mevoule had finally proven to the council that he was trustworthy enough to become a full member and the others finally revealed themselves to him. The Resistance Council consisted of Mearna; Colonel Thylus, another Royal Emperor fed up with the Overlord and Liutites; Sergeant Kima, a female Adélie, a clan who chose to ignore Antaean's edict barring females from attaining rank; Major Rayton of the Kings; K'K'Ru-ki, a member of the *feral* Emperor clan; and Pah'not, an Antarctic Gentoo.

"I just passed Liutites on his way to the rookeries. He inquired about Mearna," Mevoule informed the council breathlessly.

"Easy, Mevoule. It was expected," Rayton told him, seeing his rattled condition. "After what took place between him and the Overlord, that is."

"What happened?" Mevoule asked with apprehension.

"Liutites attacked the Overlord," Kima jumped in, eager to tell a new set of ears.

"No," said Mevoule doubtfully. "If he did, then why didn't the Overlord have him executed or kill him himself?"

"Because the Overlord *needs* him—for now," Colonel Thylus explained. "However, the Supreme Commander is becoming bolder. From what I heard, Liutites could've killed Antaean today. The time will soon come when Liutites will be ready to make his bid for power, and I fear we will not be ready to act."

"Mearna will restrain his ambitions for as long as necessary," Pah'not said.

"Is there any word from Kimmer?" asked Mevoule.

"We know he reached the human shelter where Meuseaux and the two humans are hiding and that he has left to seek out the PDA at RHC 23," Thylus answered. "We can only hope Diutes has not found him."

"The PDA's being on the move again will slow our communications," Kima stated, quickly moving the subject away from Diutes and what he would do to Kimmer if he found him.

"We have to be ready," said Rayton, trying to keep the conversation from turning to speculation about Kimmer's fate as well. "When Liutites finds the courage *and* the support to make a *true* bid for power, we must use that small opening—a moment of weakness—to overthrow the Royals."

"I doubt Liutites will make his bid until the PDA's members have been sufficiently culled," Kima said, as if she had a bad taste in her mouth.

"Then why don't we move now—while we still have the numbers?" Mevoule asked. Being new to the council, he had not been privy to the earlier discussions of upheaval and of ousting the Overlord.

"Because the Supreme Commander and Overlord are too formidable for now," said Pah'not. "When the Supreme Commander makes his move—and he will—there will be faction fighting between those loyal to the Overlord and those loyal to Liutites. At that time, we will take advantage of the division and exploit it to our benefit."

"Plus, there is the rumor of Antaean being in league with the humans," Kima added in her unsubtle way.

Thylus rebuffed her. "*That* is only rumor. We must stick to what we *know*."

Alarmed by the possibilities, Mevoule prodded Kima further. "Why would he ally with the humans? That makes no sense."

Thylus shook his head at Kima, threw up his flippers in exasperation, and walked to the back of the room.

Kima shot Thylus a look and answered, "We have heard disturbing tales that the Overlord may be working with the humans and that he has made a deal with one group in particular."

"For what reason? What could he possibly hope to gain from such an alliance?" Mevoule asked tentatively.

"We are not sure. Our best guess—if the rumors are true—is that this war against the humans would eventually render all other clans extinct, thereby making the Royal Emperors—particularly the Overlord—the sole heirs to all that would be abandoned by the extinction. And this group of humans would have exclusive access to the homeland in exchange for their cooperation." Kima looked at the other council members for reassurance and received a few nods, indicating for her to go on. "But it is as Thylus has said; this is *rumor*. But—" she leaned closer Mevoule "—it has been confirmed to some extent, by the fact that several human flying machines were seen dropping things from the sky near PIC shortly before the war began."

"It still doesn't make sense. If the Overlord is in league with the humans, why would he want to exterminate them?" Mevoule asked. He could believe that Antaean could do something so treacherous; he just wasn't convinced that he had.

"A question for which we have no solid answers," Kima responded.

"And our efforts are best spent on what we *do* know," Rayton interjected. "What we do know is that several human ships have broken through the ice and, in the absence of General Diutes, the Overlord has contacted the rogue, Warlord Talus, and put him in command of Forward Command One. With the events of the Falklands being what they were, it may not be long before the humans become the aggressors. The only thing that appears to be holding them back is the weather and the darkness, but it will not be winter forever."

The attending council members exchanged presentimental looks without saying a word. Each knew what the end of winter would mean.

"The time has come to make the hard decisions. When Mearna returns, we will further discuss what needs to be done and how soon," said Thylus to wrap up the discussion.

The other members concurred and, to pass the time, began to discuss matters that were more trivial.

CHAPTER 7

Supreme Commander Liutites roamed the rookeries and examined the latest group of fully fledged penguins. The vast rookery covered the entire upper level of Pack Ice Command and was currently full to capacity with row upon row of Royal Emperor fledglings of all ages and newly returned adults. The adults had returned for their final indoctrination. They all stood at attention as Liutites approached. As this was not a formal inspection, Liutites waved them off to be at ease. But it gave him much satisfaction to see how well the group responded to his presence; Mearna was training them well.

One particular group caught his attention. The group consisted of fifty males. All were huge, as tall as the Overlord, if not taller. Each had powerfully built flippers, without the individual *fingers* seen in other Royal Imps. They instead had a single fused grasping *hand* with a slightly underdeveloped opposable thumb, which gave them a powerful grip without sacrificing much speed in the water. Obviously, the Overlord's selective breeding program was paying off. "These are the ones. They will lead my coup," Liutites said quietly.

"You like what you see?" Mearna's voice came from behind the Supreme Commander, catching him off guard.

"Mearna," he said as he bowed his head into hers. The two made soft clicking and whirring noises in an affectionate greeting display. "Yes, I do like what I see. This group *must* be made loyal only to me."

"That may be difficult," said Mearna as she lifted her head and turned away. "The Overlord is quite fond of them as well."

Liutites impotently paced back and forth. He was near his breaking point with the Overlord. *I should have killed him.* "The Overlord has become unbearable. When winter ends, I will end his reign as well. He plans to replace me with Diutes."

"Diutes?" she asked, feigning surprise, for she had already known. "Diutes is an idiot. He lacks your wisdom."

"I know, but the Overlord knows that he can manipulate Diutes and that he will do his bidding without question."

"Your father shares this assessment of your brother?" Bringing up his relationship to the Overlord was a dangerous and touchy subject with Liutites. It was something Mearna did only to incite him further.

"My *father.*" Liutites spit out the word as if it were poison. "My father, yes, but still I had to *fight* my way to my position. All the while, he stood back and watched as I killed Temalus for his approval."

During Liutites's rise to power, Antaean would pit him against one adversary after another until the time came when he met his brother, Temalus, the one penguin to whom Liutites shared a special kinship. They were both ruthless warriors, but they had more than that in common: their mutual hatred of their father. When the time came for them to face each other, Antaean pushed them into a fight to the death with the injunction that, should either of them show the other mercy, he would be disposed of.

The fight was long and bloody. In the end, Liutites killed his brother, and as he stood over the lifeless body of Temalus, his father came down off his dais, praised him for his victory, and invested him with the rank of Supreme Commander. Liutites accepted the rank, but from that day on, his hatred for the Overlord fueled his every action. Powerless against Antaean's will, all of those under his command bore the brunt of his rage. His chest still carried some of the bloodstains of Temalus. In honor of his brother, he refused to preen the feathers.

"My father, as you say, has issued an order for me to find these hidden agitators or suffer my brother's fate," Liutites informed her.

Mearna stared at Liutites, showing no trace of fear. "The Overlord's spies have found nothing?"

"They have become somewhat unreliable. We believe they may be working for them now."

Mearna nodded slow and knowingly. "The Overlord's brutality can haunt him."

"More than he knows," replied Liutites, no longer really listening.

After a minute of silence, Mearna studied the worry in Liutites's eyes. She looked around, as if to see if anyone was watching, and leaned close to Liutites. "If you are to usurp the Overlord, you must find the dissidents."

Liutites clicked his beak in anger and frustration; if anyone else had stated the obvious, it would have cost him or her dearly. But Mearna retained special *privileges* for being the consort. "That is something I already know. What I don't know is who and where they are."

Mearna turned away. If Liutites did not find something or someone, there was no doubt the Overlord would execute his plan. She couldn't have that. They had come too far, and their plans depended on Liutites, not his flunky brother. She turned back to him and leaned in close. "Be watchful of the King, Major Rayton."

Liutites drew his head away, looked at her, and quivered with rage. "The Kings?"

"Not all . . ."

Liutites quickly spun away and fell to his stomach, sliding away as fast as he could.

Mearna watched until he was out of sight. Once she was sure he was gone, she approached the new and coveted breed of warriors. "The time is near. Be prepared."

The warriors acknowledged her with a slight nod, and Mearna exited the rookery through a secret passage, en route to the Resistance Council's meeting room. She would have to live with herself for the betrayal, but one or more life in exchange for thousands *and* her own was a small price to pay.

CHAPTER 8

After several days of swimming, Colonel Kimmer reached RHC 23. The strong pre-winter storms had hindered his travel, and that, along with the constant torment of seals, put him days behind his self-imposed schedule. Once he'd arrived near the island, he encountered a type of penguin he had never before seen—the Shadow Warrior. What was even more disturbing to Kimmer was that he spotted Diutes leading the unusual warriors. His first thought was that he had been betrayed by someone on the council, and he nearly turned to flee, but the warriors paid him no mind and continued swimming away from him purposefully.

He hid on an outcropping of rock until he was sure all was clear. When he did finally come ashore, Diutes and his minions had gone, but so had the whole of the PDA. This would make his mission to find and deliver a message to Lavour that much more difficult. He decided he had to find the Rockhopper leader to find out their direction.

He ambled over the rocks, cursing as he did. Kings are not known for their climbing abilities. "I should have gone to the Gentoo."

"And why would you want to do that?" a voice asked from behind.

Kimmer spun around in a start, nearly losing his balance as he did, to find a Rockhopper perched atop the nearest rock. "I apologize," he said, rather embarrassed. "I only meant that I am having trouble with the terrain. My climbing skills are somewhat lacking."

"What business do you have here?"

Kimmer paused. He had planned to act as if he had been left behind as to find out where the PDA had gone, but he knew there would be no deceiving this Rockhopper. "I have a message for Lieutenant-General Lavour. Can you take me to your commanding officer, please?"

"Who are you?"

After a moment of hesitation, he decided to be honest with this Rockhopper. "I am Colonel Kimmer, of the PDA."

"Under whose command?"

Kimmer had had enough of the questioning. "I just need to find Lavour. And what is your rank that you are to question me?"

The Rockhopper let out an abrasive-sounding call and dozens of Rockhoppers immediately appeared on the rocks surrounding Colonel Kimmer. "I am General Treeg, and we are no longer subjugated to the rule of the Overlord, Liutites, or Commander Diutes."

"Commander Diutes?" questioned Kimmer.

"Yes, *Commander* Diutes, and we will not tolerate his spies."

"I am not a spy—far from it," Kimmer insisted, becoming nervous from all of the apparently angry Rockhoppers bounding around him. "I just need to find Lieutenant-General Lavour."

Treeg eyed Kimmer suspiciously. "And what business did you say you had with him?"

"I have an urgent message for him from friends at Pack Ice Command."

"Since when do they use Kings as messengers?" Kimmer opened his beak to reply, but Treeg continued. "Tell me the message, and I'll see that he receives it."

"Please, General Treeg, my life will be forfeit should anyone find out. It may already be."

Treeg raised his left flipper and the Rockhoppers disappeared as suddenly as they had arrived. After they had gone, Treeg hopped down to Kimmer and led him to a depression among the rocks. "What is it?" Treeg asked him with genuine concern.

Kimmer paused before answering, but feeling that he could trust Treeg, he talked. "The humans were not responsible for the attack on Lavour's colony. General Diutes carried out the attack under orders from the Supreme Commander and possibly the Overlord as well."

"Why?"

"From what I know, to keep the Chinstraps motivated to fight the humans."

"How did you come across this information?" Treeg continued to press his inquiry; he needed as much information as possible. With his suspicions of treachery by the Royal Emperors confirmed, the war had changed even more. The threat of the Royals needed to be dealt with first.

Kimmer surreptitiously looked around as if someone were watching. "For their safety, I cannot tell you. Suffice to say they are very influential, but they cannot make change through peaceful measures."

"If what you're saying is true, none of us are safe."

"It is. I have already escaped execution, and I heard that Liutites has put a death mark on Commander T'Cuh-ka."

"The same may be true for me. Diutes came here to take control of the PDA." Treeg seemed to have more questions for Kimmer but didn't press him to reveal his sources.

"If you are truly against the Royals, know that you are not alone. I have come to rally the PDA against the Overlord. We must bring the might of the PDA against them. *They* are our true enemy," said Kimmer with a sense of urgency to his tone.

"On this island, the humans are our true enemies," Treeg said matter-of-factly.

"Are you saying that you will not join us in this uprising?" Kimmer sounded disappointed. He had heard stories of the Rockhoppers' bravery and figured them to be first in line to fight the Royals.

"I am saying that I need to make sure my colony is safe. Soon we will go to sea for the season, but we will be in contact, and if you should be in need of us, we will be there," Treeg said with all sincerity. He had already made a commitment to the Alliance of Independent Colonies to fight, but he still didn't fully trust Kimmer and didn't tell him otherwise.

"Do you know where the forces are headed?"

"They have gone west, through the straits, to give assistance to the Humboldts."

Kimmer stared away, dreading the long, hard swim he'd have to make to catch up with the PDA. "If you wouldn't mind, could I rest here for a little while? The journey, thus far, has been demanding."

"I'll do one better for you," Treeg said. His body slumped from letting his guard down. "Keerka," he called out, and Keerka immediately bounced over the nearest rock.

"Yes, General Treeg?"

"I assume you heard what needs to be brought to Commander Lavour's attention, seeing as how you were eavesdropping on our conversation," Treeg said to her, half reprimanding and half amused by her boldness.

Keerka suddenly found the pebbles on the ground very interesting as she averted her eyes. "Yes, sir," she said, slightly abashed.

"Take four others and go to Colonel Nok. Lavour is sure to be with him. Tell them what has transpired and tell them to spread the word. The Alliance of Independent Colonies will strike back at the Overlord and his followers," he said with all seriousness.

Keerka's eyes lit up at hearing that she could see Nok. She snapped a salute and disappeared to find her traveling companions.

Kimmer watched Keerka bound over the rocks, feeling a bit envious of the Rockhopper's ability. A moment later his tired mind caught up with what was said. "The Alliance of Independent Colonies? Is that what the Rockhoppers are calling themselves now?"

Treeg raised an eye the King. "No. Truth is, I wasn't sure if I could trust you. The PDA has reorganized under Commander Lavour and Kiley. The goals have changed. And it looks like they're going to change again. But we'll talk more about this later."

Kimmer nodded. Things were moving quickly and it seemed as if it would coincide with the Resistance's plans to overthrow Antaean and Liutites. He felt a certain eagerness wash over him, knowing he would be part of the change.

General Treeg saw to directing the Rockhoppers to prepare for an inevitable confrontation with the Royals. After nearly an hour, Treeg turned his attention back to Kimmer. "Now you may rest easy, Colonel. I was wondering if you could tell—" A call of alarm interrupted the general. "Diutes," he exclaimed.

"I thought he had gone?" Kimmer asked, equally alarmed, if not outright fearful. He knew Diutes's thirst for brutality.

"So did I. Rockhoppers, prepare yourselves," Treeg said to his surrounding soldiers. "This could turn bad really fast."

ΛΛΛ

"What are they?" one of Keerka's companions asked when they surfaced for air.

"Diutes's warriors," Keerka said in a panic. She had seen the Shadow Warriors at RHC 23, and before Nok left, he had told her that Diutes and the other Royals were not to be trusted. She recalled what she had overheard while eavesdropping. That and the fact that the imperial freak penguins, as she thought of them, were turning toward them, left little doubt of their intentions. "Swim," she said. "Swim like the demons are at your tail, because they are."

Without another word, the five Rockhoppers dove below the surface to gain speed and bulleted through the water with the shadows in pursuit. They didn't know why they were being pursued, only that they were. The chase continued mile after mile, and the Shadow Warriors steadily gained on them. Five shadows would move in quick bursts, while the others would fall back. And when the leaders would tire, those behind would advance to take their place. The energy-conserving relay was having an effect; the much smaller Rockhoppers had been swimming at full speed for far too long, and exhaustion was becoming a danger.

Keerka signaled for one of her companions to meet her at the surface. "Where are they?" she asked as they breeched the surface. They dove again.

"Don't know—haven't looked back," the other said as they porpoised over the waves once again.

Keerka dove and did a tight circle underwater to get a fix on the pursuers and then put on a burst of speed to catch up to the others. "Still there—gaining," she informed them quickly between breaths.

"Can't keep this up," said one of the others.

"Island's not far," said another as he flew from the sea.

"Advantage on the rocks," Keerka said quickly to let the others know the plan. "No more talk, swim," she said as she surfaced once more.

They swam harder than before, without bothering to check on the predatory shadows looming ever closer behind. All five dove in unison, their flippers burning from fatigue as they flew from the surface to gulp the precious air. When they broke the surface again, one of the Rockhoppers cried out in surprise and fear as a Shadow Warrior caught her by the foot. The others saw her panicked eyes as she was pulled below the surface by the much larger penguin.

Keerka looped back for a look and fully expected to be attacked as well, but no attack came. She saw nothing at all.

The four remaining Rockhoppers surfaced together. "Where did she go?" one asked.

Keerka didn't have an answer.

"It has Kayk," another said. "We have to go after them."

"No," said Keerka sharply. "There's nothing we can do for her now. Our message *has* to get to Commander Lavour and the others." She felt a sense of urgency that she couldn't explain. She looked to the sky; night had fallen and she couldn't believe that they had been swimming for that long. The moon was hidden behind the passing clouds, and she knew they would have little chance of seeing the next attack in the murky water. "We break for the island. It's only a short distance away, and it's our only chance." She looked at the others; they had been her friends for many years and they all knew what they were facing. "One of us has to make it. Nobody stops . . . for any reason."

CHAPTER 9

"*I demand* to be released!" Major Rayton yelled out as he was pushed and prodded forward at spear point by four elite guards.

"You are in no position to make demands, Rayton," Supreme Commander Liutites said, approaching the King.

After Mearna returned to the council room, she told the resistance that the time was drawing near, and because they had yet to hear from Kimmer or anyone else, another messenger was to be sent out to assure the message was received by the PDA. Captain Mevoule was selected to deliver the message, and K'K'Ru-ki volunteered the *feral* Emperors as escorts to the sea. He had also said he would make one more attempt at diplomacy with Antaean in an effort to end the war with the humans and avoid a bloody conflict among the clans. The other council members expressed concern with such an attempt, but K'K'Ru-ki disagreed.

The council adjourned with the understanding that they would meet again in three days. Each member took separate exits to avoid detection, and as Rayton made his way down a darkened corridor, the Supreme Commander's minions pounced.

"I am a member of the Penguin Defense Alliance, and unless you have *good* reason to detain me, I would suggest to you that you let me go on my way," Rayton demanded, standing his ground against the guard's weapons.

Liutites slowly waddled close to Rayton and stared down at the penguin. In a flash, the Supreme Commander slapped the King across the head with the backside of his flipper. "Let me reiterate, you are in *no* position to make *any* demands."

Stunned by the powerful strike, Rayton pushed himself up from the icy floor. "*How dare you.* When the Order of Kings hears of my treatment, you will regret—"

"I doubt that your *Order of Kings* will ever know your fate," Liutites said arrogantly. "Guards, take him to the Overlord. If he resists, kill him."

"What? No!" Rayton screamed as he was taken away. He wondered who had betrayed him, but he knew it could be only one. *We were so close to the end,* he thought, not knowing whether the others had been betrayed as well. "You're mad, Liutites. You won't get away with this. One day you and your Overlord will fall."

Liutites paid Rayton no mind; he had other things to think about. Satisfied that this offering should keep the Overlord's beak shut for a while, he began to put more thought into his plans to overthrow the wretch. As he mused about his plan, an Adélie penguin rushed up to him.

"Supreme Commander, sir," the Adélie said.

"Yes, what is it?" Liutites asked as if it were a bother. With so many Chinstraps away, the Adélies had taken over the duties as messengers.

"It is believed that the location of the escaped humans has been found, sir."

"And where would that be, Adélie?" Liutites asked, keeping his excitement contained. He had been fuming over the escapes for some time, and nothing would give him more satisfaction than to purge himself of the memory of past mistakes involving those humans—nothing aside from ridding himself of Antaean, that is. And to dispose of the Chinstrap would be like catching three squid at once.

"The structures where Colonel Kimmer allowed the human to escape, sir," the Adélie said with as much enthusiasm as he could muster.

"Is the Chinstrap defector with them?"

"He is believed to be, sir."

"Very good, Adélie. Dismissed." *How obvious,* Liutites thought as he watched the messenger leave, a*nd how stupid of them—hiding where they were most likely to be found.* Liutites decided today was going to be a good day, and he rushed off, filled with a new sense of malevolent purpose.

^^^

K'K'Ru-ki and Captain Mevoule exited PIC, concealed by the darkness. The winter solstice was near, and the sun made only brief appearances each day. Soon, the sun would not shine at all. As they journeyed across the vast expanse of ice, K'K'Ru-ki told Mevoule where he could find his escorts. The decision to send Mevoule was sudden, but with events beginning to unfold at an alarming rate, it was necessary. When Mevoule had expressed concern over how his disappearance would be explained, Mearna assured him that, at this point, it would not matter.

As K'K'Ru-ki gave Mevoule the Emperor blessing for a safe journey, Pah'not called out to them from the direction of PIC. "Captain, K'K'Ru-ki," she said quickly and breathlessly. "The Supreme Commander has arrested Major Rayton."

"What? On what charges?" the alarmed Emperor asked.

"We're not sure, but it is safe to say that we all may be at risk."

K'K'Ru-ki turned to Mevoule. "Go now and go quickly. Tell my clan to expect my arrival within one week. If they do not hear from me, that will mean that some evil has befallen me, and they are to gather the free clans and be prepared for flight or fight." He stopped briefly and looked around cautiously, as if expecting to find a phantom hiding on the ice. "I fear our time has come. Go now."

Mevoule didn't reply; he wasn't sure what K'K'Ru-ki meant by saying, *"our time has come,"* and he wasn't sure if he *wanted* to know.

CHAPTER 10

"Well, General Treeg, I see that you are in league with the traitor *and* defector Kimmer," Commander Diutes said in a satisfied yet evil tone. "The Overlord will be most unhappy when he hears of this," he said mockingly.

"He can be as unhappy as he wants to be. The Rockhoppers of RHC 23 have withdrawn from the PDA and we are no longer subject to the rule of your Overlord. And whom I keep company with is none of your concern," Treeg huffed. "You, of all penguins, should not talk of treachery. I know what you did to the Chinstraps. And let me assure you, Diutes, you *will* be held accountable."

"Whatever the King may have told you is a lie; he is a coward and—"

"I grow weary of your babbling. If you have a point, make it," Treeg said, cutting him off. "Soon, word will reach the Chinstraps, and soon you will pay—preferably with your life."

As the conversation progressed, several Rockhoppers leapt onto the rocks surrounding Treeg, Diutes, and Kimmer.

"Are you threatening me, Rockhopper?" Diutes snarled.

"Are you really so stupid that you have to ask?" Treeg said, turning his back on the Royal. It was a display to show how insignificant Treeg considered him to be; it was a great insult to a penguin.

Diutes ruffled himself to try to maintain his composure. While looking at Treeg's back, he smugly began to speak. "I am sorry to inform you, but your messengers will not reach their destination. Several of my warriors are in pursuit, and they will put a halt to any more subversion."

Treeg made a barely perceptible jerk at hearing Diutes's claim. He was alarmed but didn't know Diutes well enough to gauge whether he was bluffing. He kept a calm veneer, despite his worry for Keerka and the others. "I have had enough of your blather, Diutes. State your business and be on your way. I have more important things to do than waste my time with an insignificant pile of waste such as you."

Diutes quivered with anger but still tried to control himself. "*You* are subject to Pack Ice Command," he said through a clenched beak. "This island now belongs to the Overlord, and you and your *friend* are charged with treason."

Treeg continued to insult Diutes. "Spare me of your inane ramblings, Diutes, and be gone from here. I am—*we are*—not subject to your laws. Or are you too simple minded to realize that. I've told you once before, so you must be."

Diutes had heard all he could take from the Rockhopper. He let out a barely audible growl, which brought his Shadow Warriors from the shoreline and, without warning, he lunged at the offensive Rockhopper, intending to kill him in one strike. With his back still turned to Diutes, Treeg felt and heard the attack coming and quickly hopped out of harm's way, causing Diutes to fall belly first to the rocky ground.

Still standing nearby, Kimmer took the opportunity to stab at the downed commander. But Diutes was quick for a penguin his size. He rolled out of the way of the oncoming attack, and Kimmer took his spot on rocky ground. Diutes was on his feet in an instant and was ready to finish off Kimmer at once.

General Treeg saw what Diutes intended to do and immediately barked out orders to his fellow Rockhoppers. Three Rockhoppers launched themselves at Diutes from the surrounding rocks. Diutes swatted away the first with his powerful flipper, as he would have swatted an annoying insect. The second found its mark and landed feet-first against the side of Diutes's head. The third followed with an equally forceful blow, which knocked the commander slightly off balance. The infuriated and deranged penguin turned on his attackers, leaned down, and drove his elongated beak through the chest of one that had lost its footing after its attack.

Kimmer found his footing on the rocks, and after witnessing Diutes murder one of the Rockhoppers who had saved him, attacked and stabbed his beak deep into Diutes's back. Diutes cried out in surprise and fury more than pain. He spun around as Kimmer withdrew his beak for another attack and struck him with the outside of his lead flipper and the inside of his trailing flipper. The attack was so fast that it sounded like one hit.

Kimmer fell hard against the rocks and was slow to recover his senses. This time, Diutes didn't give him the chance to get up. He stabbed repeatedly at the King in a blind rage with his spike-like beak.

Being much older and slower, there wasn't anything Treeg could do except call on all of the Rockhoppers to attack Diutes.

As Kimmer lay dying, Diutes brought his face before him and stared at him with his freakish red eye. "You're pathetic, you know. Really, you didn't even put up a fight. I'm not even enjoying watching you die. I feel like I did you a favor."

In an instant, as he drew his final breath, Kimmer lunged upward and stabbed his beak into Diutes's red eye. Then he fell back and went to meet the spirits of the Ancients.

Diutes howled in pain and flailed his flippers about wildly, striking at everything within reach. The Rockhoppers ducked under his mad, half-blind assault and gave him quick bites and stabs, further infuriating the commander. From all around, Rockhoppers began to pour out of rocky crags and crevices to join the attack. The Shadow Warriors, though bigger and stronger, were outnumbered five to one and were overrun by the relentless Rockhoppers.

The Rockhoppers leapt at the Shadow Warriors, striking again and again with claws and beaks. They drove the shadows back toward the sea, but the Shadow Warriors pressed back. They stabbed and swung at anything fool enough to get close.

The battle finally reached the edge of the sea, and the Rockhoppers fought harder still. They knocked the warriors off of the rocks and were merciless once they had them down. The remaining Shadow Warriors realized they were beat and tried to break for the safety of the water. When they turned to flee, they were met by the Gentoo, who had answered the call to battle. The Gentoo and Rockhoppers fought side by side to bring down their imposing foes. In the end, only two Shadow Warriors managed to escape.

Meanwhile, Diutes struggled to stay upright under the continuous assault of the Rockhoppers. Treeg heard the victory calls of the others and called to them. He then called off the attack on Diutes and watched him stagger around on a flat, wind-worn rock until he finally collapsed to his stomach.

"You're finished, Diutes. Your warriors have fled or been killed, and very soon you will join them in death," Treeg said, taking the opportunity to taunt the Royal one last time.

Diutes lay on the ground, rasping for air while surveying his surroundings. Every escape route had been blocked. "No," he said. "I am beaten. I beg mercy. I only did what was commanded of me. Please. It was the Overlord. He intends to wipe out or enslave the inferior clans. Let me go, and I will act as a spy. Together, we can bring him down."

Treeg acted as if he were considering Diutes's words. "You are correct, Diutes. All of this *is* because of the Overlord."

Diutes let out a breath in relief, convinced he had talked himself out of death.

"I *will* show you mercy. I will relieve you of your pitiful life," said Treeg. Then he called on the Rockhoppers to finish Diutes.

"No!" Diutes screamed as the penguins descended on him.

After no more than a minute, Diutes's screams faded away, along with his life.

Treeg watched the carnage and, after making certain Diutes was indeed dead, called off the warriors. He studied the mangled remains for a second and then turned to face the others. "Rockhoppers, our messengers are in danger and are in need of our help, as are our allies. All who are able, follow me." General Treeg hopped into the churning sea with his fellow Rockhoppers in tow.

The carcass of Commander Diutes—third son to the Overlord, brother to the Supreme Commander, notorious leader of Forward Command, and murderer of penguins—was left as feed for the scavengers.

CHAPTER 11

Keerka and her remaining companions swam toward the moonlit island looming in the distance. The clouds had broken, which gave them better visibility, but it also left them exposed.

One of the Rockhoppers had doubled back in the hope of getting a fix on their pursuers. "Nothing," said the Rockhopper, surfacing alongside Keerka.

Keerka gathered the Rockhoppers to her. "They're ahead of us. They know where we're headed."

"How do you know? They could be anywhere," one asked.

"I don't *know*, it's just a feeling," she said, keeping an eye on the distant, rocky shoreline as they rode the swells. Their pursuers hadn't been seen in some time, but she knew they were trying to lure them into a false sense of security. "When we get to the rocks, we'll be safe enough. Once we near the shoreline, we'll split up again. Above all else, one of us has to reach the others. Now let's go."

The group sped forward, meeting no opposition. When the sound of the breakers could be heard, they split into two groups. Finally, as they felt the pounding of the nearby surf, the pairs separated, and they swam individually.

Where are they? Keerka wondered. She knew there was no way they had gotten away so easily. Then the attacks came. The jet-black predatory penguins had been waiting in ambush beneath the waves, and once they spotted their quarry, they launched themselves straight up at the Rockhoppers.

Out of the corner of her eye, Keerka saw one of her companions as he was lifted out of the water, firmly impaled on the beak of a Shadow Warrior. The attacking penguin struck with such force that its momentum carried it two meters above the surface of the water before it crashed back into the sea. A startled cry from the opposite direction let Keerka know that another Rockhopper had met a similar fate.

Keerka immediately began zigzagging to avoid the attackers. She banked hard to her left just as a shadow rocketed from the sea, narrowly missing her. She saw the rocks glistening in the moonlight ahead, took advantage of the Shadow Warrior's failed attack, and rode the waves in, landing hard on the shore. She quickly pressed her body against the rocks to avoid being sucked back into the water from the retreating waves.

Hopping from rock to rock, she looked back and saw that two Shadow Warriors had made it to land. She scrambled higher as another wave crashed ashore. When the wave receded, only one of her pursuers remained.

Keerka climbed higher and out of the wave's splash zone. Her legs became too tired to carry her, and she had to stop. She watched as the much larger penguin was repeatedly hammered by the pounding surf and struggled to climb the rocks. When the next wave came, Keerka saw the last Rockhopper ride it in and deposit himself firmly on the rocks. The two made eye contact immediately, and Keerka motioned toward the struggling Shadow Warrior, not a meter away from her comrade.

Two Shadow Warriors, attempting to emulate the Rockhoppers, rode the next wave ashore. The Rockhopper braced for impact. When the sea foam cleared, he saw that one of the two warriors had gone in headfirst, dying instantly. While the two shadows looked at their dead companion, the Rockhopper took advantage of the distraction and hopped toward the larger rocks and safety.

The warriors were only feigning distraction and, when the little Rockhopper took his first hop, they quickly stepped in front of him, blocking his path. The Rockhopper stopped at once, and at hearing another wave coming in, ducked and braced himself as it crashed. The wave knocked the shadows off balance. That was all the opportunity the Rockhopper needed, and he quickly bounded up to the higher rocks.

While the Rockhopper made his ascent, a larger wave slammed against the rocks and dragged the unfortunate penguin back down. The two Shadow Warriors stood in the rising tide and spotted their quarry, struggling to right itself in a tide pool. The Rockhopper paddled his flippers furiously after spotting his would-be killers. The warriors wasted no time, attacking the Rockhopper at once.

Keerka stifled a scream. She could only watch from her perch as her friend made his last splash.

The next wave came, and when the spray dispersed, the body of the Rockhopper was gone. The two Shadow Warriors stood with water dripping from their bodies, staring up at Keerka. One warrior indicated an easier climb. Keerka saw this and turned to flee.

Keerka scampered from rock to rock until she came to open ground. In the distance, she saw the faint glow of a light from a human dwelling. With the Shadow Warriors behind her and the humans in front, she decided to make a break toward the human shelter. She hoped her persistent trackers would be reluctant to follow. As she began to traverse the 200-meter space between her and the dwelling, she realized she was wrong to hope. She could hear the familiar clicking of the Royal Emperor language and turned to steal a glance. They were much closer than she had expected. She firmed her beak and ran and hopped as fast as she could, ignoring her exhaustion.

The human shelter was nestled near a low hillside and loomed like a beacon in front of Keerka. She had crossed most of the expanse and was closing in on the building when she heard the breathing and footfalls of the warriors behind her. One of the pursuers reached out with its flipper and gave her a weak slap in an effort to knock her off balance, but she managed to keep her footing. She drew closer to the shelter and prepared to launch herself against a window when a hard hit from behind knocked her off her feet.

Keerka lay on the ground and looked up to find her tormentors standing over her. The Rockhopper and the two Royal Emperors were panting from the exhausting pursuit in the cold night air. The warriors said nothing to her when one reared its head back to strike the fatal blow. No longer having the strength to fight or escape, Keerka braced for death and hoped it would be quick. A bright light illuminated the three of them.

The Shadow Warriors were momentarily disoriented and blinded. They froze in the spotlight. The distinctive sound of two gunshots rang out and Keerka opened her eyes in time to see the huge penguins drop dead beside her. Until that moment, she had never been happy to hear the sound of human guns.

The light quickly shifted to highlight another Shadow Warrior, twenty meters away, attempting to escape. Three more shots erupted, and the warrior fell dead. The light briefly scanned the horizon and then returned to Keerka. Still too exhausted to move, she awaited to be sent to the spirits as the crunch of heavy boots approached her.

"Is it dead?" one human asked another.

"Nah, it's still breathing," the other answered.

"Kill it, then," the first one said.

Keerka's eyes widened; she didn't understand much human speak, but she knew enough to get the gist of what was said.

After a few moments, the human with the gun spoke. "I don't think we should. These others were trying to kill this one. Someone should know about this."

"That may be true, but our orders are to exterminate all penguins we encounter."

"I don't need to be reminded of our orders, but this might be of interest.

Call Colonel Jenson and inform him we have a *prisoner*," the man said, sounding doubtful.

Keerka looked on and wondered why she hadn't been killed yet. She was horrified when the human bent over and picked her up. She could do nothing about it; her strength had left her and was nearly in shock from the stress of being hunted down by the Shadow Warriors. She let out a pathetic, weak call for help, and the man clasped his hand around her beak. As she was carried away, she looked at the moon overhead and wondered if Nok would ever know her fate.

CHAPTER 12

Night had fallen on the forces of the former Penguin Defense Alliance, now known as the Alliance of Independent Colonies, as they waited in the waters of the Pacific to come to the assistance of the Humboldt penguins. The journey to the Chilean coast had been remarkably uneventful. Most sea vessels remained in dock after the rumors of marauding penguins or other horrors. Those crews that tried to leave were turned back by their governments. The only ships the AIC encountered were a battle group of southward-bound U.S. Navy warships, which the penguins immediately recognized as a threat and avoided.

"Have the scouts returned yet, Commander?" Macaroni penguin General Natoo asked Commander Lavour.

"Nothing yet," Lavour replied. "Any sign of Diutes?"

"No, sir."

"He should've been here by now. Something's not right," Lavour said while staring at the night sky. While he didn't mind that Diutes hadn't shown up yet, he still was unsure about what to do next. He had to admit, however, that he did hope that some sort of tragedy had befallen Diutes.

"I'll tell you what's not right—that General Leepoh, that's what," Natoo said.

Lavour laughed. "What, besides the obvious, makes you say that?"

Leepoh usually made one of two impressions on those he met: that he was several steps down the path to insanity or that he had suffered a severe head trauma at some point in his life. Either would lead one to dismiss him, but that would be a mistake of tremendous proportions.

"While we should be planning our attack, he's prattling off about the effects these Pacific fish are having on his digestive system," Natoo said, almost angrily.

"You'll get used to him." Natoo opened his beak to reply, but Lavour stopped him. "Do not underestimate him. He may appear to be a bit *flippy*, but let me assure you he is a great warrior and a loyal friend."

Leepoh, as if he had heard his name spoken, popped his head out of the water directly in front of them. "Still waiting on the scouts, I see," he said.

"Yes, and on Diutes," answered Natoo.

"Bah, we don't need Diutes. We're better off without his negative influence. What we *need* is to get into position in anticipation of the returning scouts."

"For once he makes sense," Natoo quipped.

Leepoh did a double take at Natoo's remark.

"I agree," said Lavour.

Leepoh looked at Lavour. "With him or me?" he asked.

Lavour looked at Leepoh and couldn't help himself. "Both."

Colonel Nok floated over to join in the conversation, but before he had a chance to start in on Leepoh, Lavour began to issue orders. "Colonel, inform Commander Kiley that we will move on the human villages as soon as we hear from the scouts and when we know that the Humboldts are a safe distance from the fighting."

"Commander, are you sure the Humboldts shouldn't join in the assault? It might give them some satisfaction to see their tormentors brought down," Nok suggested.

"Whether they want to or not doesn't matter, Colonel. Their numbers are too low to risk any loss of life. They are already on the edge of extinction, and that's why we're here—to protect them."

"That's true," Nok agreed. "I just—"

Two of the seven scouts returned, interrupting the colonel. "Commander Lavour, sir," a panicked and out-of-breath Gentoo scout said.

"What is it?" asked Lavour as he looked at Leepoh, who knew immediately to put the penguins on alert.

"Squid, sir," the scout said, trying to convey his message while catching his breath.

"Squid?" asked Leepoh, perking up. "Din-ner time," he said, drawing out the words in exaggerated excitement.

"No!" the scout said quickly. "You don't understand. They're huge, giant squid."

"Then there's more to eat," Leepoh said slowly, as if talking to a fledgling.

"No, General Leepoh, *they* ate the other scouts."

All that could be heard was the sound of the sea as the leaders tried to make sense of what had been said.

"Is this true?" Nok finally asked the other surviving scout, a Chinstrap, who had been silent. He remained silent and only nodded.

"All right, calm yourselves and tell us what happened," Leepoh told the two in a surprisingly authoritarian manner.

The Gentoo took a breath and began to recount the events. "We had just made contact with the Humboldts and explained to them our plans and the circumstances of why we're here. After we concluded, it was already past nightfall, and we prepared to leave. The Humboldts became severely agitated and warned us that we should wait."

"Wait for what?" asked Nok.

"Until morning, sir," the Gentoo answered on the verge of impatience. "Apparently the humans *hunt* the squid at night, when they rise to the surface to feed."

This drew concerned looks from the others, as they looked at the night sky and began to feel suddenly vulnerable.

"We were on a schedule and, against the advice of the Humboldt leader, we decided to leave," the Gentoo continued. "As we departed, we heard the shouts of men and knew we had been spotted. We quickly decided it was best that they should not reach the shore. According to Macün, the Humboldt leader, word of the penguin attacks has reached here, and it has made life difficult for them."

"It's just as I thought," Lavour exclaimed. "Our attacks, or should I say *the Overlord's* plan, has had the opposite effect of what was intended. This could get much worse." He stopped to consider the possible future in store for the penguins and then realized he had interrupted the Gentoo scout. "I'm sorry, go on."

"There were several boats, but we attacked anyway, hoping to knock them into the water. As we attacked, we realized what their catch was and that they were not in fear of us, but the squid. The squid were huge, some as big as a human." The scout paused as if to gather his thoughts. "Once the humans were in the water and blood was spilled, the squid went into a killing frenzy and lashed out at everything they could wrap their tentacles around—including each other. Some of the squids had beaks that were larger than our heads. Tenoit and I were fortunate to have escaped," he said, indicating the Chinstrap who barely acknowledged he had just been spoken about.

"I've heard rumors of these beasts," General Natoo said. "Some of the Pacific penguins I've met spoke of them. They say the humans called them *Red Devils*. I dismissed their stories as wild tales. Apparently they're not."

"What do you propose we do?" asked Leepoh. "Should we wait to move until morning?"

"No," Commander Lavour said quickly. "We will move along the shoreline."

"With the full moon, we may be spotted," Natoo said.

"It's a chance we'll have to take," Lavour said, catching Tenoit's eye in the moonlight. "Tenoit," he said.

The Chinstrap's head dipped below the surface and didn't come back up.

"Tenoit!" the Gentoo scout called out and nudged him with his beak.

The Chinstrap's body rolled over, exposing his underside.

"He's dead," somebody cried—Lavour wasn't sure who. On closer inspection, a large wound was seen on his underside, which obviously came from a Humboldt squid or *Red Devil*. At once, Lavour noticed the water was full of blood.

"How did he make it back with such an injury?" Natoo asked.

Immediately an alarm went off in Lavour's head. "Everyone to the shallows—now!" he ordered.

As the orders were being announced, a penguin screamed in alarm.

"To the shore!" Natoo reiterated, realizing their predicament, and the water began to churn from the beats of thousands of penguin flippers.

Along with the others, Lavour followed General Natoo.

"This is ridiculous," Leepoh said to Nok as they porpoised through the water. "We should be eating these things, not swimming from them."

"In case you haven't noticed, they are eating us," Nok replied.

"Enough talk—swim," Lavour told them as he came alongside the chatty pair.

"Yes, sir," said Leepoh in mock indignation. As he looked to his left, he saw Lavour's head surface as if to porpoise, then stop suddenly and disappear below, his eyes wide in horror and surprise. "Lavour," he yelled out and came to a stop on the surface.

Nok heard the call and swam to Leepoh's side. "What is it?"

"They got Lavour," Leepoh said in a panic. "Rally the others. We're going after him."

Without any hesitation, Colonel Nok bleated out an alarm, and immediately the fleeing penguins swooped back to Nok, knowing what to do. General Leepoh was already well ahead of the rest as they dove below in search of their commander.

Lavour struggled as hard as he could against his assailant, but the powerful tentacles of the Red Devil held him tight. Each sucker on the squid's eight arms were ringed with hook shaped teeth, and those toothy appendages pulled Lavour ever closer to the squid's deadly, sharp, beaked mouth. The six-foot-long squid flashed different colors in frustration as it attempted to pull in its prey to deliver its lethal bite.

Lavour was having none of it and, ignoring the pain of hundreds of piercing teeth, swam hard in the opposite direction. He beat his wings hard but still he felt himself being pulled lower and lower by the much larger creature. A penguin can hold its breath for fifteen to twenty minutes during a dive. Lavour had not had a chance to take a full gulp of air when he surfaced, and now, as he continued to struggle, he was reaching the limits of his breath.

He could nearly feel the clicking of the monster's beak against his webbed feet, and his strength began to ebb. He looked to the surface for any sign of hope and spotted the form of a penguin silhouetted against the moonlit surface. He recognized it right away as a Gentoo and knew it had to be Leepoh. On seeing his friend, Lavour found his last bit of strength and beat his tired wings harder to stave off certain death.

Leepoh flew by Lavour in a flash and drove his beak hard into Lavour's attacker. The squid was undaunted and held tight to its potential meal.

Lavour risked reaching back and taking a nip at the beast's rubbery tentacle, but that only caused him to lose distance between him and the beaked maw. With its beak now only centimeters away, the squid clicked angrily, trying to deliver a fatal bite.

Leepoh recovered from his headlong attack, swam alongside the Red Devil, and spotted its enormous eye. He immediately jabbed his beak at the creature and repeatedly stabbed at its eye, trying to get it to loosen its grip on Lavour. The squid flashed patterned colors violently and let out jets of ink in retaliation, causing the penguins to lose sight of each other.

Enveloped in a cloud of ink and feeling his lungs burn for air, Lavour lost sight of the moonlight above him. He wasn't sure if it was from the lack of oxygen, the squid's ink, or the onset of death playing tricks on his eyes, but he saw thousands of swirling dark images spiraling their way toward him. Just as he was about to accept his fate, he realized what he was seeing: penguins, thousands of them, led by Colonel Nok, coming to his and General Leepoh's aid. The penguins of the AIC made quick work of dismembering the tentacled monstrosity and then quickly ushered Lavour to the surface. He choked and gasped for air and was escorted and assisted to shore by Colonel Nok and General Natoo.

"Thank you," Lavour said breathlessly, rolling onto his back on the sandy shore.

Nok only nodded, and Natoo went about gathering his troops. After a few minutes of silence, Nok looked down at Lavour. "Are you all right?"

After Lavour took inventory of his several puncture wounds, his mind wandered off to his lost family, and he thought of how close he had come to joining them. "I'll live," he said distantly, "thanks to you and Leepoh." It was then that he realized Leepoh was nowhere to be seen and that the last time he had seen him was during the attack. "Where's Leepoh?" he asked in concern.

Coming to the same realization, Nok spun around in a panic. He looked back at Lavour, and just as he was ready to dive into surf to go in search of Leepoh, he saw him casually strolling out of the low waves. "Leepoh," he said with tremendous relief. "Where'd you go? I was just—"

"What? I couldn't let all of that good squid go to waste," Leepoh said as if the thought was abominable.

"You ate it?" Lavour asked in disbelief as he propped himself up.

"Not *all* of it. Just the tasty bits and pieces. Do you want some? I can go and grab you a piece." Leepoh made a motion as if he were going to go back into the water.

"I'm beginning to think that rescuing me was only a byproduct of your hunger," Lavour said jokingly.

"Some appreciation," said Leepoh, feigning hurt.

"Thank you, Leepoh," Lavour told him in all seriousness.

"Bah! You would've done the same for me—right?"

"Depends on whether I would get a meal out of it," Lavour said with a nudge to Nok.

Leepoh snapped his head toward the Chinstrap in surprise. "Hah!" he bleated, and then he turned to Colonel Nok. "Send messengers to the Humboldts. Tell them we will be delayed by one day. Our commander has been injured, and we will not go forward without him. And tell the messengers to hug the shoreline. We don't need any more excitement tonight."

CHAPTER 13

Nok paced around the beach, listening to the leaders of the Alliance debate their next move. He had a feeling of wrongness gnawing at his gut ever since passing through the Strait of Magellan. Whatever the cause, he kept his misgivings to himself. He stopped for a moment to her what the increasingly brash King penguin, Kiley had to say.

"We should attack before dawn," Commander Kiley announced to the penguin leaders.

"This is a defensive action to protect the Humboldts from the humans," Commander Lavour corrected Kiley. "We will not partake in the offenses directed by the Overlord. We are here to give the humans pause, should they think to encroach upon the Humboldts any further."

"You said only yesterday, Commander, that this would be an attack," Kiley said, taking the opportunity to argue.

"True. But after hearing of the treatment of penguins by the humans in retaliation for other attacks, it was decided that this would be the best course of action. We can't risk further detriment to our kind."

Kiley turned away in a huff. "This is why there shouldn't be two commanders. Especially if one is a Chinstrap. Kings have the experience and knowledge of how to lead and get things done. Chinstraps are...too idealistic."

Lavour took a breath and turned the opposite direction to ease his irritation. Regaining his composure, he turned back to the group. "Regardless of how you feel about my kind, or me in particular, I ask that you have patience, Commander Kiley. This will work. Remember, we exist for the defense of our kind. We are not following the Overlord's edicts any longer, and we will not provoke the humans into escalating this war."

Nok watched the two commanders debate the directive. Both truly wanted what was best for all penguins, but Kiley, being more military minded, didn't see eye-to-eye with Lavour's, as Kiley described it, disastrous passivity. Suddenly longing for home, Nok walked away from the group and stared at the moon.

Nok's thoughts drifted to Keerka, as they often did now. She had admired him from a distance for some time, but the ever-dutiful Nok was oblivious to it. They had talked several times in the past, but he never took notice. Finally, after Treeg's suggestion, Nok had taken the time, and the two found each other. Nok had opened his eyes, and they had quickly made a pair pledge, the equivalent to life mates.

He watched the clouds drift in front of the winter moon and his ill-feelings turned to dread and panic. The usually steadfast Nok instantly became nervous and antsy. He began to pace along the foreign shore more vigorously, unsure as to what had increased his anxiety.

Leepoh looked away from the conversation which he, for once, was a silent observer in, and noticed his friend's nervous demeanor. He went to him without hesitation. "What's got your crest in a knot?" he asked in concern.

"Something's not right," Nok answered, without giving it a second thought and with a hint of fear in his voice.

Leepoh stared at him for a long while, not saying a word. He remembered when his little one had been taken by the humans. He'd felt something was wrong but dismissed it, until it was too late. "We'll leave in the morning—when it's safe."

"Where to? I don't even know what it is that's bothering me." Nok kicked at the sand.

"What do you think it is?"

Nok looked back to the moon. Thoughts of home crossed his mind. "Home. Something has happened. Or…. I don't know. Maybe all of this fighting is making me paranoid."

"Do you believe that? That you're just stressed?" Leepoh asked, keeping his tone serious.

Nok hesitated. He didn't want to be branded a coward, but the feelings were too strong. "No. I have to go. I have to find out if something's wrong back home."

"Then we'll go," Leepoh said, slapping Nok on the back.

"What about the others? And Lavour?"

"I'll talk to him. Besides that, they won't miss two penguins out of thousands," Leepoh reassured him. "He knows you well enough by now to know you don't act like a frightened chick for no reason."

"What if I'm wrong? What if I—"

"What if you're right?" Leepoh interrupted.

The two penguins looked at each other. They had known one another for only a short time, but they felt like brothers, and they knew there was nothing one wouldn't do for the other.

"Commander Lavour," Leepoh called out, interrupting Lavour's cyclical debate with Kiley.

Lavour gladly, if not overeagerly, excused himself. "That Commander Kiley," he said, not finishing the statement and instead leaving it open to let Leepoh fill the rest. He looked at Nok, then back to Leepoh, and concern crossed his face. "What?"

"Colonel Nok has a bad feeling about something," Leepoh plainly said without embarrassment.

Lavour stared at his new friends then at the other commanders. He stepped closer to Nok. "Home?" he asked.

"I don't know. Maybe I'm just jittery about another potential battle tomorrow," Nok said, trying to dismiss the feeling.

Lavour nodded, keeping his eyes on Nok. "All right, then, let me meet with the Humboldts. I'll leave Commander Kiley in full command, and we'll take to the sea in less than three hours."

"But, sir, you're injured and—" Nok began to protest.

"It's nothing," Lavour reassured him. "And Kiley has been a commander far longer than I have."

Nok looked away, hoping the feeling would go away, but he knew it wouldn't. "I don't want to be the cause of any problems," he said, turning back to Lavour.

"Nok," Lavour said to cut off further protest. "We're going back to RHC 23—you, me, and that Gentoo."

Leepoh looked as if he was about to say something inappropriate.

"Oh yeah," Lavour added, cutting off Leepoh's retort. "We'll also be bringing a quarter million friends."

"Are you sure about that, Commander?" asked Leepoh, genuinely surprised.

"Yes, I'm sure, General Leepoh. Diutes should've been here days ago. There was something in his demeanor that didn't seem—well, he seemed as if he had an ulterior motive, something sinister. I disregarded it as being his nature, but with what Nok is feeling—that something isn't *right*—I think we should be sure. I felt something similar when my family, when my colony was killed."

"From what I know of Diutes, I know he can't be trusted," Leepoh said in his peculiar way.

"There was something more though," Lavour said with his voice trailing away. He looked toward the ocean; something had caught his attention.

Leepoh and Nok followed his gaze.

With the first tendrils of daylight reaching from the eastern sky, they spotted several hundred penguins porpoising through the water from the north.

"Are those our scouts?" Lavour asked.

"None were supposed to be out," replied Leepoh. "Maybe Diutes has finally arrived."

"Why would he be coming from the north and not the south?" asked Nok.

They walked back to Kiley and the others who were watching as well. "Do we know who they are yet?" Lavour asked Kiley.

"We've confirmed that they're Humboldts, but we don't know why they are coming *here* and not waiting for us," Kiley answered.

"This can't be good," General Natoo said with worry in his voice.

"I agree," said Lavour. "All penguins, full alert!"

On Lavour's command, thousands of penguins went to the water's edge, and a thousand others went to the waves to intercept the oncoming penguins.

"Why didn't our scouts notify us?" Commander Kiley asked no one in particular, and no one in particular felt obliged to answer.

Just beyond the waves, the group of Humboldts turned toward the shore, and they were immediately intercepted by the penguin picket. After a brief discussion, the Humboldts were allowed to pass.

After being directed where to go, two of the Humboldts walked up to Lavour and Kiley. "Commanders Lavour and Kiley," one said, snapping a high beak salute. "I am Captain Pasillas, and this is Lieutenant Trebossas," he said, indicating the other.

"What's going on? I thought you were given specific instructions to wait for us?" Kiley said rather sternly, drawing a disapproving look from Lavour.

"Yes, sir, we were. But the humans came to our nests before dawn. They brought fire and weapons." Captain Pasillas paused. He cleared his throat as if the words were stuck. "They began to kill us. They went mad, wild— kicking, stomping, burning, and shooting all they saw."

The penguin leaders were either too stunned or too angry to respond.

"Some of us fought back. We killed two of them, but that only provoked them further. We had no choice but to flee with our lives," Pasillas said, lowering his head. "We are not cowards. There were too many, and we were too few."

"You did the right thing, Captain," Lavour reassured him. "Is this group all that survived?"

"No, there are others, but they chose not to come. They want nothing to do with fighting and nothing more to do with the PDA. Most blame the Overlord's aggressiveness for this attack on our lives. They say it was a reprisal, revenge, and that the humans did it out of fear and hate."

"How many are there, and where did they go?" Kiley asked with a little less abrasiveness.

"The last we heard, they were headed north to warn the remaining colonies and then to the Galapagos to warn the penguins there." Pasillas stopped talking and looked at the rising sun. "I fear this is the end of our kind. There are too few of us now. Too many were killed. And the humans will not leave us in peace."

Lavour stared at Pasillas, not knowing what he could say to comfort someone who knew that his whole species might soon be extinct. He looked to Leepoh and Nok, and they too stood silent. As he often did, he thought back to his lost family and colony and then to Pack Ice Command. He thought of Supreme Commander Liutites, and in that instant, his nearly forgotten ember of hatred burst into a small flame.

The Overlord, Liutites, and most likely Diutes, since he never arrived, were back at PIC, safe from death and destruction. The thought made Lavour fume. *Why are there no Royal Emperors on the front? They're the ones who were supposedly bred for this sort of thing. Why aren't they fighting?* Lavour thought back to the day his family was murdered by the humans. His thoughts were racing, but he let them go as they linked from one to another.

In his mind's eye, Lavour remembered his family's bodies and Trevot's lying next to them. *Why do I keep seeing them?* he asked himself. *The bodies.* His eyes widened in a horrifying revelation. He had nearly made the connection back in the Falklands but had dismissed it. But now he knew it was true. The world spun around him until he finally found an anchor for his mind. "General Leepoh," he snapped.

"Yes, sir," Leepoh said with concern. It was obvious his commander was disturbed by something.

"Something stinks."

"Yes, sir, sorry, sir. It's the squid."

"No, no, no," Lavour said, not really listening to the Gentoo. "Captain Pasillas, Lieutenant Trebossas, hold your heads high. Be proud; you did the best you could. Your kind is not dead, not yet, and we will find you another home."

"Yes, sir," Pasillas said, suddenly invigorated by Lavour's energy.

Kiley, Natoo, Leepoh, and Nok all looked at one another; each carrying a look of confusion by Lavour's sudden burst of anxiety.

"The bodies of my family, Leepoh," Lavour said, his mind still racing. "Their wounds didn't look like gunshots. They were too small. I've seen enough of them now to know. They looked more like stab wounds from a—" he paused, unsure as to how his assertion would be received "—a beak or even a spear." Lavour finished his accusation with a touch of malevolence that none had ever heard from him before.

Leepoh, Nok, and the others took a minute to digest the implication of Lavour's suggestion, but none refuted the accusation.

"You're correct, Commander Lavour," said Leepoh. "Something does indeed stink. And it smells Imperial."

"Commander Kiley," Lavour said with a clenched beak.

"Yes, Commander Lavour," he said firmly, not agreeing or disagreeing with Lavour.

"Take the second, fifth, eighth, and ninth corps to the Humboldts nesting grounds and search for survivors. If the opportunity presents itself, attack the humans. But I do not want a full-on invasion-style attack like in the Falklands," Lavour said with emphasis. "Harry them at nightfall. Give them pause should they think to try another attack. Leave for PIC before dawn tomorrow, and take the western coast around the cape. The rest of us will leave immediately. We will rendezvous in three weeks, west of PIC, near Eltanin Bay."

"Yes, sir," Kiley said smartly, addressing him as sir for the first time.

"Commander." Lavour stopped Kiley before he left to carry out his orders. "Are you ready for this? If my suspicions prove to be correct, it will mean full-out rebellion against the Royals."

"If your suspicions are correct, and I have no reason to doubt you, then the Overlord and his ilk *must* be removed from power."

"Very well. I'll see you in three weeks, and may the spirits of the Ancients be with us." Lavour turned away quickly. "Colonel Nok."

"Yes, sir," Nok said, snapping a crisp salute.

"We will cut through the straits once more, regroup on RHC 23, and move toward PIC from there. Does that agree with you, Colonel Nok?"

"Yes, sir," Nok said enthusiastically.

"Captain Pasillas," Lavour said, turning to the Humboldt. "I am truly sorry for your loss. I have no other words—"

"Commander Lavour," the captain interrupted. "Perhaps it was inevitable. Year by year the humans have taken a little more. This was ushered in a little sooner, that's all."

Lavour stared at Pasillas, admiring his calm at facing the end of his kind. "Stay with Commander Kiley if you like. You are not subject to *anyone's* rule."

"Yes, sir," he said, looking away to Kiley, who was standing waist deep in the surf, directing his troops.

Lavour turned to leave but stopped. "I have heard of a place, far to the north—a paradise, they say. Maybe you could go there, if it exists."

"I have heard of it as well. I have heard it is beyond a place the humans call the Bering Sea."

"Then it's real?" Lavour asked in surprise.

"Perhaps—perhaps not—and perhaps I will see you there one day," Pasillas told him as he excused himself and walked away.

"Perhaps," Lavour said quietly as he watched the Humboldt amble away. *But not anytime soon*, he said to himself. "General Leepoh, General Natoo, Colonel Nok," Lavour called out with dramatic flair. "Let's go."

The commanders nodded their approval and began to call out orders to the various divisions, and thousands of penguins headed back south, none of them, including Lavour, fully knowing what to expect.

CHAPTER 14

"Randy," Gina said, startled out of her sleep.

"Sshh," Randy whispered back to her. "Don't turn on the lights."

"What is it?" she asked with worry. While fumbling for her boots, she heard a steady tapping noise.

The winter solstice had come and gone with no sign of the King Colonel Kimmer. Several days after Kimmer failed to appear, Meuseaux told his companions he had given up hope of his return and instead hoped that the King had not betrayed them, or worse. As a precaution, Randy and Gina decided to keep the lights off, or to a minimum, in an effort to avoid attracting unwanted attention. It was the middle of the Antarctic winter and with it came twenty-four hours of darkness, which made a difficult situation even more so. The bad part of not attracting unwanted attention was that they couldn't attract the wanted kind.

"It's a penguin," Meuseaux said from somewhere in the darkness.

"What does it want?" Gina asked softly.

"I do not know. It hasn't said anything."

After a few minutes of tense silence, the group heard a barely audible warble of a Chinstrap calling through the incessant wind. Randy heard Gina make ready with her pistol.

"Corporal Meuseaux," the penguin outside called in the Chinstrap language.

Surprised at hearing his name and even more surprised by the voice that called it, Meuseaux was unsure of what he should do. "Let him in," he said after a minute of thinking.

"Are you sure about this?" Randy asked, sounding more than a little doubtful.

Meuseaux hesitated then answered, "Yes."

"Get ready, Gina." Then a thought occurred to him. "When I open the door, turn on the lights. It'll take a second for its eyes to adjust and that'll give us an advantage—just in case."

"What about my eyes adjusting? I'm holding the gun you know," Gina queried.

"Look at your flashlight first."

"Okay, boy genius, and if there's more than one?" said Gina, who couldn't help but razz him.

"Then, it's been nice knowing you? Besides, our little friend would know. Right Meuseaux?" Randy asked, shining his light on the Chinstrap.

Meuseaux gave the equivalent of a shrug.

"That's not very reassuring. And I thought you said you'd know if a bunch were out there."

"If I cannot hear something; it does not always mean something is not there."

"Great. And I thought we had a watch penguin protecting us."

"Are you ready?" Gina asked.

"I'm ready," he said after going to the door. He pushed aside the blockade and jerked open the door. "Now!" he yelled.

Gina turned on the lights, and a lone Chinstrap penguin cautiously walked in from the cold as the fluorescent lights flickered to life.

"Blinding," said Gina, looking at the ceiling as the last light hummed to life then went dim.

Randy shot her a look, took a quick glance outside, and slammed the door shut.

"Corporal Meuseaux," the newcomer said. "I had my doubts, but I am glad to see that you have survived."

Meuseaux looked at the other for a second then gave him the Chinstrap friendship gesture by rapidly flapping his flippers. "Captain Mevoule, what are you doing *here*?"

"I was sent by the Resistance Council, the penguins who saw to your escape."

Meuseaux didn't respond right away. He didn't fully trust them, especially with Mearna being a part of it.

"Things have changed, Meuseaux," Mevoule told him as he looked at the humans and acknowledged them with a nod.

Gina and Randy, after realizing the newcomer wasn't a threat, stepped away.

"Colonel Kimmer will not return," Mevoule said somberly.

"By his choice or not?" asked Meuseaux, knowing the answer and what it meant.

"It was not his choice. He was killed by Diutes."

Once again, Meuseaux grew silent. He looked at Gina and Randy and then back to Mevoule, knowing there was more.

"The Rockhoppers have risen up against the Overlord and have killed Diutes and his warriors," Mevoule continued.

"This is good," Meuseaux said. He thought further and said, "No, this is *great*." He spoke with zeal, excited at the prospect of the Overlord's third in command being dead. "Has anyone contacted Lieutenant-General Lavour?"

"It's now *Commander* Lavour. And as far as I know, he hasn't been informed about that or about the attack on our colony. Kimmer did tell you who was responsible, didn't he?" Mevoule asked carefully in case Meuseaux didn't know.

"Yes, Kimmer informed me," Meuseaux answered with contempt in his voice.

"Very soon, Liutites is going to attempt to depose the Overlord and take his place as the ruler of the PDA."

Meuseaux took the time to ponder the possible outcomes of this usurping by the Supreme Commander. "If Liutites supplants the Overlord . . ." he started, his eyes wide.

"He is even more insane than the Overlord. Fear of Antaean is the only thing that has kept him in check this long," Mevoule said, finishing Meuseaux's thoughts.

"What is being done?"

"Mearna will try to stall Liutites as long—"

"I don't trust Mearna," Meuseaux said almost angrily.

"I know, but she and the rest of the council are our only allies in PIC."

Meuseaux began to pace the floor. Things were bad under Antaean and few knew just how bad, but if Liutites took control, the Royals would become even more brazen in their brutal treatment of others. "What can I do?" he asked, not willing to let the course of events unfold without taking action.

"Can you swim?" Mevoule asked, looking at Meuseaux's flipper.

"I am not fully healed, but it is getting stronger."

"We have to find Lavour. He has the hearts of the penguins. Only with his leadership can we make a stand."

"And what of my friends and Pín?" asked Meuseaux, looking at Randy and Gina.

"If the Blue can be trusted, it can come with us."

"He trusts me. But that doesn't answer my question. I am indebted to these humans. They saved my life."

"They will be safe. More and more human machines are arriving by the day, even in the darkness. They will be found before long."

"Then we must go. We'll bring Pín with us." Meuseaux excused himself and told the Blue penguin what they were about to do. After reassuring

Pín, he looked to Randy and Gina, who had already guessed what he was going to tell them, and slowly waddled over to them.

CHAPTER 15

"Sergeant," the Overlord barked out, which compelled an elite guard to step forward at full attention. "See to it that the body of this traitor is put with the corpse of the other. It appears as if I will be amassing quite a collection."

"Yes, my lord," the guard answered dutifully, signaling for two other guards to assist in the removal K'K'Ru-ki's body.

As the guards dragged away the Emperor's remains, Supreme Commander Liutites entered the chamber. He paused briefly to look over the dead penguin and then at the sergeant. Then he turned his attention to the Overlord. "My lord, our forces have reached the encampment where the human escapees appear to be hiding."

"And what of the Chinstraps?" the Overlord asked, ignoring Liutites's breech of etiquette not waiting for the Overlord to address him before speaking.

"They are believed to be there. Captain Mevoule, the Chinstrap, was seen entering the structure as well."

"I want the humans dead and the Chinstraps brought here alive. Are your field officers clear on that, Supreme Commander?" Antaean said in his now perpetually condescending tone.

"We will have them back here before long, my lord," Liutites said, sounding as if he were bored with the conversation.

"For your sake, I hope you are correct in assuming that," the Overlord told him with smugness that made Liutites want to kill him then and there. Antaean's eyes shifted slightly, almost imperceptibly, toward his elite guards, who shifted to attention.

This didn't escape Liutites's notice, and while he wanted nothing more than to kill the Overlord where he stood, he took satisfaction in knowing that his father was being cautious in his actions, almost nervous. Liutites held his gaze for a few moments until the Overlord began to speak again.

"More human sea vessels are arriving daily, Supreme Commander. Our few brief skirmishes with the humans have been one-sided in their favor. What do you propose to do about this?"

"Talus and his band of miscreants will never be able to hold Forward Command One. They are loyal only to themselves. Plus, the bulk of the PDA has gone rogue and the Rockhoppers have turned against us. We have limitations, my lord," Liutites said reluctantly, knowing he was inviting more insults on his ability to lead.

"Diutes was an idiot. To be killed by such a lesser clan as the Rockhoppers is a disgrace. He deserved to die." Antaean obviously had no love for his third son.

"You forget that Rockhoppers also killed a platoon of Shadow Warriors," Liutites said, more to incite the Overlord than for any other reason.

"I did not forget, Commander," the Overlord snapped.

Liutites had accomplished his purpose and his eyes showed a gleam of satisfaction.

"The Rockhoppers had the advantage in numbers and terrain. That's all," the Overlord continued in a near rant. "We have an entire division of elite warriors coming ashore soon. Then we will deal with the Rockhoppers. But first, I would like a proposal on dealing with the increasing number of human forces that continue to arrive on our homeland."

Liutites stared at the Overlord for a long while. It was the Overlord's brilliant idea to send nearly the entire PDA on a crusade against the humans.

Diutes was dead. A rogue Chinstrap, with his own agenda, had assumed control of the alliance. There was no way to know where the humans were or what they were doing. There was a Rockhopper insurrection. With all of this, the Overlord had the gall to ask him what he proposed to do about the humans! *I should just kill him now,* Liutites thought. But he knew that, to make certain of his victory, he still needed the forces Mearna had promised him. *You'll be dead in soon, my father.*

"We still have the first through fifth armies available to us, plus two full divisions of elite warriors at the ready," Liutites informed him.

"Yes, with those numbers, we should have enough to drive most of them back from their inland incursions," the Overlord said, sounding unusually hopeful. "Perhaps I should send you below to seek out Lord Saeson for his assistance."

"Lord Saeson is a pacifist and only cares for the abominations you created. It's best that he remains locked far below PIC." Liutites was no fool. He knew if he sought the aid of Saeson, the caretaker of the damned, and if Saeson's brother, Aperion, still lived, he would be killed before he got his first word out. *Good try, father.* "Seeking alliances with your enemies aside, may I suggest that we send the Adélies, supported by a battalion of elite warriors?" *Elite warriors loyal to you.* "The Adélies' loyalty is without question." *That should weaken his defenses significantly.*

"Yes," the Overlord hissed as he thought over the plan. "Send the first Adélie Corp on a series of strike and fade attacks. Some of the human vessels are stuck in the ice in Marguerite Bay, and they should remain stuck for some time. Once the vessels are attacked, the humans will be forced to pull back and protect them. Very good, Supreme Commander. It is good to know that you still have enough sense about you to serve a purpose. See to it that the mission is accomplished."

"Yes, my lord," Liutites said as he turned away. Normally he'd be fuming over the insult, but no longer bothered him, knowing his plans would soon come to fruition.

"One more thing, Commander." The Overlord stopped him.

"Send two companies of warriors to kill the feral Emperors—K'K'Ru-ki's colony in particular. I will not tolerate any more ideas of rebellion—from anyone," Antaean said, looking directly into Liutites's eyes.

Liutites stood unflinching and returned his stare. "Yes, my lord." He left the room feeling confident in his planning.

CHAPTER 16

The Supreme Commander tobogganed through the dark and icy halls of Pack Ice Command, thinking about the Overlord's orders. As he approached the elite warriors' quarters, he was struck with an idea. "Captain," Liutites barked as he stood up.

The captain appeared out of the darkness. The warriors inside the chamber were loyal to Liutites alone, his personal militia. They would obey him, regardless of what he asked.

"Take two squads and go to the feral Emperor clan of the third zone. Inform them that the Overlord has executed—no, *murdered*—K'K'Ru-ki and that he plans to do the same to them." Liutites paused to make sure the captain absorbed what he had said. "After they get over their initial disbelief, make them an offer. Tell them if they pledge their loyalty to me, I will protect them. Tell them that with our combined strength, we can overthrow the Overlord and bring his tyranny to an end."

"Yes, sir," the captain said with a sharp salute. "And if they should refuse your offer?" he asked as Liutites began to waddle away.

"Kill them, of course," Liutites said without breaking his stride.

With his plans in motion and hopefully enhanced by this new opportunity, Liutites headed to the grand hall. Once there, he immediately sought out news on the capture of the two Chinstraps. His hatred of the Chinstraps was becoming an obsession, and he would love to have one to take out his ire on. But the Chinstraps had conspicuously disappeared since Mevoule had gone; there were none to be found.

The halls were bustling with penguins, as they always were. Faint light from lanterns or flashlights pillaged from human camps lightly illuminated the walls. "Any word from the assault on the human camp in zone four?" he asked.

"Yes, sir," the passing Adélie messenger said. "The forces are in position, sir."

"I know that much, Corporal," Liutites said, trying to maintain his composure. "Have they attacked yet?"

"No, sir. The commanding officer thought it would be best if he rested his troops before commencing the attack."

Normally, Liutites would have lashed out with instantaneous rage on the messenger, but fortunately for the Adélie, he refrained, knowing he may need as many allies as possible when his coup began. "Do you know why this might be, Corporal?" he asked slowly and with as much patience as he could muster.

"Because their march and the extreme storms claimed three warriors' lives, the commanding officer felt they would be ineffective in their weakened condition."

Liutites clenched his beak tightly. *I will have that officer's head when this is done.* "Very well, Corporal," said Liutites. "A good officer never puts his soldiers in harm's way unnecessarily. He always puts his soldiers first. A good lesson for you, should you attain such a rank," Liutites said, trying his best to sound endearing, but without success. "You are dismissed." *A good officer puts his soldiers first.* Liutites mocked himself as the Adélie walked away. *A good officer sees that the task is accomplished, no matter the costs. He will pay for his ineptitude.*

^^^

"Look at him," Mearna said with disdain, but also with a hint of amusement as she entered the grand hall. "He's enraged. The messenger must've made it. Hopefully it will buy Mevoule some time to escape."

The Resistance Council had infiltrated the messenger line. The commanding officer near the camp where Mevoule was had been told to hold off on the attack and to observe from a safe distance. The same messengers then sent false messages back to the Supreme Commander, and they would continue to do so until it was no longer safe.

"We, at best, have bought them only a day. Hopefully Mevoule will not delay," said Ceocilus as he walked alongside her.

"It was unfortunate we were unable to contact him. Since Kimmer's death, Liutites has become much more efficient at rooting out seditionists. We can only hope Lavour receives the message."

"Our sources have told us that General Treeg and the Rockhoppers have gone in search of them."

"True, but we don't know why. And we can't leave it to . . ." Mearna stopped suddenly. "He's coming."

Supreme Commander Liutites slowly approached Mearna, attempting to eavesdrop on her conversation with Ceocilus. "Mearna," he said when his efforts failed.

"Liutites," Mearna returned, lowering her head in greeting.

"We need to talk," Liutites said, looking at Ceocilus, who took the hint, saluted, and waddled away.

"Let's go somewhere private, then," she said, and led Liutites down the nearest corridor to the now abandoned Chinstrap quarters.

"I need the warriors you promised me. I fear the Overlord may attempt to have me eliminated before I can move against him," Liutites said, looking surreptitiously around the quarters.

"Don't worry, Liutites. Your father is confident in thinking he is safe. He needs you. As for the warriors, they will be here. And I never promised. I promised only to try. With so many human vessels about, their progress may be slow once they reach shore."

"Do we know how many have survived the trials?" Liutites asked, referring to the time when all Royal Emperors must spend two years at sea to learn to hunt, survive, and become strong.

"The last report I received was that all have survived," Mearna told him with exaggerated patience. "They will arrive soon enough and they will be armed and ready when the time comes. So I would suggest that you bring your troops here and *try* to find support from the other clans." In normal circumstances, if any penguins were less than submissive to Liutites, they would end up in severe physical distress, or worse. But Mearna was afforded special privileges. She knew the limits of those privileges. She also knew Liutites envisioned her ascending to the dais by his side.

"I have already thought of *that*," he said, mildly scornful. "And as it turns out, the somewhat less-than-omniscient Overlord just may have delivered allies to me, without even realizing," he continued with an air of conceit.

Trying not to sound overly concerned, Mearna responded to the Supreme Commander's announcement. "And who *are* these new allies?"

"Not allies—more like puppets. The overly confident K'K'Ru-ki and his companions were above joining the PDA, and now K'K'Ru-ki is dead, at the beak of the Overlord no less," he said with an air of sadistic humor.

Mearna tried not to show her surprise at hearing of the death of K'K'Ru-ki, but she knew this wasn't good, not good at all. The Emperor was a fool for trying to talk reason to the Overlord, but if Liutites thought he could manipulate the feral clans, he had another thing coming. The word of their leader's death will cause the Emperors to rise up against the Royals. She knew the resistance was not ready to take advantage of such a thing, and she hoped it would be delayed. They *had* to work together or not at all.

"I'll be seen as the conquering hero," Liutites said, snapping Mearna back to the present.

"What?" asked Mearna, missing most of what was said.

"Aren't you listening? My soldiers will bring a message offering protection to the feral clans if they assist in the overthrow. I will be seen as the penguin who stood up against the tyranny of my own father."

"And if they refuse?" Mearna asked, knowing the answer.

"Then they die," he said, sounding surprised she had even asked.

Mearna's mind raced, even though her exterior showed calm. She had to find time and a way to prevent this. If the feral Emperors attacked PIC before her plans were in place, it would be devastating, not to mention they would surely be wiped out. It would be equally devastating if they were to, *somehow*, fall for Liutites's scheme and join with him. They were too valuable to lose. "Have your warriors departed yet?" she asked casually so as not to arouse any suspicion.

"No, but they will shortly," he answered, eyeing her carefully. "Why do you ask?"

"No reason, really," she lied. "It's just that your returning warriors will travel close to their clan on their journey here. Maybe we could use that to our advantage." She made sure to use the words "our" and "we" to make Liutites believe that she meant him and her, and not what she truly meant—the Resistance.

"How so?" asked Liutites with caution. Although he was naturally suspicious, he was never one to dismiss an idea that might somehow benefit him.

"Well . . . " she stalled, making it up as she went. "If the feral Emperors see the overwhelming strength of the warriors at your disposal, they might be more likely to join you."

While Liutites silently contemplated her idea, Mearna pressed on.

"The returning warriors would need to be diverted slightly to bring them through K'K'Ru-ki's clan," she added.

"Yes," Liutites said evilly. "Then they would see for themselves the strength of my armies. Under that kind of pressure, they would not dare to resist joining me," he said as if it were his idea.

"Perhaps," Mearna said. "But it was just a thought. Besides, if you moved now and they did resist, they might take a few warriors along with them on their journey to the Ancients. You can ill afford to lose *any* warriors at such a critical juncture. If you are to overthrow the Overlord, you will need all of your resources. But, as I said—" Mearna turned away "—it was only a thought." At that point, she left it to Liutites and didn't push the idea any.

Liutites watched Mearna for a moment. "They will arrive within the month?"

"Yes," she answered without hesitation, turning her head back toward him.

"Very well," Liutites answered abruptly as he dove to the icy floor and hurriedly tobogganed away.

Mearna watched him leave and found Ceocilus as he emerged from the shadows. They exchanged nods without saying a word, and Ceocilus, too, rushed off.

CHAPTER 17

"Randy, Gina," Meuseaux said hesitantly as he approached them. "I have to leave now."

The two humans looked at each other. "Are you sure about this? Can you trust this penguin?" Gina asked him.

"No, I am certain of nothing. But we must reach our commander. Lavour is his name; he is the one you saw while being held. A revolution has begun."

"Wait a second—a revolution?" Randy asked in disbelief, looking back and forth between Meuseaux and Gina to make sure he had heard correctly.

"Yes, and we must let Commander Lavour know that the Overlord and Supreme Commander have betrayed us. We must find a way to strip their power from them."

Gina and Randy watched the little Chinstrap. Even after all they had seen and all that was revealed about them, they were still both amazed and horrified at how much penguin society had mimicked humankind. "Thank you," they said simultaneously.

"Thank you for helping me find Randy, and thank you for everything that you have done," Gina added.

Meuseaux lowered his head in humility. "Thank you for saving me." He turned to look at Mevoule, who gave him a gesture of urgency. "I must leave now."

"Goodbye, my friend," Randy said with a heavy heart, knowing he would likely never see him again. He squatted down to stroke his head. "Be careful."

Meuseaux let out a soft warble in response to the affection and went to the door.

"What about the Blue?" Gina asked.

"He'll be coming with us," Meuseaux said as Pín rushed to join him.

"Goodbye," Gina said softly as she opened the door.

Before he left, Meuseaux looked at Gina and then at Randy, who was nearly in tears. "When you rejoin your kind, ask your warriors not to destroy us. We will fix what is not right. Give us a chance for peace."

Randy thought about how such a conversation would go, and he knew that with what had already taken place, the penguins' fate was most likely already sealed. The governments of the world would stop at nothing and hunt their kind into extinction. "I'll do what I can," he said solemnly.

Meuseaux looked at him and nodded. He, too, realized extinction was a possibility. "Goodbye, my friends," he said, and the three penguins scurried out the door into the freezing night air. Meuseaux stole one final look back at his human friends and disappeared into the night.

Gina and Randy re-barricaded the door and looked around. The room suddenly seemed very empty. Feeling like parents whose only child had left home, they embraced.

"I hope he'll be all right," Gina finally said.

Randy only sighed in response, and the two began to turn off lights. Little did they know they already had drawn attention. The forward scouts of Liutites's assault force, loyal to the resistance, spotted Mevoule, Meuseaux, and Pín leave, and with them gone, the assault force was clear to attack.

^^^

Within a day, Mearna had received the message that the two Chinstraps had departed, and she approved the assault. Even though Randy and Gina had been instrumental in Meuseaux's safe escape, Mearna had no love for humans and decided to let Liutites's forces destroy them. The order to attack was welcome news to the commanding officer.

With the winter solstice passed, the sun made its first, however brief, appearance across the frozen landscape. It did not last long; the golden sliver of light was gone almost before one knew what it was. As soon as it had passed, the call to form up was given to the assault force commanding officer. Two companies fell into ranks—one Adélie and one Royal Emperor, with pikes and spears at the ready.

The Royal Emperor, Captain Astramachos, commander of the strike force, stood at the rear of the lines and gave his commands. "There is thought to be only two humans inside their dwelling. But keep in mind that these are the two who escaped Pack Ice Command. They are clever and resourceful, if not just lucky. They will most likely have weapons. Be prepared." Captain Astramachos stopped and looked toward the buildings for dramatic effect. "Sergeant Osoden will lead two squads of elite troopers to either break into their fortress or to draw them out. The troopers will be supported by the Adélie third and fourth platoons. The remaining forces will form a perimeter around the redoubt to prevent escape, should they survive that long."

Knowing their duty and the potential cost, the penguin soldiers began to move toward Randy and Gina's once-safe haven. But before Astramachos could fully muster his troops, another of Antarctica's windstorms kicked up and forced the group to huddle to avoid freezing to death. It gave the humans, unknown to them, a reprieve.

CHAPTER 18

The forces of the Alliance of Independent Colonies sped through the Strait of Magellan in no time, barely trailing behind the forward scouts. It was dangerous for them to move so quickly, as they had little warning of approaching danger, but the immediacy made it necessary.

As they neared open water and went out of the strait, a Gentoo scout swam to Lavour, stopping him along with Leepoh, Nok, and Natoo.

"Commander Lavour, sir, we have made contact with General Treeg's forward scouts," the Gentoo informed him.

This alarmed Colonel Nok immediately. "General Treeg? What's he doing out here?"

The Gentoo looked to Lavour, who nodded for him to answer Nok; there would be no punishment for a simple breech of etiquette under his command. "We're unsure as of yet. All we know is that the whole of RHC 23's Defense Ministry is trying to reach us."

"Something's happened—something bad," Nok said in a panic.

"We don't know that," Leepoh said, trying to reassure his friend. "They might just want to join in and bolster our forces."

"Agreed," Lavour said and then looked at the scout. "Thank you, Corporal. You have done well. Fall into the main group, swim slowly, and rest yourself."

"Yes, sir," the scout said in surprise and with respect. He was not used to such treatment, having served under Liutites for so long.

Lavour and the others resumed their swim and continued for nearly a half hour before they swam into General Treeg's Rockhoppers. "General Treeg, what brings you out here?" Lavour asked with Nok waiting impatiently at his side.

"Greetings, Commander—I take it by your question that our messengers have not reached you," Treeg said, stealing a quick glance at Nok.

"Not that I am aware of. What's happened?" Lavour asked, sounding worried.

Treeg didn't answer right away. Instead he began to bark out orders to his Rockhoppers, telling them to begin searching the surrounding islands for any sign of the messengers. He turned back to Lavour and again caught the eye of Nok as he did.

Nok's heart skipped a beat. He knew at once that something worried Treeg, and that it involved him.

Leepoh and Lavour also seemed to pick up on it and gave Nok a wide berth as he swam closer to the Rockhopper general. "What? What is it?" he demanded of Treeg, bracing himself for more tragedy.

Treeg looked at him, knowing all of the hardship the young Rockhopper had already experienced in his life. He didn't want to add to it, but he had no choice. "Keerka was one of the messengers," he said regretfully.

Nok could say nothing; he just stared at Treeg, trying to absorb what he had just been told. *Not again. I can't do this again,* he thought. "We have to do something. *I* have to do something,"

"We are, Nok. We're doing what we can." Treeg tried to reassure him.

"But why did you send her out here? What was so important?" Nok asked.

"Because she is one of the best and I can count on her," Treeg answered and then looked to Lavour. "After you left, Diutes returned, along with his warriors. It was Diutes—under Liutites's and probably the Overlord's orders—who attacked your colony. It was not the humans."

Lavour's body sagged under the weight of having his suspicions confirmed. "Lanerra. What must she have thought when they came?"

"Don't let your thoughts rest on that, Lavour. It will destroy you from the inside," Leepoh said.

"How do I not?" Lavour asked through a clinched beak.

Leepoh didn't have an answer.

Lavour paddled in a circle, coming back to Treeg. "Did Diutes tell you this?"

"No, I learned it from Colonel Kimmer. He explained all he knew, just before Diutes attacked." He finished the sentence by looking at Nok.

Nok started to panic. He mimicked Lavour's nervous action by swimming in circles, not knowing what to do next. "We have to find her," he urged Lavour.

"We will, Nok. We will," Lavour told him calmly. "We need more information first," he said, turning to Treeg. "What happened next?"

"Diutes killed Kimmer, and a battle ensued."

"Hold on a moment," Lavour interrupted. "Isn't he a King? He was Diutes's puppet at Forward Command."

"Not when I met him—apparently he belonged to a subversive organization at PIC. What it is, I am not clear. All I do know is that a close friend of yours is involved and that Kimmer died to bring you this message."

"What about Diutes?" Leepoh asked while Lavour floated in silence, pondering over who this friend was.

"We killed him, along with his warriors," Treeg said boastfully.

Lavour took in all that he had heard. He looked at his panic-stricken friend and then at Leepoh. "Nothing can be done about my family. But we can help Nok's mate and the others. General Leepoh, issue a command to our entire force. We will search every direction and every island between here and RHC 23. We will search until we find them or know their fate."

Colonel Nok looked at Lavour in appreciation.

"Nok, my friend," Lavour said with sincerity. "We have nearly a million penguins at our disposal. We will find her."

Returning to his stoic form, Nok only nodded.

"General Treeg," Lavour continued. "After the search, we will move against the Royal Emperors. Will you be joining us?"

Treeg straightened himself as well as he could. "It would be an honor, Commander."

"Very well. Let's find your missing Rockhoppers and be on our way," Lavour said, and the AIC dispersed to begin the search.

CHAPTER 19

ASMALL AMERICAN MILITARY OBSERVATION POST ON THE ISLAND OF ISLA SOLA, ON THE ATLANTIC SIDE OF THE STRAIT OF MAGELLAN: "It won't stop making that *rumbling* noise," an agitated soldier, Private Jenkins, told his sergeant.

"So?" Sergeant Turnbull asked, equally annoyed with the private. He stood and dragged his hand over his shaved head down to his thick neck.

"So, it's bugging me," said Jenkins, stepping over to the sergeant, his lithe frame shadowed by Turnbull.

"Sergeant, no disrespect intended, but why are we keeping that thing alive? If all of these reports are true, shouldn't we just kill it?" a voice asked from behind Turnbull.

Turnbull crooked his neck to look at Corporal Guerra, who was leaning back in a chair in the corner of the room, examining his knife.

"Because it may prove to be invaluable," someone said from behind the private before the sergeant could answer. "You saw what happened, Private Jenkins."

"Yes, sir, Captain," he answered sharply.

"The bigger black penguins were trying to kill this one. And we're at this outpost to report just such a thing. For all *we* know, it may be only a few or even one species causing the problems. What is needed are live samples, and that's what we have here. I have already informed the commander that we have one. I also have informed him about the events leading up to its capture," Captain Logan said. He walked to the cage holding the

Rockhopper and stooped down to see inside.

Turnbull and Jenkins looked at Logan expectantly, while Guerra feigned disinterest.

"They'll be here in the morning for the samples," the captain finally said.

Turnbull saw something else in his expression and began to worry. They had been at the outpost for over a month. He hoped this meant a break, but Logan's face said otherwise. "What is it?"

Logan straightened and faced his men. His lips parted, but transformed into a pursed frown, losing their color enough to nearly disappear against his exceptionally white skin. "The reports are real. Everybody on the Falklands has been killed and, presumably, everyone on the Sandwich Islands *and* Antarctica as well."

Guerra sat forward in his chair and looked at his captain. "There were thousands of people on those islands. There're only twelve of us here, Captain."

"Which is why I am going to push for extraction," Logan said before any debate or argument could begin.

The weeks of close quarters and miserable weather had caused tension to grow among the soldiers, and spats were beginning to break out over the most trivial of things. This, however, wasn't trivial.

Turnbull stared out the window on the other side of the room, at the darkness beyond, suddenly feeling vulnerable.

"Sergeant, get everyone up, armed, and ready," Logan told him.

Turnbull didn't respond; he instead kept his eyes fixed on the window as if looking at a specter.

"Sergeant!" the captain said more forcefully to bring the man out of his haze.

He looked at Logan and Jenkins, as if seeing them for the first time. "Yes, sir," he said and then looked at the corporal. "Guerra, rouse the rest of the sleepyheads."

Guerra stood and sheathed his knife, giving the sergeant his perpetual angry glare.

Keerka sat in her cage nearby, listening. Even though she understood little human and what she did understand wasn't English, she nonetheless sensed the sudden elevation of stress among them.

CHAPTER 20

Waves from a winter's gale pounded against the shore of Isla Sola with increasing ferocity. Clouds hid the moon and prepared to drop their cargo of freezing rain on the tiny island at a time most inconvenient for man and penguin.

A group of fifty penguins from five different species scurried from the shore. Each group used its special terrestrial strengths as they crossed the landscape. The Rockhoppers deftly hopped over the rocky shore and perched themselves as lookouts; the Gentoo sprinted across the open ground to take their position as forward observers; the Macaroni scurried through the sparse tusset grass to hide their numbers; and the Kings stood on the shoreline as silent sentinels to guard the rear. The Chinstraps boldly strode toward the human shelter to ascertain the situation. The light from the shelter shone like a beacon in the night.

Just an hour before, they had confirmed the presence of one of the missing Rockhoppers inside the structure. With a series of clicks and low grunts, barely audible to human ears but definite to a penguin, Keerka had communicated with the search party since the time they had arrived on the island. Communicating this way, she was able to inform those outside about the humans' movements inside the outpost.

The outpost itself was small, consisting of two all-weather portable shelters joined together, made up of a canvas-like material. One was for barracks. One was for operations. In addition, there were two latrines, an ammo dump, and generators. The penguins strategically positioned themselves within feet of each structure.

On hearing that his beloved was the lone survivor of the Rockhopper messengers but that she was being held captive by the humans, Nok sped away from his group and headed for the island. He ignored the calls of his friends urging him to wait. Commander Lavour didn't blame him; he had done nearly the same thing when he heard about his colony. He immediately called on General Treeg to follow his troops.

"General Natoo," Lavour said, and the Macaroni responded with a salute. "Send word to the other search groups. Tell them to regroup with us at the designated island." The Macaroni general sped off without saying a word. "General Leepoh, any word from Commander Kiley?"

"Not yet, sir," Leepoh said without his usual mirth. Something had been pressing on his mind, a sense of foreboding or perhaps something else. He dismissed it as anxiety over the impending rebellion.

Lavour picked up on his friend's morose behavior and was about to comment on it when a scout interrupted him.

"Sir, messengers from Pack Ice Command," a Chinstrap said.

"Pack Ice Command?" he asked and looked at Leepoh with concern.

"It's Captain Mevoule, sir," the Chinstrap said, excited to see survivors from their colony, "and Corporal Meuseaux."

"Captain Mevoule," he said, at once excited and worried, remembering their last conversation.

Mevoule and Meuseaux, trailed by the Blue penguin, Pín, swam over the swells of the increasingly angry sea to greet Lavour.

"Commander Lavour," Mevoule said. "The last time I saw you, you were *just* a lieutenant-general."

"Mevoule, what are you doing out here?" Lavour asked with genuine happiness at seeing his old friend. "And Meuseaux," he exclaimed when the Chinstrap popped his head from below the surface. "When we left, I feared you were dead. I can't tell you how relieved I am that you're not."

"I am equally relieved—if not more so," Meuseaux said blankly, drawing a laugh from Leepoh.

After their initial greetings, Lavour remembered his friend's seemingly questionable behavior. "What brought you out here, my friends?" he asked cautiously.

Mevoule took a breath. "You know what happened to our home?"

"I do, and I know that Diutes was responsible," Lavour answered, completely stoic.

"Then Kimmer did reach you?" Mevoule asked hopefully.

"No. Diutes killed him before he could. And then the Rockhoppers killed Diutes," Lavour said, hoping to flush out a sense of Mevoule's loyalties.

"Lavour, there is more happening at PIC than you realize."

So he's the one, thought Lavour. *Mevoule is the insider.* "What is it, Mevoule?"

"I," Mevoule started, but then he looked at Meuseaux, who returned his stare. "*We* are part of a secret organization working to undermine the Overlord."

Lavour kept his eyes blank, but inside he was ecstatic. This was what they needed, someone working from the inside while they worked on the outside.

"There are several high-ranking officers within the PDA who are working together under the name of the Resistance Council," Mevoule said as he returned Lavour's gaze.

"How high?" asked Leepoh.

"Very high," Mevoule answered as he looked to Lavour for reassurance about Leepoh. Lavour responded with a nod. "The Supreme Commander's consort is the head of the council."

Lavour and Leepoh looked at each other worriedly. "You can't trust her," Lavour said firmly. "She is nearly as bad as Liutites."

"I agree," Meuseaux jumped in, looking at Mevoule. "But she saved my life—more than once."

Unconvinced, Lavour looked at Mevoule.

"It's true. She is eager to be rid of Liutites as well."

"But she is a *Royal Emperor*. She will never turn against her own kind," Lavour insisted.

"Time will tell. But she has connections with the free Emperors, the Kings, and other clans. The Resistance Council commands a good portion of the forces still at PIC. Mearna herself commands at least one full brigade of elite warriors." Mevoule looked directly into Lavour's eyes. "Even with our resources, it won't be enough. The Overlord and Liutites have amassed a huge army of Royals and those still loyal to the PDA. We need you and the forces you now command."

Lavour thought about it. He didn't trust Mearna, but he was going to fight against the Royals regardless of the Resistance's involvement, so he might as well hope to have the help. "How can I talk to Mearna?" he asked.

"When we return it will be arranged, but we haven't much time," Mevoule added.

There's always a catch. "Why is that?" Lavour asked suspiciously.

"There's more," said Mevoule.

"I figured," replied Lavour dryly.

"The humans have amassed a large number of war vessels around the homeland. Plus, Supreme Commander Liutites is planning to overthrow the Overlord." Mevoule let the news sink in before continuing. "If Liutites succeeds in his coup, the results will be terrible. He is even more insane than the Overlord."

"It will be the death of us all," Lavour said with haunted eyes. "He is too proud to give in to the humans, and the war will continue. I've seen what they can do. They are too powerful to be beaten. We *must* end this war."

"We are fortunate to be experiencing a harsh winter. Otherwise the humans might have moved against us more quickly," Mevoule added.

Lavour looked up as the storm clouds let loose their contents and rain fell on the rising sea. He wondered about his fate, the future of the Chinstraps, and the future of all penguins. How had he gotten to this point? He felt as if the burden of the future of penguins everywhere rested on his back. As he looked at the faces of those around him, and the throngs of penguins who followed him, he realized that it just might be so. "General Leepoh," he said. "Gather a messenger squad. Have them seek out Commander T'Cuh-ka of the Magellanics; tell him what has transpired and what our plans are. Ask if he will join us in our fight against this evil."

"Yes, sir," replied Leepoh. "And what is next for us?"

Lavour looked at Mevoule and Meuseaux. "First we rescue a captured Rockhopper. Then we bring down the tyrants."

CHAPTER 21

"Something doesn't feel right," Gina said quietly to Randy, who had nearly dozed off.

Randy squinted with one eye. "Strong in the force, this one is—" he joked as he lay on the couch of the central room before Gina cut him off.

"Shut up, Randy. I'm serious," she said, tilting her head as if she were trying to hear something.

Seeing her reaction, Randy sat up. "What?"

"I don't know," she said, walking to the nearest window. "I can't see a damn thing. Just a curtain of snow against black. These storms haven't let up in I don't know how long."

Randy looked at Gina in the faint light of a glow stick. Something definitely had her on edge. He dropped the stick between the cushions and walked to her side. He put his arm around her as they stood at the window. Gina didn't respond to his touch. Instead she stood motionless, taking shallow breaths. Randy watched her. In the faint light he could see wide eyes dart back and forth, searching for something in the shadows and wind-driven snow. The expression of fearful concentration she carried caused a chill to crawl up his spine.

After several long minutes, Gina leaned into Randy. "There's something out there," she whispered.

Randy strained his eyes to try to focus. "Where—I can't see anything," he whispered back.

The two stood in silence a minute longer as the gusts repeatedly slapped something which had broken loose against the outer wall, further dulling their senses.

A brief wisp of a slightly darker form in the night caused Gina to jerk. "There!" she blurted, making Randy jump.

"What, where—I don't see it," he said, instantly panicked as his eyes scanned the outside.

"A penguin. It's small, but I saw it," she said. "It was there and gone."

"Maybe its Meuseaux," Randy said, hoping against hope.

"If it was, why wouldn't he have just come to the door?" she asked with her eyes still fixed out the window.

"Yeah," Randy scratched out through his suddenly dry throat.

"You have the gun?"

"Yeah," he said, mimicking Gina's stare. He handed the pistol to Gina, whom he trusted to shoot more accurately. He did not take his eyes from the storm.

Two more shadows briefly scurried into view and then disappeared just as quickly.

Randy took a step back. "They're here," he said with his heart racing. "I think they were Adélies."

"I'm not really interested in what kind they are, just how many," Gina said, her stress increasing.

"Sorry," Randy said, suddenly too nervous to be offended or to construct a snappy retort.

^^^

In the weeks since the Chinstraps had left, Captain Astramachos's assault on the human base was postponed by a series of Antarctica's windstorms. The storms came on rapidly, and his forces had to huddle together to keep from succumbing to the cold, because even a penguin can freeze to death in such brutal conditions. But he sensed that the intensity of the storm was waning and rallied his troops to, once again, begin the assault.

ΛΛΛ

"The wind is dying," Gina said, hearing the steady banging on the outside of the building slow. "Now I wish it *wouldn't* stop. I'll be right back," she said as she walked to where the glow stick was lying. She checked her weapon.

Randy remained standing at the window, trying to see something as the blowing ice finally slowed. In a break between gusts, he saw it. "Oh my God," he said, backing away from the window. He looked at Gina, his eyes wide in fear.

Gina was on her feet in a flash. "What?" she asked, frightened by Randy's look.

"Outside—hundreds—or more—the big ones—the Royals," he said, fear making him unable to complete a sentence.

"Reinforce the door," Gina said, taking charge until Randy came to his senses, which she knew he would. She reached over and flicked on the lights.

"What are you doing? They'll see us," he said as he dashed for the light switch.

Gina put her hand over the switch and then on Randy's hand. "Do you really think they don't know we're in here?" she asked with exaggerated calmness.

Randy stopped and looked at Gina, looking like someone who had just gotten off a cheap carnival ride as he got his bearings. "Yeah, I guess you have a point," he said, sounding a little embarrassed.

They went from room to room, turning on the lights, half-expecting penguins to pop out of the shadows as they did. Whatever furniture was movable, they put in front of the door to reinforce their barricade.

Gina checked her weapon one more time and patted her coat pocket, feeling the weight of extra ammunition for reassurance. "Remember, I only have one clip—so it'll take a minute to reload."

"I know," Randy said. He zipped up his jacket and picked up a fire axe for defense. "Let's just hope it doesn't come to that, all right?"

"You ready?" she asked nervously.

"Yeah," Randy said, looking around the room. "Time to sit and wait."

Randy was right; there was nothing to do but sit and wait for the inevitable. Gina sat on the sofa and thought about her fortunes. It all seemed more than just a little bit unfair. To have improbably survived all she had, to have unexpectedly found the man she knew she could love forever, just to have it end like this—back where it all began, trapped, with possibly thousands of murderous penguins outside, wanting to get inside—and no genuine hope of being rescued.

Randy seemed to sense what Gina was feeling, put his arm around her, pulled her chin up, and kissed her. It was a soft kiss, filled with the love he felt for her, a kiss to last an eternity—because they knew it might have to.

The first pecks of the invaders against the wall startled the couple, and they prepared themselves for what was to come.

CHAPTER 22

PERU, NEAR THE CHILEAN BORDER: Commander Kiley's armies floated offshore near the quiet fishing village of Cabo Redondo. The hand-to-mouth existence of the inhabitants had led to the near destruction of the Humboldt penguin colony. After hearing rumors of attacking penguins, the frightened villagers sacked the Humboldt nesting grounds, displacing them once and for all. Although Commander Kiley's orders specified a defensive posture, Kiley had a different idea—revenge.

"Commander, sir," Captain Pasillas said after swimming from shore. "All of the troops are in position, and it appears as if the humans are in slumber."

"Very good, Captain," Kiley said. "After we are done here, I am taking my forces to *possibly* deal with the Royals. You are more than welcome to join us," he said almost as an afterthought.

"Thank you, Commander, but we will be going to the Galapagos to search for survivors. We have good relations with the Galapagos penguins, and the humans do not bother them. Perhaps we can work out an arrangement with them. Remember, if you ever find your way this far north again, you have a friend."

"Thank you, Captain Pasillas, I will," Kiley told him before he left to join the other Humboldts. "This is it," he said, turning to the generals.

"The plan is simple. Each of you will take your divisions ashore. Surround the human township and, once the signal is given, attack. Remember that these humans are to blame for the death of an entire race of penguins. Show them no mercy, give them no quarter, and leave none of them alive." On Kiley's mark, swarm upon swarm of penguins descended on the quiet village.

The village was quite small, nestled between the hills and the sea, with barely fifty inhabitants. It was a community in its death throes. Too far to the south to enjoy the lucrative tourism trade and too isolated, with only one road in or out, to sustain any real commerce. The people were poor and uneducated. With most of the younger people gone to seek opportunity in the cities, those who remained were mostly older. They stubbornly held on to the old way of life. The nearby penguin colony was, at first, an exploited resource, as their guano was a rich fertilizer. But as rumors of penguin attacks from traveling fishermen made their way north, it became an object of fear and hatred.

Thousands of webbed feet moved from the surf toward the hapless village. Although the armies under Commander Kiley were marching without uttering a noise, the sheer number of penguin feet crunching across the ground created a steady din, which increased as they reached the hard-packed dirt roads of the town. The sound roused sleeping birds from their roosts, and they squawked and chattered as the penguins passed underneath.

The first of the penguin marauders moved into position between the hills and the village, effectively blocking Cabo Redondo's only road. A light flickered to life inside one of the well-weathered shanties, and at once, all of the penguins came to a sudden and silent halt. The night became still and unearthly quiet, with the distant waves the only sound.

A squeak of a rusty door hinge broke the silence, and a middle-aged man stepped out onto his old wooden porch and lit a cigarette. He stood under the moonlit canopy then squatted on his haunches and took a deep drag of his tobacco. Squinting through the smoke, he stopped before taking another puff. The glowing ember of his cigarette fell to the earth as fear paralyzed his body. "Dios nos ahorra," he muttered quietly at first and then louder. "Dios nos ahorra!" *God save us.*

The man quickly ducked back into his little house, frantically shouting as he rummaged through his wardrobe. He stepped back onto the porch brandishing an old lever-action rifle and continued to shout. "Los pingüinos han llegado." *The penguins have arrived.* He shouted continually, and he fired his first shot. Throughout the village, lanterns ignited and windows lit up as the commotion awakened the people.

The penguin generals, seeing their carefully orchestrated attack plan begin to crumble, called out to one another and the order to attack was given. Penguins poured into the village by the hundreds and down what passed for the main thoroughfare.

The curious people filed out of their homes to find the cause of the disturbance and were horror stricken to see the yelling man engulfed in a roiling swarm of penguins. The penguins used the lessons learned at the Battle of the Falklands to bring down their victims.

The fearful onlookers did nothing, could do nothing as the gun-wielding man was brought down and his pleas for help extinguished. The penguins turned their attention to the bystanders, and it was then that the villagers snapped out of their stupor and realized their peril.

Calls and screams of warning filled the air. Some of the villagers ran back into their homes and returned brandishing machetes, hatchets, and other tools, thinking they could fight the penguins. They didn't know that the penguins they could see were only the beginning and that thousands more waited in the darkness for their turn to attack.

The men hacked and cut at the penguins with little effect. The women and few children who were there took refuge indoors, thinking they were safe from the carnage outside. Most of the able-bodied men were cut off from one another by the throngs of penguins that filled the spaces between the homes. The penguins stabbed, pecked, bit, and slashed their way past the machete-wielding men in a matter of minutes and trampled over the bodies to lay siege to the homes.

Hundreds of birds pecked madly at the wooden doors. Inside the dead gunman's house, the penguins knocked over a kerosene lantern, and the old wooden structure burst into flames. Several penguins dashed from the fire with their bodies ablaze, squealing in pain as they died in the road.

House by house, doorways crumbled under the sheer number of penguins hacking with their beaks. Inside, the women, the last defenders of their homes, fought back with knives, iron skillets, brooms, or whatever they could find. But they only postponed the inevitable. In other homes, children and the elderly cried out; unable to defend themselves, they succumbed to Commander Kiley's vengeful plan.

Roosters crowed and livestock called as the first rays of dawn appeared. Unaware of the carnage surrounding them, they awaited their masters' hands to feed them. The smoldering homes held no survivors, and no one had escaped. No one would come for the animals, and those who were not taken by the fighting would go hungry.

As the orange of the morning sky transformed into blue, Commander Kiley decided to come ashore. He found Captain Pasillas at the center of town, comforting the wounded. Groups of penguins worked together to drag the dead to the sea for a proper penguin burial. The badly wounded went to the sea as well, to await their time to be called to the Ancients.

Captain Pasillas looked at the devastation wrought by the penguins and felt a bit overwhelmed by the amount of destruction. Until recently, he and the other Humboldts had never considered fighting back. And their recent thoughts were purely out of self-defense. But now things had changed, and now he wished it had happened sooner. It would have saved his clan.

"What you have accomplished here—this retribution—is a great thing," Pasillas told Kiley. "We are grateful. I am grateful."

The two started to walk, but Commander Kiley stopped to examine the brutalized body of a dead human. "Their faces are quite expressive, aren't they?" Kiley said in mock fascination.

Somewhat nonplused, Captain Pasillas only nodded in agreement.

"When we attacked The Falklands," Kiley began, "we thought we had achieved total victory. Thousands of humans lost their lives, but the penguins paid an even greater toll. We were wrong about the victory. When the battle was near its end, their reinforcements arrived. Flying machinations with horrible weaponry began to lay waste to our brave fighters. Thousands died before we could escape."

"You fled?" asked Pasillas, trying to see where the conversation was going.

"Yes," Kiley answered flatly. "We swam for our lives. Had we stayed, as the Overlord commanded, we would all be dead—every last one of us. That is why we are no longer associated with the PDA. To think that we can defeat the humans is foolishness to the extreme. Today, these are the victories we can achieve—strike hard and disappear back into the sea. Others feel the same, yet others just want to wait and *then* strike back."

"But you achieved a great victory today—" the confused Pasillas started before Kiley cut him off.

"No, Captain Pasillas, my friend. It was not a victory, but revenge— nothing more. And vengeance is all that we'll ever have. And *that,* my friend, is what I intend to carry out," Kiley said, issuing his own decree. "I will continue to do so until we arrive at the Northern Paradise."

Pasillas stood in silence, surveying his surroundings. The euphoric feeling of victory had waned. "I don't care what you call it. Vengeance, victory, it doesn't matter. The humans received what was due to them. And from this day on, you are *Mi Caudillo,* my leader."

Kiley stared at the smaller Humboldt. "Remember that when I return," he said.

Commander Kiley gathered his forces and began barking out orders. Soon after, they disappeared into the surf, leaving Pasillas and his small group of Humboldts. Feeling suddenly vulnerable, Pasillas called the group together and made a dash for the sea.

CHAPTER 23

ISLA SOLA: The squad of soldiers was sitting around the operations room listening to Captain Logan explain the circumstances in which they found themselves.

"Why don't they just send somebody right now?" asked PFC Reyes, a stocky man who wore glasses. His glasses made him appear to be looking down his nose when speaking.

"There are no resources close enough," Logan said pointedly, as though he were repeating something he did not quite believe.

"How about the British or Argentineans? They're close," Jenkins said.

"With the recent events at the Falkland Islands, their governments have become suspicious of each other. They have their own problems."

"So that's it? We just sit and wait," Reyes said, exasperated.

"Jeez, Reyes, quit being such a wuss," a particularly large man, Specialist McPearsons, said. "It's just a bunch of stupid penguins. Grow some—"

"That's enough, McPearsons," Captain Logan interrupted. "These *stupid penguins*, as you call them, overran a British military base and subsequently wiped out all human life below sixty degrees low latitude."

"Whatever you say, Cap," McPearsons whispered under his breath as he walked toward a corner of the room.

The rest of the soldiers stared at the captain in silence, not *quite* sure if they should believe what they had just been told. There was no way penguins could do that. They knew something big had happened and that penguins were involved, but everybody? That didn't seem possible.

"We are a team, and we will continue to act as one," Logan said forcefully. "We'll have a flight out of here at zero-seven-hundred hours. So, until then, keep your heads and stay alert."

The briefing concluded, and the men began doing weapons checks. But Reyes sat staring at the caged Rockhopper. "Captain," Reyes said as Logan walked by.

"Yes?"

"What if they come looking for that one?" asked Reyes, pointing to the cage.

"I'm sure they won't, Reyes," Captain Logan answered, a little troubled by the question but not letting on that he was.

"I mean, they're smart. They have to be, to do what you said they did. And don't animals have, like, a sixth sense?"

"I doubt they'll come looking for just one. Just relax. You worry too much. We'll be gone in eight hours."

"Still," Sergeant Turnbull butted in. "Don't you think it'd be wise to get rid of it? Not necessarily kill it, just let it go."

"I—*we*—have orders, Sergeant," Logan sighed.

"Yeah, we should get rid of it, Captain," McPearsons jumped in. "So Reyes will quit being such a crying little wuss."

In a flash, Reyes was on his feet. "I'll show you who's a wuss," he said, reaching for his knife as Sergeant Turnbull restrained him.

"That's enough!" Captain Logan shouted.

McPearsons looked at Reyes with a mocking smile.

"One more comment out of you, McPearsons, and you'll be on latrine duty until your tour is over."

McPearsons stared at Reyes for a second longer. It wasn't that he didn't like Reyes. He just enjoyed antagonizing him. "Yes, sir," he finally said.

"And the rest of you—we have orders to bring back a live specimen.

That's why we have the cages. You will do your duty and follow orders. Is that understood?"

The men all looked at each other, surprised by the captain's outburst. He was usually rather subdued. "Yes, sir," they said almost in unison.

Logan took a breath and sat down. The sound of the soldiers checking and rechecking their weapons filled the room.

Keerka was sitting with her back turned toward the humans when she heard something unexpected but very welcome. She perked up instantly. She replied to the sound with a low rumbling click in her throat. The men stopped everything and looked at the Rockhopper. She resumed her silence at once. The soldiers exchanged a look. Instinct told them something was wrong, and they quickly began to load their weapons.

CHAPTER 24

"This is where we tracked them. There is a human outpost nearby," one of the penguins from the search party informed Colonel Nok, walking alongside of him as he came ashore.

Nok hopped up the rocks and saw the light from the encampment shining through the night and rain. He made a low guttural noise and then stood motionless. After a few seconds, his head perked up. "She's here," he said excitedly. "She's definitely here. Let's go."

"Colonel Nok," General Treeg called out after coming ashore behind Nok. "Halt!"

Nok came to a quick stop.

"Just hold on there, son," Treeg said in a fatherly voice.

"But she's in there, General. We have to save her," pleaded Nok.

"We will, but right now we have to wait. The rest of our forces are on their way. Be patient."

"But they have her locked up. She told me. We have to—"

"If she's locked up, she'll be fine," Treeg interrupted the anxious Rockhopper.

Nok stared at the outpost, wanting nothing more than to rush to her rescue. He turned away instead, knowing Treeg was right. "I don't want to lose her, Treeg. I . . ." Nok stopped himself and lowered his head.

"You won't," Treeg said, knowing that Nok had lost nearly everyone he had ever cared for. "Think about it, Nok. If we move now, with so few of us here, we might all end up dead, leaving no one to save Keerka. Since she's still alive, they obviously don't plan to kill her. Now, which way would you like it?" he asked, leaving the decision and the responsibility to Nok.

Nok took a deep breath and looked at the light one more time. "All right, we wait," he resigned. "What will we do when the others arrive?"

"I suggest a diplomatic solution," a familiar voice said from behind the two Rockhoppers.

"Coming from anyone else, that might be a suggestion I would take seriously," Nok said to General Leepoh as he came forward.

"That *truly* wounds me, Nok. *Truly*," Leepoh said in a less-than-serious voice. "But I *am* serious. What other choice do we have?"

Nok looked at Treeg in disbelief, and Treeg appeared to be considering what Leepoh had said.

"You know, he might be right," Treeg said thoughtfully. "If we attack them full on, we don't know what their reaction might be. They might kill her."

"You can't be serious!" Nok exclaimed, not believing what he was hearing.

"I am serious," Treeg said.

Nok looked back and forth between the two. He thought the plan was asinine, but he had little choice. He didn't want to risk Keerka's life on a foolhardy rescue attempt. "Fine, diplomacy it is. But who'll be the diplomat? I don't speak human," he said, looking at Leepoh.

"Don't look at me," Leepoh said. "I'm just the brains of this operation."

"In that case, we're all doomed," Nok said, looking at Treeg.

"Not me," Treeg said, shaking his head. "I'm too old, and I only speak one of the human languages. We don't know which one these speak."

"Well, then, who?" asked Nok as he looked around for prospects.

The first wave of the AIC came ashore, and with them came Commander

Lavour, Captain Mevoule, and Corporal Meuseaux. "This is the place?" asked Lavour as he waddled toward his friends.

"Commander Lavour," said Leepoh. "We were just talking about you."

"Why don't I like the sound of that?" he asked, looking at the others.

"We are in need of a diplomat, and you're just the penguin for the job," Leepoh told him overly upbeat.

Lavour looked at Leepoh silently for a very long moment. "I don't think so, General."

"But, sir," Leepoh urged and then went into a lengthy explanation as to why Lavour would be the best penguin for the situation.

Lavour listened intently to everything Leepoh had to say. "You're correct, General Leepoh. Under the current circumstances, diplomacy *would* be the best policy. But it would take somebody with an enormous gift of gab. And *I* know just the penguin."

Leepoh looked at Lavour with his beak agape. "You're serious, aren't you?" Leepoh asked, considerably less enthusiastic now.

"Of course I am."

"But . . ." Leepoh began to counter.

"Think of it as your moment of glory, your moment in the sun," Lavour mockingly encouraged him.

"Need I remind you, sir, that it is, indeed, night," Leepoh said with a righteous indignation.

Leepoh and Lavour looked at each other, enjoying the moment of frivolity.

"Fine," Leepoh finally said. "If I get killed, I'm going to pluck your tail feathers," he added and began to stomp off toward the outpost. He passed Nok and looked down at him. "You'd better appreciate this. The things I do . . ." He continued to grumble until he reached the clearing before the camp.

In the meantime, Lavour ordered the rest of the penguins to surround the small island, which didn't take long.

Once all penguins were in position, Leepoh began to walk forward again. He stopped midway there and, taking a guess as to which language to use, called out in his best human. "Hello," he said, which to him sounded perfect, but to a human it sounded a bit like a parrot, only more guttural. "Hello," he called again.

CHAPTER 25

Inside the outpost, the men were engaged in quiet but nervous conversation.

"But if we're closer to Ushuaia, why are they flying out of Punta Arenas?" Reyes asked, worried about more delays.

"As I already explained, the Argentinean government is being less than cooperative and we are officially in Chilean territory…I think" Captain Logan said, sounding a bit annoyed.

"Wait," Sergeant Turnbull suddenly said. "Shut up!" he said more forcefully when nobody listened. Logan turned to say something, but Turnbull silenced him with a gesture.

All of the men were silent and motionless.

"What is it?" Logan mouthed.

Turnbull stood with his head cocked.

"*Hello.*"

Although barely audible through the wind and rain, they all heard the call this time.

The captain and sergeant locked gazes. "Is everyone accounted for?" Turnbull asked, looking around the room. Seeing that everyone was, he looked back at the captain. "It shouldn't be the extraction team yet. We would've known if they were coming early. Hell, we would've heard them land."

Logan motioned for his men to prepare for action.

"Orders, sir?" Turnbull asked.

"Let's just see who it is. We're way too jumpy. It could just be a local."

"At this time of night?" the sergeant asked doubtfully.

"Could be a fisherman who ran aground," Logan replied. "There is a storm."

Turnbull shrugged as if he hadn't thought of that. Logan was right; they were all getting too jumpy. "I didn't know the locals spoke English," he said. He looked at the caged Rockhopper, who also was becoming fidgety.

The sergeant motioned for two members of the squad to stand by the door. He went to a chest and pulled out a large handheld spotlight. "On my mark," he said. "One . . . two . . . go!"

Reyes and McPearsons barged out the door, guns at the ready; Turnbull followed, ducked out, and flipped on the spotlight as he took a knee. He swept the light across the landscape but saw no one. On his second pass, he thought he saw something. He stopped the sweep brought the beam back and spotted a form through the rain, standing in the night, not more than thirty yards away.

McPearsons brought his weapon up into firing position.

"Hold your fire," Turnbull shouted. "Hold your fire."

The lone Gentoo penguin, standing in the light, noticeably exhaled. "Hello, humans," Leepoh called out once more.

The three soldiers looked at each other, confused.

"Who's out there? Show yourself," Turnbull demanded.

"I'm out here. My name is Leepoh, and I *am* showing myself."

Turnbull motioned for the rest of the squad to come outside and take up defensive positions.

Captain Logan came out and kneeled next to Turnbull. "What's going on?" he asked, looking at the penguin in the spotlight.

"Not sure, Captain," Turnbull said quietly. "All we can see is that penguin, but someone is talking."

"Will you kill me if I come closer?" Leepoh asked nervously, becoming frustrated.

"Identify yourself first," Turnbull told him.

"I have already done so," Leepoh told them, even more annoyed.

"Right. Leepoh is it?" Logan said, taking over the conversation. "Please, just step into the light."

Leepoh looked around, feigning confusion. "How much more in the light would you like me to stand?"

"No, don't upset them, Leepoh," Lavour said quietly, watching from cover in the nearby rocks.

"He has a tendency to do that, you know," Nok responded from Lavour's side.

Logan and Turnbull gave each other disbelieving looks.

"It doesn't sound like a person," Reyes said. "More like a parrot. A weird parrot."

Logan didn't reply to the unspoken suggestion. It was too much; he couldn't make himself believe it. He watched the Gentoo and took a deep breath. "Take two steps closer," he said hesitantly, and Leepoh obliged. "Whoa, holy . . . " the astonished man exclaimed. "A little closer," he said after regaining his composure.

"Give me your assurance that I will not be harmed, and I will," Leepoh replied, using caution.

Logan and Turnbull exchanged looks again. "Everyone, stand down," Logan ordered. "Hold your fire, and that means you, McPearsons," he emphasized to the hotheaded man.

McPearsons looked at Logan sideways and slowly lowered his weapon.

"No harm will come to you," Logan assured Leepoh after seeing everyone had complied with his order.

Leepoh took several slow steps across the open ground. He stopped just out of the humans' reach, in case they should try to nab him, to make a collection of captured penguins.

The two sides stood silently, each appraising the other. "Who are you?" Logan finally asked, fully expecting to have the source of this prank revealed.

Leepoh lowered his head. "These creatures really aren't too bright, are they?" he muttered to himself. "My name is Leepoh, and I am here to request the release of the penguin you have taken captive," he said with exaggerated patience.

Logan took a few seconds to regain his composure. He felt lightheaded at the revelation that this really wasn't an elaborate hoax. He looked at his squad, whose expressions ranged from curiosity to horrified disbelief. "What makes you think we have a penguin here?" he asked, not knowing what else to say.

Leepoh sighed. "Do you really want our first diplomatic encounter to begin with a lie?"

"Hey, Reyes," McPearsons said, leaning across the captain and sergeant. "That freak speaks better English than you."

"Shut it, McPearsons. Last warning," Turnbull said threateningly.

Logan tried to ignore the squabble and directed his attention to Leepoh. "Very well, my name is Captain Logan," he said, falling into conversation with the Gentoo with remarkable ease, almost alarmingly so for his taste. He looked at Turnbull and gave a slight shrug. The sergeant returned the gesture. "Why should we release the penguin? After all, didn't your kind just kill thousands of our kind?" the captain asked, probing for the truth or confirmation of what he had been told.

"That is regretfully true and unfortunate," Leepoh conceded. "But your kind has killed millions of our kind for generations."

Logan had no defense. For over one hundred years, people had killed these birds, albeit considerably less in recent times, never stopping to consider that maybe they might be sentient, that they might have intelligence or that they could even have a society. That would be impossible, for only man was endowed with the divine spark. Logan thought about it all. He was a well-educated man and knew the history of the region. He relinquished the debate. "Reyes," he said. "Get the cage." He paused. "And release the penguin."

"Yes, sir," Reyes snapped and went inside immediately to fetch the bird.

Leepoh let out a sigh, relieved that violence had been avoided.

"Are you sure about this?" Sergeant Turnbull asked. "What about the orders you were so keen on following not an hour ago?"

"Sergeant, an officer's job is to assess the situation at hand and to act accordingly, right?" he asked, hoping for support with the decision. "What we just learned gave us insight as to the reason for the attacks. Therefore, as a gesture of goodwill and to possibly prevent future tragedy, we will release the penguin."

"This is bull," McPearsons butted in.

"That is all I will hear from you, Specialist McPearsons. Consider yourself on report," Logan snapped at the petulant man.

"I'm sorry, but this is bullshit," McPearsons continued, ignoring his captain. "A talking penguin—you can't actually believe that. It's gotta be remote controlled. There's somebody out there laughing at us right now."

"Then how'd it know we caught one?" Jenkins asked.

"We caught it outside, didn't we?"

"He's right," Jenkins told Logan, sounding surprised that he actually agreed with McPearsons.

"And what if he is—or worse, isn't?" Logan asked, irritated. "The point is that these things wiped out the entire population of the Falkland Islands, which included a British military base. If there's more than just this one out there—and I, *we,* have to assume there is—what makes you think we'd stand a chance against them? I am doing what I think is best. This is not a democracy. You will follow orders without argument."

"If you let it go, you're getting rid of our bargaining chip," Turnbull said quietly to the captain.

"Do you really think it matters, Sergeant?" Logan asked, leaving

Turnbull confused by what he meant. Reyes came back out holding the cage. "Is this who you're looking for?" Logan asked.

Leepoh looked at the cage. "Are you all right?" he asked in penguin common.

"Yes. I am very hungry though," replied Keerka, sounding relieved at nearly being free.

"Yes, this is the one," Leepoh said, turning his attention back to the humans.

"Release it," Logan said, and Reyes immediately obliged.

Keerka poked her head out, looked both directions, and then cautiously took her first steps toward freedom. She surveyed the armed men, saw it was safe, and ran to Leepoh. The two exchanged a few words, and Leepoh gestured toward Nok, who was hurrying out of the darkness.

Leepoh directed his attention back to Logan. "Thank you, Captain Logan. I wish I could offer you more than just our gratitude, but that will have to suffice."

"You could answer one question for me," Logan said as Leepoh turned away. "How did you learn to speak our language so well? Do all of you speak it?"

"That's two questions, Captain," Leepoh joked, taking Logan aback. "Your kind has been among us for many years. We do have ears and brains. No, not all of us speak human, but a lot do. Goodbye, Captain Logan," he said and walked away.

Logan, dumbfounded, stood looking at the Gentoo. "Goodbye, Leepoh."

"That's *General* Leepoh, Captain," he commented, not bothering to look back to see the reaction.

Logan stared at the penguin, not sure of what to make of his last comment. The soldiers watched the penguins in the spotlight as several gathered in what was obviously a greeting.

"What do you think?" Sergeant Turnbull asked Logan as he came to his side.

"I think the world is a lot different than we thought it was," Logan answered, keeping his eyes fixed on the penguins.

"Yeah, I think you're right, Captain," Turnbull said. "Turn out the light and lets bring it in," he said to the rest of the men.

"This is all a bunch of garbage, Sergeant," the perpetually irked McPearsons said. "Penguins don't talk. It's a trick."

"That is enough, McPearsons. Not another word," Logan said with as much authority as anyone had ever heard from him.

"I said turn that light out, Jenkins," Turnbull demanded.

"Can't we watch them for a minute, Sergeant?" Reyes asked. "This is amazing!"

McPearsons looked at everybody as they disregarded his rants about tomfoolery and he became more agitated. "This is a bunch of crap. They're fakes. I'll prove it," he yelled and brought his weapon up to firing position.

CHAPTER 26

"Keerka!" cried Nok as soon as he saw her walking toward him with Leepoh at her side. He rushed to her at once, and the two began an elaborate ritual of greeting, equally happy to see each other.

"Job well done, General," Lavour told Leepoh as he joined them on the plain.

"Humph," Leepoh grumbled. "Sending your friend into the enemy's den, while you stand safely behind the rocks," he said as if he were upset.

"We were with you in spirit," Lavour joked. "Besides, I needed someone I could trust," he said more seriously.

For once Leepoh didn't have a dry response. He acted like he was truly touched by the compliment. "Thank you, Commander."

General Treeg, trailed by Mevoule and Meuseaux, approached the happy reunion. "Fine work there, Gentoo," is all the craggy Rockhopper had to say.

"Bah, it was nothing," Leepoh replied.

"Might I suggest we take this somewhere a little further from the enemy. We're too close for my taste," Treeg said, staring into the spotlight.

"I agree," said Nok, finally prying himself from Keerka. "You're always right, General Treeg."

"No, I'm just experienced. You don't live this long in this world by not being cautious."

The group started to head back to the shore when they heard a shout from one of the humans, followed by a gunshot.

^^^

"No!" shouted Captain Logan.

McPearsons pulled the trigger and the others watched in horror as one of the penguins flew to the ground in an explosion of blood and pinfeathers.

"Damn it, McPearsons!" yelled Turnbull. He swung the butt of his rifle into McPearsons jaw and watched him fall to the ground, unconscious.

"Keep that light on me," Logan ordered, and he ran to the fallen bird.

^^^

In a moment of confusion, the stunned group turned and saw one of the humans being brought down by another and then looked around to find General Treeg lying on the ground, gasping for air. In the brief span of a second, Nok's jubilation was replaced by devastation and shock as he stood over the fallen general.

"Nok," Treeg rasped. "Be well and live long, my son."

Nok's heart ached in a newfound way while struggling through his emotions. His heartbreak at losing his surrogate father, his warm feeling at knowing that Treeg considered him his son, and the overwhelming hatred he felt for the humans threatened to consume him as he watched Treeg slip away. "Go in peace to join the Ancients, my father," he whispered.

"Watch out," Lavour called when he spotted Logan running toward them.

The man fell to his knees in front of the dead Rockhopper and saw nothing could be done. "I am so sorry," he said to Leepoh. "This was not by my orders."

Nok listened to the man babble in his language, feeling his simmering rage beginning to boil over. "Keerka," he said, barley containing his anger. "My love, you must go to safety. Go now; I will join you soon."

"But, Nok," she began to protest. Keerka was a proud warrior herself but an intelligent one as well. She hadn't eaten in days. She was weak from her ordeal and knew she would be a hindrance to Nok if a battle began. She gave him an affectionate nudge and scampered away.

"I'll be with you before long." Nok's eyes followed Keerka until he was sure she would go to safety. With her gone, he turned to his friend. "Commander Lavour, something must be done."

Lavour looked at Nok, then at Treeg's body, and then finally at Captain Logan, who was pleading his innocence to Leepoh. Nok was right; something had to be done. He lowered his head and glanced back at Nok and Leepoh and saw their eyes watching him expectantly. He locked eyes with Mevoule. Mevoule closed his eyes. "Sound the call to battle, Colonel," Lavour said with little enthusiasm.

"Yes, sir," Nok said immediately.

Mevoule, Meuseaux, and Leepoh watched Lavour. "It is my responsibility. The lives lost will rest on me."

Leepoh nodded, his body slumped. Mevoule stood silently and stared at Treeg's body.

Nok began to make a loud, braying call, which startled Captain Logan.

"What's going on? What's happening?" Logan asked, his eyes wide. He spun on his heels as Nok's call was answered by the call of thousands of penguins in the darkness.

Leepoh looked to the shadows, and then back at Logan. "I am sorry, Captain—I truly am."

"What, why?" he asked, but he received no response.

"Let's go," Leepoh said to the others. They left Logan standing alone in the spotlight.

CHAPTER 27

ogan stood alone for a second until his sense of self-preservation kicked in and he sprinted back to his squad. "Get a light on those rocks right away," he demanded.

"Oh my God," one of the men said, which was followed by a chorus of swearing from the rest.

"What do we do?" Guerra asked nervously.

"Sergeant, get on the radio. Tell them we need immediate extraction. Let's get inside. I'm not sure what they intend, but I'm sure it's not good."

"What about McPearsons?" Jenkins asked as he shut off the light.

"Leave his ass out here. This is his fault," Reyes said as he stepped over McPearsons' unconscious form.

Logan looked at the man on the ground and briefly considered it. "Private Tanner, give me a hand," he said with a sigh. The two dragged McPearsons inside.

Once inside and secure, Sergeant Turnbull handed the headset to Captain Logan so he could hear the bad news for himself. Despite the captain's explanation of the situation, 07:00 was still the earliest possible extraction time. He set the headset down with exaggerated care, trying to remain calm, and looked at his watch—05:23.

"What now?" Turnbull asked.

Logan looked around the room. "Let's get as much ammo as we can before we can't reach it. I doubt they can get in, but let's blockade the doors anyway. We'll gather all the supplies we need to weather out the next couple of hours. Then we'll blockade off the barracks—it'll be easier to defend from here—just in case."

The canvas-like buildings were designed for rapid deployment. They were tough and able to withstand seventy-five mph winds and temperatures as low as minus seventy. Even though they had faced wind gusts up to eighty mph on the small island, the shelters held their own. But what they didn't plan for, despite what command knew, was a penguin onslaught. This was supposed to be an out-of-the-way outpost. It was only there to track anything suspicious.

"Why aren't they coming?" asked Reyes plaintively.

"Well," Logan hesitated. "Apparently there's been another attack, this time in Peru. So everybody is scrambling right now. I think there's something bigger going on that we're not privy to," he said.

"Like what?" Turnbull asked, motioning for one of his men to push a table in front of the door.

"I don't know, but what I do know is that Jenson has been replaced by a guy named Maycotte, from D.C.," Logan told him, becoming more distant as he spoke.

"There's something else, isn't there?"

Logan turned to look as crates of ammunition were stacked in the middle of the room. "We have to keep the penguins here as long as we can," he said, distracted by a thought.

Turnbull watched but noticed the others were trying to eavesdrop on the conversation. "Okay, get back to it," he said and followed the captain to the corner of the room. "They're gonna hit the whole island, aren't they?" he asked quietly.

Logan stared straight ahead. "Yes," he said without emotion.

"We're not getting off of here, are we?"

"I . . . I'm n-not sure. I don't think so," Logan said, coming to the realization that this might be his last day.

"Did they say that?" Turnbull asked, rubbing his bald head.

"Not in so many words," the captain said, snapping out of his stupor.

"Tell them the penguins have gone. Then they won't need to," Turnbull urged, trying to find a way out of their situation.

"They're watching. They know. They said there are approximately half a million penguins surrounding us. And I . . . I told them they talk," Logan said, looking away. "I thought that might change things. They said the airstrike would commence at oh-seven-hundred. I asked if they meant airlift, and all I got in return was a noncommittal '*yeah*.' Logan looked at Turnbull and then looked away.

"Strike a deal," Turnbull said, rubbing his head more persistently. This didn't escape the notice of the others and they gathered closer.

"I doubt they would listen."

"Not with the brass—the penguins."

Captain Logan grabbed a chair and sat down heavily. He put his weapon on his lap and leaned back, shaking his head. "Yeah right, Sergeant. I think that piece of—" He stopped himself. "McPearsons sealed our fate."

As if to emphasize his point, the cacophony of calling penguins moved closer to the building and the first sound of beaks scraping against the thick fabric could be heard.

"If these are the same penguins that attacked the Falklands, they know what an airstrike is," Turnbull said, throwing any idea out there he could as he became more desperate.

Logan sat for a minute longer without saying a word. He lifted his head looked at the sergeant. "What the hell, why not?" he said. "Either way—" he said, not finishing the statement. He knew no matter what they did the outcome would most likely be the same.

"It's worth a shot. Either way," Turnbull said. He knew what *either way* meant as well.

CHAPTER 28

"Concentrate on the entrance. It may prove to be the only weak spot," Colonel Nok ordered a group of Macaroni penguins.

"What's happening, Colonel?" asked General Natoo as he approached Nok.

"We thought we'd make short work of the structures, sir. They seemed rather weak. But that hasn't been the case. The walls give, but they don't easily tear."

"We don't need this to turn into a siege, Colonel. The troops are at your command, but the commander said it is imperative we be on our way soon."

Nok looked at the general, understanding what was said. Lavour had given Nok control of this battle, but it had to be resolved in a timely matter. The commander didn't want the massive loss of life like previous skirmishes. "Double your efforts on the entrance," Nok shouted.

The penguins thrust and pecked with all of their ability against the door, but it remained firm in its frame.

^^^

"Persistent little bastards, aren't they?" the now conscious McPearsons said sheepishly while gently touching where he had been hit.

It took every bit of self-control Captain Logan had to keep him from knocking the man to the floor again.

"No thanks to you," Reyes yelled over the chattering and unremitting scraping of claws and beaks against the fabric walls. "It's just a matter of time before there's a breech."

Logan looked at his men and then cautiously peered out a chest-high window. The penguins were leaping toward the window without effect. "General Leepoh," he yelled. "I need to speak to General Leepoh." The response was more hammering against the walls. He tried again with the same results.

"They can't hear you, Captain," Turnbull told him. "*I* can barely hear you."

Logan eyed the sergeant for minute as he tried to think of a way to communicate with the one penguin he knew would listen. "Reyes, get me the two-ways," he said, and Reyes ran to the communications table and grabbed the radios. Logan checked them both to make sure they worked, went to the window, pulled back the window flap, and tossed the radio out into the mass of penguins. "Let's hope this works," he said to no one in particular. The penguins, realizing there was an opening above them, began to jump toward the window and Logan promptly shut it.

The penguin attackers scattered as the device flew toward them. They had seen enough to know that the humans had a myriad of weapons at their disposal. The penguins looked at it curiously when Colonel Nok appeared. "What is it?" he asked no one.

"*General Leepoh,*" a voice called out of it, which sent the penguins scattering in fear. The voice called Leepoh's name repeatedly.

"It's a human," one of the few Jackass penguins said. "A tiny human inside of a thing," he continued.

Nok looked at the Jackass and shook his head in disbelief. "Someone get me General Leepoh. I don't speak human and I want to know what its saying."

A Chinstrap hurried off to find Leepoh and returned with him in less than a minute.

Leepoh heard his name being called out of the box. "What's this?" he asked in idle curiosity.

"Seeing as how I don't speak human, I was hoping you could tell me," Nok said impatiently.

"It's a communication device, and the human commander is calling to me," he said as if it were no big deal. Leepoh had a habit of making the important things seem trivial, which was the only thing he did that actually got on Nok's nerves, even though he acted like *everything* Leepoh did got on his nerves.

"How do you know he wants you specifically?" asked Nok, his voice straining to sound patient.

"Because that's my name in human-speak he is calling out," he said plainly.

"General Leepoh, if you can hear me, please come to the entrance of the building," the captain called through the walkie-talkie.

"He wants me to go to the structure entrance," Leepoh said, looking at the outpost and the swarms of penguins surrounding it.

"Why?" Nok demanded.

"He didn't say," answered Leepoh distantly, listening to the repeated request.

"It's a trap," Natoo added to the discussion.

"I doubt it. If they wanted to, I'm sure they have enough weapons in there to kill hundreds, if not thousands of us, but they haven't."

"Yet," Nok added.

"Correct," Commander Lavour chimed in, after listening to the discussion from afar. "It's your call, General."

"General Leepoh, if you can hear me . . . Please, we haven't much time," Logan urged through the radio.

Leepoh looked at the arched structure. "I'll find out what he wants."

"Well, you're not going alone this time," Nok said, stepping in line with the Gentoo.

Lavour looked at the others and joined Nok and Leepoh.

Leepoh and Nok looked at Lavour questioningly, who threw up his flippers in a 'why not' gesture.

"Colonel Nok," a Rockhopper soldier said excitedly, approaching the colonel. "We've made a small breech in the wall—we'll be in, in no time."

"Very good, Private—now stand down," Nok said, followed by another braying call. After the call all of the penguins forces halted their attack.

"Sir?" the Rockhopper said, confused by the sudden change.

"The human commander wishes to negotiate a surrender," Nok said, drawing a quick look from Leepoh and Lavour. "You never know," Nok said to the other's questioning eyes.

∧∧∧

All of the soldiers had their weapons trained on the small tear in the wall, when everything went silent outside. The heavy breathing of men and the pattering of rainfall was all that could be heard.

"Captain Logan, what is it you wished to discuss?" a familiar penguin voice called from outside.

"Thank you for coming, General Leepoh," Logan said while looking at Sergeant Turnbull and shrugging his shoulders. "We, you, all of us are in imminent danger. Our leaders have decided we are expendable. That we should be sacrificed in order to destroy you and your . . . army."

The formal announcement of this caused a stir among the men, for obvious reasons, and Turnbull had to shout to settle them down.

"We are all expendable in war, Captain Logan. That is the nature of it," Leepoh responded.

"I understand, General Leepoh," Logan said, amazed that what he was hearing came from a penguin. *How many wars have these things fought?* "But there's just a dozen of us in here and thousands of your kind out there. Who do you think will make the bigger sacrifice?"

Leepoh looked at Lavour and Nok for guidance. "How can we trust you? And how will we be destroyed if there are only a dozen of you?"

Logan lowered his head. How could they trust him after what McPearsons did? "I guess you can't trust me. You'll just have to believe me. As far as how—from the air, a weapon called a missile. It causes massive destruction."

Leepoh jerked in alarm. He explained to the others that what happened toward the end of the Battle of the Falklands was about to happen again. Nok still wasn't buying it. Leepoh growled in frustration. "You have to understand, Captain Logan, the penguin your rogue soldier killed was a general. He was well respected and very old. He was a friend to us all. That can't just be forgotten."

"I do understand, General. But this will be the death of us all. If you leave, you can save yourselves and we might be able to escape this."

After Leepoh translated, Colonel Nok was vehement. "He's lying. They're done for and they know it. They're just trying to save their featherless hides."

Leepoh relayed Nok's thoughts to Logan who, in turn, gave him his assurance that they weren't lying. Nok's eyes narrowed with an idea. "Tell them to give us the one who killed General Treeg. If it was truly a rogue as they say it was, then we will issue its punishment. Then we'll leave."

"Out of the question," Logan replied at once without thinking after Leepoh relayed the message.

"Suit yourself, Captain," Leepoh said and started to walk away. He stopped when he heard an argument break out inside.

"Give him up, Captain," Reyes shouted. "This is his fault. Why should we all have to die because of him?"

"Go to hell, Reyes," McPearsons said defiantly.

"That's enough," Turnbull demanded. "It's a trick. As soon as we open the door, they'll rush in. We're all as good as dead anyway."

"To hell with that. I'm not going to die for this piece of trash," Reyes said, becoming increasingly irate.

"Just calm down," Turnbull said, walking toward Reyes, who was pacing back and forth. "There's nothing we can do about it now."

"Yeah, Reyes," McPearsons said, antagonizing the man again. "Quit being such a wuss and take it like a man, like the rest of us."

"Really, McPearsons?" said Turnbull, turning toward the soldier. He threw his hands in the air in exasperation, disbelieving the man could be so stupid.

Reyes glared at McPearsons with hate in his eyes and fear of dying. Before anyone could react, Reyes brought his weapon up and fired, dropping McPearsons with a shot to his abdomen.

CHAPTER 29

"Damn it, Reyes!" more than one voice called out as McPearsons fell to the ground, screaming. Reyes kept his gun at the ready, keeping everyone at bay.

"What are you doing?" Turnbull asked with exaggerated slowness, keeping his eye on the weapon.

"I'm saving our lives. If those things want him, we give him to them. It's our only chance. Now stay back," Reyes demanded as he moved across the room to where McPearsons lay. "Jenkins, Walker, drag him to the door," he ordered, motioning at the men with his gun.

The two hesitated, looking to Captain Logan.

"Do it!" Reyes yelled as he moved closer to the door. The two men complied and pulled McPearsons toward the door. "Good. Get rid of his gear too," he said, and the men obliged, not looking at McPearsons, who was writhing and moaning in pain. "Penguin!" Reyes shouted. "What's the penguin's name?" he asked Logan.

Logan didn't respond at first. He had lost everything. Not just the battle and most likely his life, but control of his unit and self-respect. He conceded, deciding that whatever happened from this point didn't matter. "Leepoh," he answered softly.

"Leepoh, are you still there?" Reyes shouted without taking his eyes off of Turnbull or the others.

Leepoh waited for a second before answering. "Yes," he said, looking warily at Lavour and Nok.

"I'm Private First Class Reyes. Captain Logan is no longer in command and I have the one you want. No tricks, right?" asked Reyes, sounding a little unsure of his plan.

"No tricks," answered Leepoh after translating for Nok.

"And you'll leave immediately?"

"Immediately after our punishment is dealt, yes," Leepoh said, looking at Nok, who received translation from Lavour and then nodded his head in agreement.

"Okay, I've wounded him. Clear the entry and we'll drag him out."

"Damn you, Reyes. Damn you," McPearsons cursed between gritted teeth.

"Get him out of here," Reyes ordered the others.

"No. No, don't. C'mon, guys—don't do this," McPearsons whimpered, appealing to Jenkins and Walker.

"He's the reason we're in this situation," Reyes implored the others. "This is our only chance." Reyes stooped down next to McPearsons, putting his mouth close to his ear. "C'mon, McPearsons, take it like a man."

As the men reached for the door, Logan stood up. "No! I am still in command here. We are soldiers and we will not sacrifice one another, regardless of the circumstances. We have dignity and honor. I will not allow this. We live together, we fight together, and we will die together."

Reyes's shoulders slumped and his helpers watched, not knowing what to do.

"Nice speech, Cap," McPearsons said cockily between labored breaths. "Now you be a good boy, Reyes, and do what your captain told you."

Logan looked at the wounded man, confounded by the soldier's arrogance.

"I'm sorry, Captain," Reyes said and then looked at Jenkins. "Get the door."

"Stop," Logan shouted as he brought his weapon to bear on Reyes.

Reyes saw him and pulled his trigger first. Logan fell to his knees, his eyes wide in surprise and his forehead covered in blood, and fell face forward to the ground.

"No!" shouted Turnbull, seeing the captain die. He pointed his weapon toward Reyes and pulled the trigger. Reyes took a bullet to the arm and fell to the ground, but not before squeezing off a burst of his own. Sergeant Turnbull fell dead instantly.

The other soldiers watched in disbelief at the chaos that was taking place. Reyes got himself up, pointing his weapon at the others. "Get him outside, now," he demanded of Jenkins and Walker. "Don't even think about it," he told Guerra, who had ducked for cover during the shootout and looked like he might make an effort to stop them. "Stand clear," Reyes shouted breathlessly through his pain.

Leepoh told the others, and the surrounding penguins began to chatter nervously. All were on edge after hearing the gunfire.

The door flew open and Jenkins and Walker threw the strenuously protesting McPearsons to the ground. The severely wounded man tried to crawl back to the door but his head was met by Reyes's boot. "Here's our part of the bargain. Do what you will, but do it quickly, before we all die."

Reyes stumbled back to the door and looked back at McPearsons. McPearsons screamed a torrent of obscenities at him. The two men locked eyes and, for a second, McPearsons thought the other would change his mind. Then Reyes slammed the door shut.

"It's all yours, Colonel Nok," Leepoh said, turning away.

"Commander Lavour, please take the others. But tell the Rockhoppers of RHC 23 to remain. We will avenge the death of our leader, our father. Get to safety, my friend, in case they *are* telling the truth."

Lavour didn't say a word but got straight to work on gathering the forces, leaving Nok to deal with his loss and his retribution.

"He was a good penguin," said Leepoh before heading out.

"That he was, Leepoh. A remarkable penguin," Nok said, looking away. "Now get out of here—we'll catch up to you before you hit the cape."

Leepoh nodded his head and began to walk away when McPearsons mouth started again. "You're leaving? Ha," he laughed. "Oh, thank God. I knew this was a load of bull. That idiot Reyes is gonna pay for this."

Leepoh stopped and looked back at the man as he tried to get to his knees while holding on to his profusely bleeding gunshot. "I'm afraid your thanks to your deity are premature, human. Your time of judgment is upon you," Leepoh said and then scampered away. He turned his head from the look of horror in the doomed man's eyes.

After Lavour called the others to sea, over a thousand Rockhoppers from RHC 23 came out of the darkness. With Keerka leading the way, they rallied around Nok and the hapless man.

"My fellow Rockhoppers," Nok spoke solemnly. "We had reached an accord with the humans and in an act of cowardice, this human broke that accord. He shamefully killed our leader and friend, General Treeg. Honor dictates that Treeg must be avenged and we must send this human to the depths of the underworld. Be as the Petrels—leave no flesh on his bones."

McPearsons knew his time was up when Leepoh walked away. He had stopped applying pressure to his wound, allowing the blood to flow more freely. He was barely conscious when the attack came and only managed a few gargled screams before it was over.

Reyes watched from the window and the others listened as the penguin calls filled the air. They heard scuffling noises and what they thought was McPearsons screaming. In a matter of minutes, it was over. Once again, only the rain could be heard.

Jenkins cautiously peered out the door and saw nothing but the nauseating mass of what used to be Specialist McPearsons. "All gone," he said and rested his hands on his knees, weakened by what he saw.

Reyes rushed to the communications center and called their commander. "Yes, they're all gone, sir." He paused. "Killed in the assault, as well as

Sergeant Turnbull and Specialist McPearsons," he said, looking at the others. "Yes, sir, we'll be waiting, sir. Thank you." Reyes looked at the others once again. "I told you we'd get out of this. Colonel Maycotte said to expect relief shortly. Now we're going to have to stick together on what happened here."

"What're we gonna say?" Jenkins asked as he sat down.

"It doesn't matter," said Guerra as he walked to the door and looked at the breaking clouds. "The satellites saw everything."

"We'll tell them it was McPearsons," Reyes said, ignoring Guerra. "It's close to the truth."

Jenkins ignored Reyes, his eyes following Guerra. "What is it?" he asked, hearing a distant roar.

Just before the first missile struck the small island of Isla Sola, Guerra and Reyes locked eyes. "I guess they *really* wanted to make sure," Guerra said.

ʌʌʌ

"Looks like they *were* telling the truth," Leepoh said to Lavour when Nok and Keerka arrived.

They all watched from a safe distance in silence, riding the swells of the South Atlantic as Isla Sola was repeatedly hammered by explosions.

"I think the Overlord seriously underestimated these creatures," Leepoh said to no one in particular.

"No," Lavour corrected him. "I don't think he did at all. I think he knew *exactly* what he was doing," he said distantly, but with a determination in his voice. "Are we ready?" he asked after a prolonged silence.

"Ready here, Commander," announced Leepoh proudly before disappearing below the surface of the water.

"We're ready as well," Nok said with Keerka by his side.

"I'll follow your lead, Commander," Mevoule added.

"If I may ask a favor, Commander?" asked Meuseaux tentatively.

"Yes you may, my friend," Lavour told him with the utmost sincerity.

"Could we go by way of the camp, where I left the humans? To make sure they got away safely—they did save my life."

"Absolutely, Meuseaux—providing it's safe," said Lavour. "Captain Mevoule, once we arrive back on Antarctica, contact the Resistance Council—I'm sure Liutites has a death edict on me."

"For me as well. But I'm sure we'll be contacted before we have to go in search of them."

"What do you say we dispose of a despot?" Leepoh said, popping his head up from below the surface.

"Very well, then," Lavour said enthusiastically. "Lead the way."

Leepoh twitched his head in surprise. "Very well. Onward, brave penguins, to the shores of destiny, where we shall satisfy our gullets with the blood of our enemies," he said with far too much enthusiasm and cheerfulness before paddling away.

"Is he all right, Commander?" Meuseaux asked Lavour of Leepoh.

"You know, I get asked that quite a bit," Lavour responded without answering the question. He too swam away.

Meuseaux looked at Mevoule, who gave his best shrug, and the two hurried to catch up to Lavour and the others.

CHAPTER 30

Randy and Gina sat down after checking and reinforcing the door blockade. The persistent pecking and scratching had continued for days on end, yet the penguin marauders had had no success at gaining entrance. Although the two humans were relatively safe, the noise was beginning to wear on their nerves.

"Do you really believe they killed *everybody* in Antarctica?" Randy asked, trying to make conversation to distract them from the noise. "I mean that's somewhere around a thousand people or more. Plus, I was thinking—if they can't get inside here, how'd they get inside *everywhere* else? I think that penguin was lying."

Gina looked at Randy with tired eyes. "One big difference, genius . . ."

"What's that?"

"We knew they were coming and what their intentions were. The others didn't."

"You're so smart," he said mockingly but with his usual jocularity. "I have to use the facilities—yell if you need me."

"Of course," she said with a tinge of amusement.

Randy headed off toward the restroom, grumbling along the way about the layers of clothing he had to remove to accomplish the task. Since the siege had begun, the two of them thought it would be wise to wear their cold gear at all times.

Gina sat back with her gun in her hand and became oblivious to the steady rapping of beaks. She wondered how long she and Randy could keep each other going, how long they could remain holed up in these cramped quarters, and if anyone would ever come. Then her mind drifted away, toward home and her parents. She wondered what they would think of Randy, and what he'd think of them. Her thoughts turned to dreams—dreams of a wedding in the hills near the Central California coast. Then Gina heard Randy bemoaning putting back on his gear, and she laughed at his less-than-convincing cantankerous mood.

Gina sat up as Randy rushed back in. Sometime during her daydream, the pecking had stopped. "What happened?" he asked while he struggled to put back on his top layer.

Gina shrugged, confused by the sudden silence as well.

They both walked slowly to the window and peered out. The sun was making longer regular appearances, but still for no more than an hour. It was high noon, and what they saw took what hope they had and resoundingly crushed it. What was once a siege of only a hundred or more—now were innumerable. A countless horde of penguins stretched out as far as the light would permit the eye to see.

Gina and Randy looked at each other with their hearts in their throats and resignation on their faces.

CHAPTER 31

"I thought I'd be glad to be home," Corporal Meuseaux complained as they trudged over icy outcrops.

"If I made this place my home, I wouldn't come home," Leepoh remarked after picking himself up from slipping on the ice.

Pín, the Blue, who had become Meuseaux's constant companion, chirped in agreement with Leepoh.

"Well, I usually stick to the coastal areas," Meuseaux said defensively.

"Hey, watch it there, little fella—I think you hurt your daddy's feelings," Leepoh told the Blue.

Pín barked an unmistakable insult at Leepoh and hopped to Meuseaux's side, glaring at the Gentoo as he did.

"You sure have a way with penguins," Nok said to Leepoh as he and Keerka clambered over the icy crags.

"That I do."

"You still don't get sarcasm, do you?" Nok followed up.

"Bah, I would if I heard it."

"What's that supposed to mean?" asked Nok, looking at Leepoh while climbing over an ice cleft.

"It means it looks like we might be facing our first battle of this revolt."

"Huh?" said Nok, sounding confused until Keerka guided his gaze to the expanse of ground ahead of them. On the edge of the ice floe was the human base surrounded by Royal Emperor elite warriors and Adélie penguins. "Oh," was all Nok could say.

Lavour stood stoically in the vague sunlight with Mevoule at his side. Meuseaux, Pín, Leepoh, Nok, Keerka, and Natoo soon joined him. They walked toward the forces which besieged the humans. They were followed by the Alliance of Independent Colonies. As they approached, a large Royal Emperor took notice and called his elite warriors to his side.

"Is that Liutites?" asked Natoo.

"No," answered Leepoh. "It's just one of his underlings."

Lavour looked at his friends for a last bit of reassurance and Mevoule gave him a nod. Lavour then looked at the Royal Emperor commander. "Leader of the Penguin Defense Alliance forces, I am Commander Lavour of the Alliance of Independent Colonies. You must stand down immediately."

Captain Astramachos stood unfazed. "Adélie," he snapped. "Take a message to the Supreme Commander. Tell him that the Chinstrap deserter has returned and that it is experiencing delusions of superiority." The messenger departed and Astramachos called for another Adélie. "I will not lower myself to speak to this miscreant directly. Go and ask him why we should stand down and on whose authority?" he said in his most condescending voice.

"Yes, sir," the Adélie said and hurried off to Lavour.

"Sir," one of the elite warriors whispered to Astramachos. "Maybe we should surrender to him."

The captain looked at him sideways. "And why would I do that?" he asked angrily.

"Because that might get us close enough to him to *kill* him," he said sinisterly. "Think of the praise and adulation you would receive from the Overlord. You may even be promoted—perhaps even to fill Diutes's spot as commander—and you could take me along with you."

The Royal Emperor mulled it over. "Yes," he hissed. Commander Astramachos liked the sound of it. Without hesitation, he stabbed his long beak into the warrior's throat and the horrified subordinate fell to the ground, gasping for air. He pulled his beak free and looked him in the eye. "Thank you for the suggestion. I just might use it. But I can't let anybody else take credit for my idea," he said and stabbed the penguin one more time for good measure.

∧∧

"Commander Lavour," the Adélie said, snapping a salute. "Mearna will be pleased to find out you have finally arrived."

"Excuse me?" Lavour said, surprised.

"I apologize for my informality, sir, but I am pressed for time. I am Sergeant Gichi and I am a member of the Resistance."

"Oh," said Lavour. "I'm pleased to meet you. What about the Royal. What did he say?"

"The usual elitist babble—*on whose authority do you act, you're a lesser penguin,* and so forth. But be cautious—do not take him prisoner. He will betray you. The Adélies are with you. What message would you like me to bring to the Resistance Council?"

Lavour looked at Mevoule, unsure about what to say. "Tell them we will begin our march toward PIC tomorrow and I would like to coordinate our efforts with them."

"Yes, sir," Gichi said and snapped a salute as he began to leave.

"And tell that bloated pile of guano that I act on the authority of free penguins everywhere, and tell him to stand down or prepare to die."

"With pleasure, sir," the Adélie said and took his leave.

In the fading light of the fleeting day, Commander Lavour walked along the front of his command and gave the order to prepare for battle once again. There was no need for grand speeches; each member of the AIC knew what needed to be done and they believed in their cause enough to have no doubts.

Astramachos listened to Lavour's message, trembling with fury as Gichi spoke. "He also mentioned something about your head being buried so far up Liutites's backside that when you—"

"That's enough," the captain howled, cutting off the Adélie's embellishment. "Kill him. Kill that Chinstrap," Astramachos screamed maniacally. "Kill them all."

The Adélies were placed on the front line and were forced to lead the charge, with the Royal Emperors in the rear. Lavour remained in front of his soldiers and they all braced for the first impact of battle. Just before contact between the opposing forces was made, the Adélies, along with the few Kings who followed, stopped their advance and bowed to submit to Lavour's authority.

"We are at your command," one of the Adélie told Lavour.

"As I hoped it would be. Fall in, my friends," replied Commander Lavour.

"What? What are they doing?" Captain Astramachos screamed at one of the elite warriors. He surveyed the field and knew there was no way to win. He decided to implement his acquired plan. He had no other options; if they retreated, he would die at the Supreme Commander's beak, if not the Overlord's. If he cut the head off the beast, then the body would die with it. *Take out their leader and I would be a martyr for the ages,* he whispered to himself. He explained his plan to his cohorts and walked out to meet Lavour.

"Commander Lavour, I submit and surrender," Captain Astramachos said, bowing his head.

Lavour approached the captain. He kept Sergeant Gichi's warning in his mind and stayed a safe distance away. "That's far enough," said Lavour as he stood looking up at the large penguin. "Do you truly submit to our authority, Royal Emperor?"

"Yes," Astramachos said slowly, shifting his weight slightly.

Lavour studied the Royal Emperor in the ebbing light. He detected the movement and that small hint of deception and duplicity was all he needed. He turned his back on his enemy, trusting the others to protect him, and walked a meter further away. Lavour turned to face him once more. Astramachos was looking for an opportunity to attack. Lavour looked him in the eye. "You lack integrity," Lavour said plainly. "Kill them."

Astramachos's eyes widened in surprise as the forces of the AIC tore into the Royal Emperors. The captain was gone within minutes, but the warriors fought to the last. They stabbed and swung viscously with staff, spear, and beak. But with only a hundred warriors against countless others, they too were dispatched in minutes.

"May the Ancients forgive us," said Lavour as he watched the mêlée wind down.

CHAPTER 32

"If they breech the . . ." Randy said, looking at Gina and not wanting to finish his sentence.

"You mean *when* they breech the door," Gina corrected him, placing the gun in his hand. "It'll be quicker. I can't do it myself."

He wrapped his hand around hers without saying a word. In a million scenarios of possible deaths, he never could have imagined it would end this way. A few short months ago, this was the beginning of something exciting—an adventure to talk about for a lifetime. In a way, it was still true and he decided, as he took Gina in his arms, there was nobody else in the world he would rather have at his side when all things ended.

While whispering *I love you* to each other, in what they guessed would be their final embrace, they heard a tapping at the door—not the persistent attempt at a forceful entrance, but more an *'excuse me, hello,'* polite tapping. Gina and Randy pulled away from their embrace, looked at the door, and then back to one another. They both carried concerned expressions as the tapping began and stopped again. They slowly walked hand-in-hand to the door and listened closely.

"Randy, Gina, it isss Meuseaux. If you are safe, please open your door," Meuseaux's voice said, nearly flooring them with surprise.

The two looked at each other in disbelief and then quickly began to move the barricade from the door.

"Wait," Randy said, halting the progress. "What if it isn't Meuseaux?"

"It sounds like him," Gina said, resuming her work.

"Yeah, but there's millions of penguins, I'm sure to us all of their vocalizations sound similar. I mean we can barely tell them apart by looking at them, if even then. They could be trying a different tactic."

"Okay, you're right—so let's make sure," she said, turning her attention back to the door. "Meuseaux, before we open the door, we have to make certain it is you."

"I underssstand," Meuseaux called back.

"If it's him, he's dragging his S's again," Randy commented.

"He probably didn't have much opportunity to speak *human* while he was away," Gina said dryly. "Meuseaux, what happened the first time we met?"

"Do you mean after you fell off your vehicle?"

"Open the door, Randy," she said, convinced.

Randy gave her a questioning look, which she ignored. She had never told him all of the circumstances of their first meeting.

The two pulled the rest of the barricade out of the way and then cautiously opened the door. Meuseaux, followed by Mevoule, Pín, Lavour, Leepoh, Nok, and Keerka walked across the threshold. Randy and Gina had to step back as the entourage entered as if the building was their own.

"It iss good to sssee that you are alive," Meuseaux said as he greeted them.

"We almost weren't," Randy said, looking outside. "I guess we owe you another thank-you."

"It is Commander Lavour whom you should thank. He obtained the victory," Meuseaux said, indicating Lavour.

"Well, then, we thank you, Commander Lavour," Randy told him.

Gina bowed her head in appreciation.

Lavour stood silently at first, but after a moment's hesitation he shuffled toward them. "I am glad to find that you escaped from the Overlord and had such a capacity of forgiveness to assist a distressed fellow creature, such as Meuseaux was."

"He is a remarkable penguin and our friend," Gina told him.

"Indeed he is," Lavour said, looking at Meuseaux and maintaining his air of authority. "I am pleased to have met you, Gina. Meuseaux has told me much about you. Your paths should be safe now. Those who tormented you will no longer do so. There is a . . . much human presence nearby," Lavour said, getting his phrasing confused. "We have assured their safety, Meuseaux—now we must be going," he said to the corporal in penguin.

"Yes, sir," Meuseaux said, sounding a little forlorn. "My friends, this isss our farewell," he said, raising his head to look into their eyes.

Gina and Randy both stooped down and stroked his back and head affectionately. "We wish you luck, and stay safe, my friend—we will never forget you," Randy said for the both of them.

"And may good fortune be with you as well."

Gina squeezed the tip of his flipper gently as he was escorted away by Nok, who was noticeably wary of being in such close proximity to the humans.

Gina held the door and they all began to file out, when Leepoh came to a stop. "Wait," he said and approached Randy. "I have a question for you."

"Okay," Randy said, somewhat unsure of what was to come. He squatted back down to the penguin's height and awaited his question.

"Several seasons ago, you, or a human who looked very similar to you, came to my island, doing what you called *taking pictures*."

"Possibly," he said hesitantly, not sure of where this was leading. "Like I told you before, I've taken pictures of a Gentoo colony."

"Leepoh stared at the man, briefly hesitating before continuing. "When you or they departed, they took a Gentoo with a lame foot. Was that you, and if so, what have you done with him?"

"Yes, it was us," the man answered. "We knew the little guy would struggle to survive with his foot being the way it was. We took him to a facility in California—to take care of him."

Leepoh stood with his eyes wide, paralyzed by the answer. He was scared, angry, and hopeful all at once. Shaken to his core, he fell to his belly and the others came to his side. "That . . . that was my fledgling, my son. He is alive?"

"Yeah, definitely," Randy said proudly. "He's strong and healthy, and I see him several times a year. He swims with the other penguins and—"

"He swims, in the sea?" Leepoh asked excitedly.

"He does swim, but not in the sea—it would be too dangerous for him. I assure you—no, I *promise* you, he is well taken care of and he is loved. He will live a long, healthy life," Randy said, smiling at seeing the penguin's outburst of emotion.

Leepoh's head swam and he felt as if his world was turned upside down. The years of hatred he felt for the humans were unfounded for him personally, until he thought of the loss of his mate and her heartbreak at not knowing. But even then, nothing could squelch his joy at hearing that his little Mee'oni was alive and well. He felt pangs of guilt for his friends, knowing their losses would never have a happy ending. But there they stood, watching him, with genuine happiness for him showing in their eyes.

Leepoh felt his life was complete as it would ever be. His lost son was found. His friends were his family now. He would go with them, to fight by their sides against the forces of evil and if necessary, to die for or with them. And he would, one day, take his journey to join the noble Ancients complete. "Hah!" he exclaimed. "Very good, Randy. When you travel to this California again, please give my love to my Mee'oni."

"I live in California and I will," Randy said happily.

"Hah! He lives in California!" Leepoh shouted to his friends joyfully as he walked away.

The rest of the penguins followed Leepoh. Lavour took up the rear. The commander stopped and looked back at the humans, who were watching them walk away, and gave them a nod of appreciation.

Randy waved and had a realization. "My camera!" he announced. Gina ran and brought it back, and he was able to take a few shots before they were gone. With the moon now illuminating the icy landscape, they watched them disappear into the night.

CHAPTER 33

"**S**upreme Commander Liutites, sir," Lieutenant Antilodon announced when he entered his command room.

"Yes, what is it?" Liutites snapped.

"We have . . . unfortunate information, sir," the lieutenant said, trying to ease the news.

Liutites had fire in his eyes instantly but said nothing; instead, he let the moment simmer in the silence. "Well, Lieutenant?"

"First, the—" Antilodon began before getting interrupted.

"Wait, Lieutenant, let me understand this—there's a first? So that means there has to be a second," Liutites said, sounding half crazed.

"Yes, sir," Antilodon said, looking like he wanted nothing more than to take a few steps back but not daring to.

"Guards, find me something to kill—preferably a Chinstrap," shouted Liutites. Two of his four guards immediately left the room in search of a victim, leaving the unfortunate Lieutenant Antilodon alone to face Liutites's ire. "You were saying, Lieutenant . . ."

"The Adélie forces are being decimated by the humans, sir. The entire fourth army is gone, including the Royal Emperor advisors."

Liutites only reacted with a slight twitch, and only when Antilodon mentioned the Royals. "Go on," he said, knowing he was being eased into the worst of it.

"The same is happening to the first and fifth, but the third is faring much better."

"I don't care about the Adélie armies, Lieutenant. They are expendable," Liutites said slowly and malevolently. "Tell me the rest—I don't have time for this."

"Captain Astramachos's attack force at the encampment, where the escaped humans are hiding, has been destroyed . . . by the Chinstrap, Lavour's, army."

Liutites brought himself up to full height and stood still and silent for a few tense heartbeats. The Supreme Commander exploded into a blind fit of rage. He attacked the lieutenant, viciously slapping him with his flippers. "Do you know what this means?" he screamed at Antilodon and sent him flailing to the ground from a hard slap. Liutites paused in his fury and looked around the room madly. "Mearna," he growled throatily. "Guards, summon her at once."

Lieutenant Antilodon struggled to get to his feet to escape his commander's wrath.

"Where are Lavour and his co-conspirators now, Lieutenant?" Liutites asked, turning his attention back on the subordinate.

"Unknown, sir," Antilodon told him and braced himself for the next attack, looking like he would fight back this time.

"Unknown?" Liutites growled even more maniacally than before.

"Yes, sir," the lieutenant said. Any thoughts of fighting back turned to looking for an escape.

"Unknown, you say? Unknown," he began to say the word as if it were a mantra. "Unknown . . . unknown . . . unknown." He continued as he advanced toward the lieutenant.

^^^

In the corridor near the Resistance Council's hidden chamber, Mearna was stopped by two elite guards. "The Supreme Commander demands your presence at once, milady."

At least they were cordial, even if she did hate being called milady. *So, Liutites was having another one of his tantrums*, she nearly said out loud. "Very well," she said reluctantly. "Where is he?"

"His command room," the guard answered.

"I will be there at once—you're excused," she told the guards, who seemed to be waiting to escort her.

Once the guards disappeared, Mearna turned to Ceocilus who, as always, was waiting in the shadows. "I don't have time for him," she said as if it were a mere annoyance.

"That didn't sound like a request," Ceocilus said.

"Which means he might be on the edge of losing control," she said, concerned about her plans. "Tell the Resistance Council it is too dangerous for them to remain here and to gather their forces and join Lavour. I'll deal with Liutites."

"Understood," said Ceocilus with a touch of worry for her safety.

"I have to meet my warriors as they return from sea. I'll be a day's journey behind them," she reassured him. "Go now—see that they leave safely."

"And if Liutites tries to kill you in the meantime?" he asked her.

"He won't. And if he does, I'll have the Overlord's warriors kill him, but that would severely disrupt my plans. I *need* Liutites to kill the Overlord. Antaean's forces are loyal to him, and in the event of his death, they are loyal to me. Liutites has to do it. He is the only one who has enough warriors strictly obedient to him," she said as she began to walk away.

"Until now," Ceocilus said conspiratorially.

Mearna just fixed him with a look.

"Be careful, Mother," he told her.

"Go," was all she said, waving him away.

CHAPTER 34

In a low depression, near the mountainous area known as Heritage Range, two groups of penguins stood in the night. The moon hid behind clouds and had not presented itself to illuminate the proceedings, which suited them fine. They discussed a treaty, albeit one-sided. Liutites's emissary, Captain Leotholis, presented his offer and the other reacted.

"The clan of K'K'Ru-ki would never consider the idea of joining in an alliance with a penguin as mad as Liutites," Kra K'K'ki-ro, the newly appointed leader of the *Free* Emperors told the Royal Emperor. Leotholis had brought Liutites's message of forming an alliance to overthrow the Overlord. The Free Emperors however, had been forewarned and were told by Resistance Council messengers of K'K'Ru-ki's death.

"It is a generous offer, Kra. Together, we can bring peace back to penguinkind," Leotholis said with a hint of warning in his tone.

"We had peace before the Overlord," Kra K'K'ki-ro countered. "If only K'K'Ru-ki were here to direct us in such matters," he said accusingly.

Leotholis shifted uncomfortably under his gaze.

"But he can't be here, can he? Can he, *Royal Emperor?*" Kra K'K'ki-ro asked angrily of Leotholis, who said nothing. "What are our options, should we choose not to join you?"

Leotholis answered with only a hard glare.

"Wait, let me guess. Could it be perhaps . . . death? Are you and your legion going to kill us all, Captain?" Kra K'K'ki-ro asked, mocking the Royal Emperor. "Were those your supreme commander's orders? Answer me!"

Leotholis stared for a moment longer. "If that is what you choose. The *new* Overlord will have little use for an inferior race of penguins such as yourselves. It is unfortunate that you will not live long enough to see the end of your kind." The captain signaled with his flipper, and his elite warriors brought their weapons to bear and began to march toward the group of unarmed Emperors.

"Predictable," Kra K'K'ki-ro snorted. "I may not survive this battle, but at least I will die knowing the arrogance of your kind will be your deaths."

"What are you spouting off about, Kra?" Leotholis asked, angrily turning back toward the Emperor.

"Did you or your master really think we didn't know you were coming? Prepare to meet *your* end, *Royal* Emperor. You will not find a place of honor at the side of the Ancients."

After news of K'K'Ru-ki's death had reached them, the members of his clan gathered the other free clans and united with them for this moment. They remained hidden in the nearby hills until Kra K'K'ki-ro called them to battle. While watching the Royal Emperor carefully, Kra K'K'ki-ro made a low sub-sonic grunt, calling the Free Emperors to arms. Nearly three thousand Emperors answered his call from atop a nearby rise. The answering calls created a harmonic tone which filled the night air.

Leotholis watched the darkened forms of the Emperors as they slid down the icy slope. He looked back at Kra K'K'ki-ro and narrowed his eyes. "It means nothing," he spit out and then lashed out, furiously slapping at the Emperor with his flippers.

Kra K'K'ki-ro endured the initial assault and returned the attack with his beak, stabbing at Leotholis's chest repeatedly. The Royal Emperor's thick layer of fat and muscle kept him from sustaining serious injury from the smaller penguin's attacks. Although his wounds were superficial, it was enough to infuriate the captain.

Leotholis pushed the Emperor away with his beak and stabbed wildly at his neck, grazing him. Kra K'K'ki-ro fell back from the force of the attack and looked up to see the Royal become further infuriated at not delivering a killing blow. He flipped to his stomach and began to toboggan away.

Kra K'K'ki-ro saw Emperors and Royal Emperors fully engaged in battle ahead of him. The Royal Emperor warriors stabbed and swung with their spears, and the Emperors attacked en masse with their beaks. Their tactics cost them dearly, however; for every Royal Emperor killed, three Free Emperors fell.

Kra K'K'ki-ro risked a look back to see if he had lost his pursuer. He spotted Leotholis coming at him, running faster than a penguin of his size should be able to.

Leotholis hissed evilly before diving at the prostrate Emperor. Kra K'K'ki-ro dug his claws into the ice and gave a hard kick to propel him just out of reach of Leotholis's attack. The captain landed face-first on the spot where his target had just been.

Kra K'K'ki-ro scooted away, smiling inwardly with satisfaction, and attempted to make his escape. Leotholis began tobogganing as well, and the now completely enraged Royal quickly closed the gap between them. Kra K'K'ki-ro cursed himself for taking the time to gloat.

Kra K'K'ki-ro attempted to slide away, but his path was blocked by the body of a dead Royal. As he tried to stand, he heard the maddened scream of Leotholis behind him and knew there was nothing he could do. He could fight, he would fight, but in the end, the much more powerful and hate-filled Royal would make quick work of him. He resigned himself to death.

At the last possible moment before contact, several Free Emperors slid into the captain and knocked him to the ice as he stood. They righted themselves quickly and stabbed feverishly at the downed Royal Emperor until he no longer moved, and went in search of another.

Kra K'K'ki-ro thanked the Ancients for such good fortune and ambled over to Leotholis. "Are you still alive, you pathetic excuse for a penguin?"

Leotholis tried to respond but only managed a raspy hiss.

"Good. I wanted you to live long enough to see your mighty elite warriors lose to a *lesser* clan."

The captain only rasped another hiss but eyed him with malevolence nonetheless.

"You see, Captain, you can't—" Kra K'K'ki-ro stopped mid-sentence as a sudden burning and searing pain overwhelmed him. He looked down and saw a Leopard Seal's tooth protruding from his chest. It took a couple of moments before he realized what he was looking at. The spear-tip was pulled back from where it came. Kra K'K'ki-ro looked down at Leotholis, whose eyes belied a great sense of satisfaction as he hissed a gurgled laugh. Kra K'K'ki-ro fell forward and drove his beak into the Royal Emperor, silencing him at last, and died with his beak buried in his enemy.

CHAPTER 35

Mearna entered the command room of Supreme Commander Liutites and found him, panting and standing over the bloodied corpse of Lieutenant Antilodon. His guards stood motionless by the door, eyes forward.

"Liutites," Mearna called out, getting no response. "Liutites," she called out again, more forcefully.

He snapped his head toward her, spraying tiny droplets of his victim's blood across the room. "You . . ." he hissed in a low, demented voice.

Mearna took a step back, unsure if maybe she had overplayed him or if he had finally completely lost his mind.

"Where are those warriors you promised me?" he growled.

Mearna waited before answering as she tried to gauge the depths of his madness. She watched him until she saw a tiny spark of rational thought in his eyes. She took a noticeable breath of relief. As long as he held a single strand of sanity, Mearna knew she could manipulate him. But she also knew he wouldn't hold on to his stability much longer. "They are expected tomorrow."

"Tomorrow may be too late!" he barked out.

"Why would that be?" she asked, already knowing the answer.

"That Chinstrap has returned, and he has control over *my armies*," he grunted, never taking is eyes off of her.

"There is nothing to fear—"

"Did I say I was afraid?" Liutites screamed at her. "I want the Chinstrap dead! I *need* those warriors."

Normally, Liutites would never dare raise his voice to her. It was an indication of how close to the edge he had gone. Now she had to be stern with him and give him something to occupy his mind. "Does the Overlord know Lavour has returned?"

"Most likely," he said, finally taking his eyes off of her.

"Then now is your opportunity," she said, a little quieter.

"Now?" he asked, disbelieving, thinking there couldn't be a worse time to act.

"Yes, Liutites—don't you see? He will be distracted by Lavour's impending attack. Kill him and we'll be rid of two problems," she said, letting him draw his own conclusions as to what she meant by *two problems*.

"I still haven't heard from the feral Emperors. They might still join me, or, at the very least, I'll have Leotholis back to assist me," Liutites said, more to himself. With his mind now on other things, he had calmed down considerably. He looked through half-mad eyes. "I will act tomorrow. Take a battalion of elite warriors loyal to Antaean with you and go meet the returning warriors. Your new warriors will act as reinforcements. By the time you return, I will be the new Overlord and Antaean will be dead."

"Yes, my lord," she said to stroke his pride.

"Be cautious of the humans," he said, dismissing her.

"Yes, as we all should be," she said, exiting the command room. She turned down the corridor and headed straight for the Overlord's chambers.

CHAPTER 36

Gina and Randy sat, dozing in their chairs. The time since the AIC left had been the most relaxing they had experienced since before they arrived in Antarctica. There was no research to do, no major storms, no lost friends, no escaping peril, no battles, no sieges, and no threats. With little else to do except wait and hope for rescue, they began to look at their time as a vacation.

The two relaxed in separate recliner chairs in the common room. Gina lazily opened her eyes, thinking she had heard something. She listened, decided it was the wind, and closed her eyes once more. A distant *'whump, whump, whump'* noise made its presence known, and this time, both Gina's and Randy's eyes opened.

They looked at each other as the noise grew louder. "Helicopter!" they exclaimed in unison and jumped from their seats.

"The flares," Randy told Gina. She was a step ahead of him and was already grabbing them off a nearby shelf. "It's getting closer," he said, stating the obvious as always.

Gina leaned into Randy and gave him a congratulatory kiss as he struggled with his gloves. He looked at her and smiled. They threw on their hoods and ran into the dim midday sun. Gina struck a flare.

It became quickly apparent that the flare was unnecessary. The helicopter was already low enough to indicate that the base was its intended target all along. Gina dropped the flare, and then she and Randy went back inside to avoid the wind and ice kicked up by the powerful rotors.

"I wonder who it is," Randy said aloud.

"I don't care, as long as we get to go home," Gina said, pushing the door closed. "Probably some corporate advisor for GT—nobody else would be stupid enough to fly in these conditions."

"Don't you mean *bold* enough?" Randy remarked. "Regardless, let's greet them as liberators," he said after hearing the rotors wind down. He opened the door and was surprised to find several soldiers and Vance Lyons, founder, president, and CEO of GT.

Gina saw him and her reaction was immediate. "Bastard," she yelled and punched him solidly in the nose.

Vance grabbed his face and cussed as he stumbled backwards. The soldier next to him restrained Gina from further violence. "It's all right," he said as more soldiers came forward and directed Gina and Randy inside. "I guess I deserved that," he said with a cocky smirk, looking down his bloodied nose at Gina. "I wish I could say it's good to see you, but . . ."

"You son of a bitch," Gina said, cursing Vance again, disgusted by his arrogance. "Do you *know* who you're dealing with, what he's done and attempted to do?" she said to the soldiers.

"He's done a lot more than what you know of, ma'am," one of the other men said as he walked into the room.

Gina straightened in surprise. "I know of quite a bit," she said, unsure of how to take the man.

"Allow me to introduce myself. I am Colonel Maycotte," he said, taking her hand in greeting after pulling back his hood. The colonel was in his late fifties, with a stocky build and average height. With olive skin and a thick mustache, he was an otherwise nondescript man. But as he greeted Gina, his eyes belied a greater knowledge than his outward appearance showed. "We are surprised to find you alive. So far, you are only the third group of survivors who have been found."

"In all of Antarctica?" asked Randy.

"We still haven't heard from the Russians, but it doesn't look very promising," he said, looking at Vance.

"How about the Falklands?" Randy continued.

"As far as we know, only one family survived, and no one survived in South Georgia, the Sandwich Islands, even as far north as Peru there's been—wait," Maycotte said, narrowing his eyes at Randy. "How did you know about the Falklands?"

"They talk, you know," Randy answered. He turned away from the colonel, looking at Gina while shaking his head. He didn't need to say anything for Gina to know that, without a doubt, no matter what they said, the penguins' fates were sealed.

Colonel Maycotte looked at Vance sideways. "So I've heard."

The look didn't escape Gina's notice. "What was that? That little look you gave him?"

Randy stared at Vance as long as he could stand to and came to a realization. "It means he, or they, or somebody knew about them, Gina— before we were even sent down here. Am I right?"

Vance looked at Gina. "Yes, we knew," he said unapologetically.

"You sent us down here, knowing these things were going to attack?" Gina huffed. Her face was flushed with anger.

"You and Randy were the legitimate front for GT," he said after looking at the colonel. "Speaking of which—I thought you were dead?" he said, looking at Randy, his tone as condescending as the posture he carried on his tall fame.

"Looks like I'm not. Sorry things didn't work out for you in that regard."

"Anyway, certain government agencies expect results from expeditions. That's why you were given only the best equipment. And, Randy, you just kind of . . .fell in our laps. You were eager and, to be honest, a little naïve. But we were hoping you would document the whole thing. You weren't supposed to go missing and be presumably killed."

Randy rolled his eyes and turned toward Gina, who was awestruck by what the man was saying. He looked back at Vance with a little more venom in his eyes. "Were you the one who ordered Gina to be killed?"

Vance hesitated and took a step back from Gina. "You have to understand," he said, putting his hands in front of him. "It's like I told these guys—this goes beyond GT. This goes way up the ladder. Way up."

"You didn't answer his question," Gina told the man with more than a hint of a threat in her voice.

"All you had to do was be a team player and go along with things, Gina. I honestly thought you were smarter than that. If you hadn't been so headstrong about getting your boyfriend's photos to the *world* . . ." he said mockingly. "With his disappearance and your persistence, our operation was in danger of being compromised. So, in answer to your question, yes. We couldn't have any witnesses; you were to be tossed overboard once you got in the ship. Dan was too soft to do it himself."

"I got this one," Randy told Gina.

"Got what?" Vance asked condescendingly just before Randy punched him in his already broken nose. He fell to the floor, groaning in pain.

Colonel Maycotte stepped between the man writhing in pain on the ground and Randy. "Okay, okay, that's enough. Not that he doesn't deserve it—he does, but I can't have you beating a prisoner."

"Do you have any idea what this man has put us through?" Gina asked, barely restraining herself from kicking Vance as he stood up.

"Yes, Gina Rosedale, I do. But you survived and a lot of people didn't. You're fortunate," Maycotte told her.

Randy put his arm around Gina to try to help her settle down.

"So how is GT involved in this?" Randy asked. He felt a little better after punching his boss in the face.

"I'll let him explain it," the colonel said, looking at Vance.

Gina walked to the kitchen area, grabbed a towel, and threw it to Vance to help slow his bleeding; not because she wanted to help him—he could've bled to death for all she cared—she just wanted to hear his unobstructed explanation.

After a minute of applying pressure to his nose, he began. "Did Dan or Lawrence explain to you the reasons we were down here to begin with?"

"Davis did, just before he tried to kill me," Gina said spitefully.

"Speaking of Ferdinand—do any of you know what happened to the others?"

"Not me," Randy spoke up. "After I was captured by the penguins, I—"

"Wait, wait, wait, *wait*," Maycotte said rapidly. "Captured?"

"Yeah, but Gina helped me escape—well, with Meuseaux's help."

Maycotte was confused. "You helped him? Were you taken prisoner too? Who is this Meuseaux? Another survivor?" he asked, looking toward the back of the room.

"No, I wasn't taken prisoner. Meuseaux is a Chinstrap who helped me find Randy and helped him escape," she explained.

"Chinstrap? As in Chinstrap *penguin*?" Vance asked, genuinely surprised.

Gina looked at him in disgust and turned back to Colonel Maycotte. "Yes, a Chinstrap penguin. Not all of them are against us, you know. They're quite intelligent."

"Yes, we're aware of their intelligence," Maycotte said.

"And deceptiveness," Vance said quietly.

"And in answer to your question, Mister Lyons, I assume they're all dead. As a matter of fact, Davis died right about where you're standing," Gina continued.

Vance looked down and took a step to his left.

"The penguins saved my life that day. Randy and I put Davis's body about fifty yards behind the shop, if you want to see it."

Vance stared at her without responding.

"You can continue," Gina said, motioning with her hand for him to get on with it. She turned her back on him, unable to stand the sight. She hated the man. He was everything she despised: rich and arrogant and never accountable for his actions. Ordering people to do his dirty work, never giving regard to the lives he altered or destroyed, and all just for profit. The past couple months of emotion welled up inside her and threatened to overcome her with hate.

Gina took a breath and looked at Randy, who was sitting back in the chair with his arms crossed, casually waiting for Vance to continue his tale. He looked up at her and gave her his half smile and she felt some of the hate dissipate. Gina walked over and stood beside Randy. She rested her hand on his shoulder and listened to Vance talk.

Vance pulled the blood-soaked towel from his nose, deciding the worst of the bleeding had stopped. "We came here over two years ago, to survey the best possible sites for drilling and possibly mining."

"But the treaties," Randy protested.

"Will expire in less than about twenty years—we're not the only ones, you know. Do you honestly believe that *all* of these research stations being built down here are for studying climate or wildlife? C'mon, Randy. Anyway, what everyone was looking for, we found. But in order to act, we had to find a way around those treaties and, as it turned out, we stumbled onto it—or it stumbled onto us."

"Dan, my brother Val, and I were traveling back in a crawler from the site—" he paused and looked at Maycotte "—where we staked the claim, so to speak."

"It's in the area claimed by the French," Colonel Maycotte explained.

Randy snorted a derisive laugh.

"We had mechanical problems," Vance continued. "While we were out of the vehicle, Val came across a huge opening in one of the ice monoliths. We heard noises coming from inside and curiosity got the better of us. Once inside . . . you already know what we found." He waited for Gina or Randy to respond, but they only looked at him stoically. "What we found obviously shocked us, and we were escorted, rather roughly, to Antaean, who subsequently ordered us to be executed."

"Yet you're still here," said Gina, sounding more than a little disappointed.

"Very observant," he said snidely. "We made a deal. This penguin Overlord wanted the human presence gone from Antarctica and so did we—well, everyone except us. The penguins were already very organized and showed signs of becoming even more so. They really are remarkable," he said with near adulation.

"So what was this deal?" asked Gina. She was getting a bad feeling about where the talk was headed.

"We gave them the location of every base, camp, or known settlement in Antarctica, and provided them with arms, so to speak."

"What kind of *arms*?" Randy asked, alarmed.

"The metal tips you've probably seen on their beaks. We showed them how to apply them, given the limits of their dexterity—and, in exchange, they were to drive everyone out of Antarctica and leave our operation alone. That obviously didn't happen," he said, standing up. "We didn't expect them to be so efficient," he added, almost as a side note.

"What about the Falklands, and everyplace else?" asked Randy.

"That wasn't part of the deal. Antaean obviously had his own plans."

"But you must've known that the sudden disappearance of one or two thousand people would arouse somebody's suspicion?" Randy continued questioning. Gina began to silently fume again as she listened.

"Of course, that was the whole idea. The U.S. military did respond."

Colonel Maycotte shifted almost imperceptibly.

"The military had to respond to the threat, and by doing so, they—" Vance waited for Randy to answer.

"Broke the Antarctic treaty—the Madrid Protocol, which prohibits a military presence in Antarctica by any nation," Randy said dejectedly.

"Rendering it void and leaving GT, and our interested party, open to drill and to eliminate the penguin problem as well. That was the way it was supposed to go. What we didn't count on was Antaean's aggressiveness," Vance concluded.

"You used them," Gina said exasperated. "You used the military, us, the penguins . . ."

"That's business, Gina. You use whatever tools necessary to get the job done."

"That's bullcrap, Vance," Gina countered.

"That's life," he snapped back. "Like I said, the Overlord wanted the humans and other penguin species gone, and we wanted exclusivity. It was an agreement of convenience for both parties."

Randy watched their heated exchange grow, and then quietly interjected. "So how did Dan and Val feel about this?"

Vance hesitated as he dabbed his nose again. "Dan was all for it. The prospect of becoming richer than he had ever dreamed was very appealing to him. Val on the other hand was less than enthusiastic. He protested during the negotiations with Antaean repeatedly. It threatened to ruin everything and get us killed in the process." Vance abruptly stopped talking.

"So what happened to your brother?" Gina asked, even though she felt she already knew the answer.

"I asked him to leave the talks," Vance said while looking at Maycotte. "I never saw him again."

Randy scratched the back of his head, looking at the floor. "I did," he said disdainfully.

Vance lifted his eyebrows slightly in surprise. "You did? I'm surprised. I had given him up for dead."

"Oh, he's dead. I think your brother's skull is on display in the Overlord's trophy room," he said with an uncharacteristic callousness. Vance, however, was not human, or humane, enough to seem to care.

Colonel Maycotte's eyes shifted from person to person, as if gauging their reaction.

After a long silence, Vance spoke again, and Gina and Randy wished he hadn't. "Just as well," he said coldly. "He lacked vision."

Gina and Randy were amazed by the man's lack of compassion over his own brother's death.

Vance looked at everyone watching him. "Like I said, this is bigger than GT. In the end, I'm just a pawn as well."

"Well I'm *really* heartbroken for you, Vance," Gina said derisively. "Why did you come back here, anyway?"

Randy perked up at the question. It had become apparent that this wasn't a rescue mission.

"When we lost contact with Lawrence and Dan, we knew something had gone wrong, especially after Jack e-mailed us those pictures. You know, the ones you were so keen on showing the world," he said, looking at Gina.

Gina clenched her fist, but Randy put his hand on hers to restrain her.

Vance saw the movement and, knowing he had angered her again, gave her a cocky smirk. "This is bigger than you, Gina," he said, stepping back in case she swung at him again. "We came here to get the geographical coordinates of the penguin stronghold."

"Wait, you're telling me that in the whole of your corporation, you kept only one copy of something and you kept it here?" asked Gina disbelievingly.

"Sometimes you have to keep an ace in the hole. Without me, they'll be searching this big ol' continent for months, if not years, to find that base. And, as it turns out," he said, looking at Maycotte. "For my cooperation, I'll get reduced time, if I serve any at all," he said with even *more* arrogance.

Gina and Randy looked at Colonel Maycotte with astonished expressions.

"I'm just in charge of the mission," Maycotte said with his hands up. "I have nothing to do with prosecuting this piece of—"

"Ah, ah, ah, Colonel," Vance said, wagging his finger at him. "Any insults to my character could be construed as abuse and, therefore, psychological torture of a prisoner."

"Tell it to your attorneys, asshole." Maycotte had had enough of the man and told his troops to take him to search for the documents.

"So, if he was so careful, how'd he get caught?" Randy asked after Vance was escorted away.

"I'm not entirely clear on the circumstances of his arrest. I think one of his associates had left evidence with his wife, to be revealed in the event of his death," Maycotte said, looking down the hall at Vance. But something in his eyes made Gina believe he knew more than he was letting on. "Regardless, it looks like you two get to go home. Consider yourselves lucky—extremely lucky. You had contact with the penguins and you survived," he said, then walked back to check on Vance.

Randy and Gina took deep sighs, relieved that their ordeal was finally over. They heard Vance speaking to someone on a phone but paid him no mind. They heard things crashing around and decided to get their personal effects packed before their ride arrived.

Randy and Gina couldn't help but to worry about Meuseaux and his safety. Randy passed up Colonel Maycotte in the hall and stopped him. "What are you going to do with those coordinates once you have them? Is there going to be some kind of interspecies dialogue?" he asked him, leading him to the central room.

"We're going to eliminate the threat," Maycotte said, as if Randy should have known.

Randy lowered his head and let out a long breath. "But, Colonel, the penguins . . . There's more to it than this."

"How so?" the colonel asked, becoming slightly irritated.

"They have their own social structure, politics, and they have risen up against their leader, the Overlord. They were *used* as well. Most of them just want to be left alone," he urged.

"Listen, son," Maycotte said, trying to sound patient. "I understand that you may have developed an attachment to these creatures. But they have killed thousands of people. You haven't seen what they are truly capable of."

"Because of that man in there," Gina said accusingly. "And he's going to receive leniency."

Maycotte looked at Gina and something in his stare told her not to pursue the subject any further. "I'm sorry, but this truly is out of my hands," he said, looking at the two of them as his radio chirped. "It looks like your ride is on its way."

"There's nothing you can do, Colonel?" Randy asked one more time.

"I'm sorry," he said more sternly. "Be thankful that you're leaving here with your lives."

It was a barely veiled threat, and Gina knew it by the way he looked at them. She pulled Randy away. "We are, Colonel—thank you."

Maycotte saw that she got the message, nodded, and walked away to make sure Vance was being cooperative.

Gina and Randy sat back in the chairs, feeling somewhat defeated. There wasn't a thing they could do to save the penguins, and they knew whoever it was they were going up against was too powerful to be swayed. It was like the colonel had said; they got to go home and they were thankful that they had indeed made it out alive.

After roughly thirty minutes of searching, Vance was successful at finding what he was looking for. The thumping of chopper blades could be heard. Randy and Gina grabbed their packs and walked calmly to the door. They hoped no one had noticed that Gina had put the memory card from Randy's camera in her pack. Vance and Colonel Maycotte approached them before they left.

"I know it doesn't mean much, in light of things," Vance Lyons said. "But I've arranged for *compensation* for the two of you, in exchange for your discretion," he said, looking at Maycotte. "Your checks will be waiting for you at the Santa Monica office."

Gina looked at Vance in disgust. "I don't care for southern California."

"Suit yourself, but they will be there and they are *quite* considerable."

"Have a safe journey home," Maycotte told them.

"Thank you, Colonel," Gina told him, and Randy shook his hand.

There was the slightest pause by Colonel Maycotte as he looked at Gina. "We will be leaving shortly. We have all we need. Don't you want to tell your boss goodbye?" Maycotte said. There was a hint of malevolence in his tone and in the way he looked at Gina.

Gina's eyes widened as she got his meaning, but she knew better than to say anything to protest it. Randy was oblivious to his meaning and chose not to say anything to Vance. Gina just looked at Vance.

"What?" Vance asked, sounding as if he were annoyed. "Your ride is here. Go home and get your money," he said contemptuously and as arrogantly as ever.

Gina said nothing. She snorted derisively and smirked as she walked away. "C'mon, Randy, let's go home."

As the helicopter took them away, Gina leaned against Randy and both looked out over the vast, icy landscape and hoped for Meuseaux's safety. But in the end, they wanted nothing more to do with this place.

CHAPTER 37

"Commander Lavour!" a Gentoo penguin called from behind the line of officers as he tried to make his way through the masses.

Lavour didn't hear him at first; the Gentoo's voice was drowned out by Leepoh babbling nonsensically about the dangers of swallowing too much ballast, and how he once knew a penguin who had swallowed too many ballast stones and sank to the bottom of the sea. Most of the others were paying him little mind, including Leepoh himself, who rarely stayed on a subject for long.

"Commander Lavour!" the Gentoo called out again, close enough this time for Lavour to hear him.

Lavour stopped to let the Gentoo catch up.

"Commander Lavour, sir," the Gentoo said breathlessly. "I have brought Private Cho'ka with an urgent message for you." She stepped aside to reveal a Magellanic penguin.

Lavour stifled his surprise at seeing a Magellanic. Although messengers were sent to appeal for T'Cuh-ka's aid, he had little hope of him actually responding after the debacle at the Battle of the Falklands. T'Cuh-ka had reason to be angry; the Magellanics, along with the Kings, Gentoo, and Rockhoppers of the Falklands, had lost their centuries-old breeding grounds. With no safe haven for breeding and the current environment toward the penguins, they were a race marching toward extinction.

"I have a message from Commander T'Cuh-ka," Cho'ka said proudly while saluting.

Lavour returned the salute. "At ease," he said calmly, trying not to seem too eager to hear the message. "What can we do for you?"

"Commander T'Cuh-ka has come to understand that you are no longer a part of the Penguin Defense Alliance."

Lavour glanced at Leepoh and Natoo. "That is true."

"And you intend to bring down the Overlord and his ilk."

"True as well, Cho'ka."

"Then, as liaison for Commander T'Cuh-ka, he offers the remaining forces of the Magellanics to assist you in your endeavor to defeat this tyrant." Cho'ka made the offer, standing tall and proud.

Lavour looked at the penguin and wondered what was meant by *remaining forces*. Was there a division amongst the surviving Magellanics? He didn't even know how many had actually survived the Battle of the Falklands. He wondered how badly they had been persecuted after the battle. Lavour decided these were questions best left for another time. "We would be honored to have you among the Alliance of Independent Colonies."

"On behalf of the Magellanic Union, thank you." Cho'ka bowed at the waist with his head extended forward in a gesture of friendship.

Commander Lavour and the others returned the gesture. "Where is Commander T'Cuh-ka? I could use his advice about the upcoming confrontation."

"If you don't mind me being forward, Commander, from what we've seen and heard, you seem to be doing a capable job."

Lavour looked at him, slightly abashed. "You are only as good as those you surround yourself with," he said, deflecting the praise to the others.

"Commander T'Cuh-ka is not far. He took the only approach he knew would be safe, near the Emperor colony by the Heritage mountains," said

Cho'ka.

"Then our paths should cross very soon; our journey to PIC will take us very near there. Colonel Nok," Lavour said, turning to the Rockhopper, "send scouts ahead to inform them of our arrival."

Nok didn't hesitate and dispatched a group of messengers straight away.

"Well, Private Cho'ka, welcome," General Leepoh said and introduced himself and the others to him. "So, tell me, Cho'ka," Leepoh continued, drawing a look of protest from Lavour, "you ever eat a squid bigger than me?"

"No, sir, I can't say that I have," Cho'ka answered, a little confused and looking to the others.

"I have, and it was quite a tasty treat—although I was discouraged to do so by these other penguins. But it was ripe for the eating, and the way I see it, a squid is a squid is a squid. And even though it was trying to eat my friend there—" he indicated Lavour "—it made my stomach grumble with anticipation of a well-deserved meal. So I ate it. Not the whole thing, mind you—just tiny bits. Lotsa tiny bits.

"So if you ever find yourself in the warm waters of the West, it'll do you good to be cautious. But bring your appetite. Which is why I always say— *it's not how a penguin puts food in, but how it comes out.* So always, always, *always* swallow a good stone or two to help with the digestion . . . *makes things pass easier,*" he said in a whisper. "Plus the stones can help you gain diving speed, but be careful not to swallow too many. I knew a Rockhopper who did just that and sunk to the bottom of Half Moon Bay—just like that."

Cho'ka looked to Commander Lavour for assistance, feeling more than a little bewildered by Leepoh's stream of babbling.

"You'll learn to pass it off as background noise, just like the rest of us," Lavour told the Magellanic, shaking his head at Leepoh, who hadn't seemed to notice the insult as he was too busy talking still.

CHAPTER 38

Mearna entered the Overlord's chambers with Ceocilus following two paces behind. Ceocilus had taken it upon himself to return to PIC after seeing the Resistance Council safely away. The two marched up to the Overlord's dais, where their path was blocked by the spears of Antaean's praesidiarius, his special elite guards. "Do you feel vulnerable, even before me, my lord?" she asked calmly.

"At ease," Antaean said while eyeing her intently. "The consort to my son comes to my chambers unannounced, with her offspring in tow," he said, sneering at Ceocilus. "And boldly strides up to my dais—during these turbulent times, no less. I have to wonder where her loyalties lie." It was not a question.

"Ceocilus has your features, does he not?" Mearna said, meeting his gaze and causing Ceocilus to shift uncomfortably. *Good,* she thought, noticing the shift. *It serves him right for returning here after I explicitly told him to wait for me.* "I have information and a warning. If you care not to hear it, then I will excuse myself," she said, backing away. She had to be cautious. She knew if she overplayed this she would end up dead.

The Overlord stared at her coldly. "What is this information and this *warning?*" he finally asked, sounding somewhat disinterested.

Relieved to have finally piqued his interest, Mearna told him. "The forces of the PDA have returned. They seek to overthrow you."

"Yes, I know," Antaean said dismissively. "*Commander* Lavour is far too overconfident in his rebellion. But I would expect nothing less from a Chinstrap. Do you have any information that I do not already know?" he asked contemptuously.

Mearna knew Antaean hadn't already known, or, at least, hadn't had confirmation; she had seen the subtle twitch of surprise when she told him. "Apparently I do not, unless of course you do not know that Liutites will make his bid for power in two days' time."

"What?" the Overlord barked out.

Mearna stood back, satisfied with the results this time. The mighty Antaean, Overlord of his would-be penguin empire, was scared. With Lavour's forces bearing down on him, Liutites starting a coup of his own, and the human military decimating what loyalists he had left, they both knew he would fall.

"Where are those warriors? I will need them," the Overlord demanded.

"That is the other reason I came, my lord. As we speak they are returning from the sea. I must go to them."

"You? Why?" he asked suspiciously.

"My reasons are two-fold, my lord. Liutites also knows of their arrival and desires to claim them as his own. I also must take a full battalion of loyal warriors to defend them should they encounter Lavour's forces," she told him, hoping he would believe the lie.

"Why must *you* go?" Antaean asked again impatiently, taking small steps toward her.

Mearna had to tread carefully. If Antaean suspected the slightest bit of deception, she would be dead within minutes. "Because all of the hatchlings were imprinted to me and will obey me, even over Liutites and his commanders." She paused as she waited for the Overlord to absorb what she had said. "But I must go at once—they are in jeopardy."

Overlord Antaean watched her silently, as if he were peering into her soul, searching for a sign of disloyalty. "Very well," he said. "Go and bring them to me. Take one full battalion with you."

"Yes, my lord," Mearna said and turned to leave.

"And, Mearna, if I find that you have been anything less than forthcoming, your fate will be the same as Liutites's," Antaean said, glaring evilly at the back of her head.

Mearna stopped. "I would expect no less, Antaean," she told him, not bothering to look back.

CHAPTER 39

The Alliance of Independent Colonies made its way across the ice plains, steadily marching toward Pack Ice Command. Ice plains was a term used loosely and by no means indicated that the entire terrain was flat. Rolling moguls of ice, six feet high or more, deep depressions, crevasses, fissures, and juts of ice were everywhere. The terrain was difficult to cross for a million penguins, but not impossible. There were other passes, but the humans occupied most of the more easily accessible areas.

Many penguins of the AIC had died from the extreme conditions in Antarctica. It became obvious it was the non-natives who were struggling with the conditions. Lavour ordered the non-native clans to the center of the huge mass of penguins to benefit from the heat generated from so many bodies. The plan had worked, they were stronger, and morale was boosted significantly.

When the sun made its appearance, the AIC commanders spotted a procession of a couple hundred penguins headed in their direction. The scouts had spotted them during the night, but they had been ordered not to make contact with them until they knew which penguins they were dealing with.

"It's the Emperors the scouts told us about," Lavour told General Natoo, who stood alongside him. "The true Emperors, not the Royals," he clarified.

"I believe they're the group I talked to before I left," Captain Mevoule said, stepping to Lavour's other side. "Something's wrong—they're leaving."

"Maybe they are coming to join us." Natoo threw out the possibility to the others.

"Maybe . . ." Lavour said, distracted. Something seemed out of place. There were too few Emperors traveling together. The times he had seen them before, there had always been a lot more. "You said you knew them?" he asked Mevoule.

"They helped me on my way from PIC, but I don't really *know* them."

"Quit your chattering. You'll know them soon enough because they're coming this way," said Leepoh, drawing looks from everyone within earshot. ". . . sir," he added, shifting uncomfortably under the stares.

"Lead the way," Lavour told Mevoule after turning his attention back to the matter before them.

Mevoule gave him a sideways glance and headed down a slight slope toward the Emperors. Once they arrived, Mevoule greeted the lead penguin. "Hello, I don't know if you remember me. I am Captain—"

"Mevoule," the female Emperor finished for him. "Yes, I remember you. I was there when you brought us the warning."

"Where is Kra K'K'ki-ro?" Mevoule asked, looking down the line of penguins.

"He is dead," the other said bluntly.

"Oh," Mevoule said, looking to the ground. "I am sorry to hear that."

"Don't be sorry, Mevoule." The Emperor relented her crass tone. "Liutites's thugs came to us, just as we were forewarned. When we did not yield to their command, they tried to destroy us."

"Where are they now?" Corporal Meuseaux asked as he came to Mevoule's side. The corporal appeared both nervous and eager at the prospect of meeting the forces of the Supreme Commander on the field of battle once again.

The Emperor looked down at Meuseaux. "Dead, my friend—all but two, that is," she said, looking back at Mevoule. "We wanted to make sure Liutites got our answer."

After a minute of silence while the Emperor contemplated the past and the AIC officers did the same for the future, Commander Lavour came forward. "We would be honored if you would join our cause. That is an offer, not an ultimatum."

"You must be Lavour," the Emperor said. "I'm sorry, but we are through with wars and fighting. Life is a struggle enough without searching for ways to die. We are the *Free* Emperors and as such, will remain so."

Lavour nodded, agreeing with the Emperor's wisdom. "I understand—I wish it were the same for me," he said, looking at the diffused sun behind a haze of clouds.

"It is, Lavour," the Emperor said and then paused to let the statement sink in. "One day you will see it for yourself. But in the meantime, you have a job you were called to do."

Lavour looked back at the Emperor, thinking back on how he came to be where he was. Right then, he should have been at sea, swimming in the open water with his colony, with no burdens but that of catching his next meal and preparing to meet Lannera on that little strip of beach. But he wasn't; he was where he was, and his colony was gone. He knew he would never return to that rocky stretch of coast and he would never again hear the voice of a hatchling at his feet.

Lavour looked at his friends and then at the thousands of penguins on the horizon. All of them looked to him for leadership. All were united for a common good. *What if I just left and never looked back?* he thought to himself, feeling suddenly overwhelmed. But then he looked at the faces of his friends: Mevoule, Meuseaux, Leepoh, Nok, Keerka, and the others. They had all sacrificed so much to get to this point and they all supported him. Even though he didn't fully understand why, they followed him, they believed in him, and he believed in them. "I suppose I do have a job to do," he finally said. "What will you do?"

"We will return to the sea—our crèche is lost this year. We will try again next year and hope that when we return, all will be put right."

Lavour looked at the Emperor, wishing he could assure her it would be. "Have a safe journey, my friends."

"You do not wish for the spirits of the Ancients to be with us?" the Emperor asked.

"Who am I to presume to tell the Ancients what they should do?"

The Emperor studied Lavour, said nothing, and only nodded.

"If things do not go well for us, I have heard tales of a Northern Paradise," Lavour began to say.

"Lavour." The Emperor stopped him. "Paradise is where you believe it to be."

Each penguin who heard the Emperor only watched as she turned and followed the procession of departing Emperors. When she was nearly out of sight and with Lavour still watching, she turned to look at him. "Commander Lavour, remember the prophecy of the penguin whom all would look to in times of trouble. It said nothing of it being a Royal Emperor." With that said, the Emperor disappeared over the horizon and into the rapidly approaching night.

Leepoh looked at Lavour intently. "What do you suppose she meant by that?" he said as he walked away. "Let's go, Nok. Our friend needs some time to think about things."

Lavour watched his friends walk away and then turned back to find no trace of the Emperors. Penguin after penguin passed him by as he stood. "*Prophecy,*" he said quietly to himself. "Prophecy, fate, destiny—those are things best left for greater penguins. We just need to be done with this once and for all."

As the penguins continued to pass by him, trudging their way in the bitter cold, Lavour came to a realization: this was no longer solely his quest for vengeance; it truly was a quest for freedom. Although he had heard the words spoken a hundred times, only now did he understand. How many clans had endured what his had in order to be brought into line? The penguin clans had all been manipulated by the Overlord and his kind. Now they were at war with the most powerful species on Earth— the humans—and it would mean the death of all the penguins if it were allowed to continue.

"Now we must put an end to it," Lavour said to himself. "The only way to save our kind is to be rid of the Royal Emperors—they brought this on us." Lavour raced back to join the others, stopped, and looked at Colonel Nok. "How long do you plan to keep this from me?"

"Excuse me, sir?" Nok asked, stealing a look at Keerka.

"Did you honestly think I wouldn't know Keerka was with egg?"

Nok just stared at Lavour for a moment. "I'm sorry, it's just that—"

"Enough of that, Nok," Lavour interrupted. "Keerka, do you wish to continue on with us? It will be dangerous, and I'd hate for anything—"

"Commander," she said, taking a turn at interrupting, "the Royals must fall. And I will honor Treeg's memory by doing my part."

"And you, Nok?"

"Your fate is our fate, Commander," he said with his chest puffed up proudly.

"Very good, General," Lavour said. He then turned toward Leepoh.

Nok looked between Lavour and Keerka, not knowing if Lavour had made a mistake or not.

"Sir," Leepoh said. "If you don't mind my saying, if you're going to give out promotions to just any ol' penguin, it kind of diminishes the title and my rank."

Nok realized that Lavour hadn't misspoken and looked at Leepoh with his beak agape. "Thank you, sir," Nok told Lavour. "But Leepoh is correct, it's not much of a mark of distinction if I'm in the same class as this," he said, looking the Gentoo up and down smugly.

"Are you two done yet?" Lavour asked lightheartedly.

"Bah!" Leepoh barked. "As done as he'll ever be."

"What?" Nok asked, confused. "That doesn't even make any sense."

Once again, the two friends started bickering, joking, and jabbing at one another, and Lavour led them toward the inevitable, secure and comforted by the friends with whom he was surrounded.

CHAPTER 40

"Everybody halt!" Mearna called out. Ahead of her company lay the remains of the Royal Emperor and Free Emperor penguins who had fought just the day before. "Ceocilus, come with me."

With his spear at the ready, Ceocilus led the way as the two moved cautiously forward. The dead lay all about them, frozen combatants forever locked in battle. "Who do you think won the battle?" Ceocilus asked while he absently prodded the frozen body of a dead Emperor.

"Liutites's warriors were defeated," Mearna said without hesitation. "However, the feral Emperors took significant losses. Liutites is a fool," she spat. "By now I'm sure the other colonies have been warned not to trust the Royals. They have fled, returned to the sea for who knows how long."

"How do you know?" Ceocilus asked.

"Look around you—they have abandoned their nesting site." Mearna continued to survey the site when something caught her attention.

"Maybe they joined Lavour," Ceocilus said, not abandoning hope that the Emperors would still join them.

Mearna seemed distracted as she stood over the body of an Emperor. "No, Ceocilus, they have not joined Lavour, they will not fight again. That idiot Liutites saw to that," she said angrily after a long pause.

Ceocilus came to her side to see what had caught her attention.

"This is the body of Kra K'K'Ki-ro and with both him *and* K'K'Ru-ki gone, they no longer have a strong leader and they will forever keep to their feral ways."

"That is unfortunate."

"It is more than unfortunate!" Mearna snapped. "The feral Emperors are the true masters of this land. They had the skills we needed to secure the homeland while we were away. *They* were better suited for it than the Adélie . . . or us. Therefore, it is not unfortunate; it is devastating."

"Perhaps we should be on our way, then. The warriors will be arriving soon," Ceocilus said, trying to placate his mother.

"The warriors are of little concern right now. They are already loyal to me and they were instructed before they left for their trials to report directly to me upon returning. Their path should not intersect with Lavour's. Their only real danger is encountering humans, and we are powerless against that." Mearna surveyed the battlefield once again. "If we had more time I would've liked to study the battleground to see how elite warriors lost to an inferior, unarmed opponent."

"That is an easy question. Leotholis was an overaggressive fool with no leadership skills or tactical knowledge," Ceocilus told her as they trudged back to the others.

"To put it simply," Mearna said before she approached the company under her command. She gave Ceocilus a sideways glance and began to address her warriors. "Loyal soldiers of the Overlord," she said as mightily as she could. "What lies before you, what we have observed and discovered, is a tragedy, a crime of immense implications. The Overlord has sent us here to gather evidence, and we have found it. Supreme Commander Liutites has turned on the Overlord and the Penguin Defense Alliance." The news caused a brief stir among the highly disciplined troops.

"I have recalled the forces of the PDA to help us deal with the threat from within," she continued. "Liutites and those loyal to him are now enemies of the Overlord. I ask you to remember *your* loyalties, first to the

Overlord and then to me."

At once, all of the Royal Emperor elite warriors offered a salute to their new field commander, Mearna.

A warrior standing in the front line looked past Mearna and then grounded the butt of his spear into the ice, coming to full attention. "Milady, a group of penguins are approaching," he announced strongly.

Mearna and Ceocilus spun around and saw several smaller-sized penguins standing atop the low hill on the far side of the imperial battleground.

"Who are they?" Mearna asked quietly as she signaled for her warriors to stand ready.

"From here they appear to be Magellanic," Ceocilus answered, even though Mearna was actually talking to herself.

"They *are* Magellanic," she said, a little confused. "But they abandoned the PDA after the Battle of the Falklands. What are they doing here?"

More and more Magellanic penguins gathered on the hill and, as they did, Mearna looked at the bodies lying on the ice around them, and then back at her soldiers. She spat out a curse, startling Ceocilus. "Stand ready," she ordered her warriors, who immediately brought their spears forward into attack position.

"But—" Ceocilus began to protest until Mearna cut him off.

"Look around you, Ceocilus." He obliged, and when she saw his expression turn to realization, she continued. "If this *is* Commander T'Cuh-ka, he left the PDA before Mevoule made contact with Lavour."

"So he doesn't know of the Resistance Council or you," Ceocilus said, clutching his spear.

"Correct. And to him it looks as if we just slaughtered over a hundred feral Emperors. Come with me," Mearna said as she watched more Magellanics appear. "We *must* try to settle this peacefully. They appear to drastically outnumber us, and I don't want a repeat of what happened here."

ᴧᴧᴧ

"Where are the Adélies?" Supreme Commander Liutites shouted at his guards after finding the Adélie quarters vacated. "How could they just leave without anyone noticing?" he fumed impotently. He desperately wanted something to lash out at but could no longer afford to lose any more of his own. Out of the corner of his eye, he spotted something—one of his Blue penguin spies. "You there—halt," he commanded.

The Blue knew she had been spotted and stopped immediately. Since becoming members of the Resistance, the Little Blue penguins had become invaluable as information gatherers. The members of the Council were able to know exactly what the Supreme Commander and, to a lesser extent, the Overlord were doing on a daily, hourly, and if necessary, minute-by-minute basis.

With that knowledge, Sergeant Kima, the Adélie member of the Resistance, was enabled to get the Adélies out of PIC unseen.

"Ah, my loyal spy," said Liutites in the language of the Blue, sounding as if he were once again dancing on the razor's edge of sanity. "Where or what has become of the Adélies?"

The Blue chattered nervously and informed him they had left the previous day out the north passage. When Liutites asked why he wasn't informed, the Blue told him they didn't know it wasn't authorized.

Liutites wanted nothing more than to crush the Blue penguin under his foot, but he refrained. Unlike his father, he knew the value of the Blue penguins and that he could not afford to lose their loyalty. It took all of his restraint to maintain his composure. It didn't help that, as much as he hated to admit it, he needed the Blues, even if they were a lesser clan. "Very well. In the future, however, I want to be informed of all movement by any group. Is that understood?" he asked, still forcing calm on himself.

The Blue acknowledged with a salute, backed away, and quickly ducked out when dismissed.

Liutites skulked off, brooding over the Adélies' departure. Was it a move by the Overlord to deny him resources? Or something to do with the

Resistance, as he had heard it was called. Just thinking about it increased his anger.

Liutites made his way to the main hall and, once there, was met by two of his loyal elite guards, who were escorting two survivors from the battle with the Emperors. He knew at once that things had not gone as expected. "Where is Captain Leotholis?" he asked in a low hiss, already knowing the answer.

The two warriors remained silent for the briefest of moments, bowed their heads slightly, exchanged quick glances, and looked at the Supreme Commander. "He is dead, sir," one of them said at last.

Liutites glared at the two and, once again, resisted the urge to strike. "Explain," he said, his voice unsteady, teetering on the edge of self-control.

"It was a trap, sir," the same warrior as before spoke. When Liutites said nothing, the warrior continued. "When we arrived, the feral Emperors brought several hundred fighters to bear on us. They were forewarned of our arrival and we were vastly outnumbered. We were defeated."

Liutites quivered with rage and turned his back on the duo. "How is it that you two managed to survive and return here?" he asked, turning back toward them quickly, causing the pair to flinch slightly.

"We were allowed to live to deliver a message," the second warrior spoke.

Liutites waited for the message, and when the warriors were not forthcoming, he demanded it. "The message—now!" he spat out.

The warrior straightened himself and took a noticeable breath before beginning. "They said *they* are the true Emperors, the lords of this realm, and they would never join abominations such as us, especially with leaders who are skirting the edge of sanity." The warrior then lowered his head and waited for the inevitable attack, but it never came. He looked up and saw Liutites glaring over them.

"Very well," Liutites said with unexpected coolness. "Get your wounds treated and join Major Hyodon's company. We are expecting an attack very soon, and I will need everyone at full battle readiness."

The two surprised warriors offered a proud salute and hurried off to fulfill the commander's orders, thankful to be leaving with their lives.

With the Emperors out of the equation, which was, after all, what he had wanted, Liutites decided to focus on more pressing matters. "Come with me," he barked at his guards, who escorted him everywhere now. "It is time I should get fitted."

CHAPTER 41

"Be ready!" Commander T'Cuh-ka shouted to his fellow Magellanics. "General Kih-T'Gik, spread right and flank their left. We may outnumber them, but they have the advantage on this terrain and they have weapons."

"Understood, Commander," Kih-T'Gik acknowledged and took his battalion to perform the maneuver.

"Well, Cuh-trük, what do you think?" T'Cuh-ka asked the nearest penguin.

Cuh-trük was the advisor to the commander, and it was under her persuasion that, after receiving General Treeg's message, they sought to rejoin the reformed PDA, now known as the AIC. The Magellanics had run out of options. After leaving their home in the Falklands, they had tried to nest at various locations along the coast of Argentina but were persecuted along with the native Magellanics and joined with the natives in fleeing.

Everywhere they went, from as far north as Brazil to the peninsula of Punta Tombo, which was once a penguin nature preserve until recent events, they met with heavily armed human militia, who decimated their numbers. Unable to find a safe haven for breeding and nesting, they took to the sea, where they had a chance encounter with an AIC messenger. With all other options closed to them and under Cuh-trük's urging, T'Cuh-ka decided to join Lavour's forces, simply for the purpose of retaliation against the Overlord.

"This *is* what we came for," she said without any real emotion behind her words.

"Yes, but I was hoping to do it with the assistance of the AIC," T'Cuh-ka said, sounding a little disheartened as he surveyed the landscape.

"For all we know, they may not want our help any longer—our messengers still haven't returned," she said stoically.

"If that *is* the case, it was a mistake to come here. We've lost so many to the cold already," the commander said, scanning the horizon one more time for any sign of Lavour and his armies. He did not want to face this foe with what he had. Magellanic penguins are from a relatively warmer region, and the cold had been brutal on them; dozens had died already.

The opposing forces maneuvered and jostled for position as the rapidly disappearing sun took what ambient warmth it had with it. The Magellanics were forced to huddle close together to benefit from each other's body heat. The Royals did the same, but to a lesser extent.

In the fading light, T'Cuh-ka saw the form of two Royal Emperors coming their way. "What do you think they want?" Cuh-trük said from T'Cuh-ka's side.

T'Cuh-ka didn't hesitate; he threw his head back and let out a loud call that started in a low guttural honk and ended up in a high-pitched squeal.

^^^

After hearing the call, Mearna and Ceocilus stopped their advance.

"Why are we stopping?" Ceocilus asked.

"That was a warning cry, that's why," she said impatiently. "Ground your spear into the ice—show them that we are no threat."

Ceocilus stole a sideways glance at his mother, not wanting to relinquish his weapon, but he reluctantly did as he was asked. The pair resumed their walk, carefully avoiding the corpses on the battlefield. They were greeted by a second call from the Magellanic commander. The call was similar to the first, only louder, and with a pronounced click at the end. They stopped again.

"They obviously don't want us to come any closer," Ceocilus said, sounding frustrated. He did not like being without his weapon.

"And we won't," said Mearna. She observed the Magellanics further positioning themselves on the advantageous high ground. "Commander T'Cuh-ka!" she called out.

ᴧᴧᴧ

Commander T'Cuh-ka stiffened at hearing his name called. "How do they know me?" he asked himself quietly.

"You *are* the commander of the Magellanics. How could they not?" Cuh-trük reminded him.

"I thought the Royal Emperors were commanded by males only—this one is clearly a female."

"That could be a good sign. Perhaps they have suffered enough losses for them to turn to their females for leadership," Cuh-trük said, sounding unusually hopeful.

"Commander T'Cuh-ka, please respond. We do not wish to fight an ally," Mearna called out once again.

"An ally? Who does she think she's fooling? The Royal Emperors are no one's ally," Cuh-trük said indignantly.

"Quiet," T'Cuh-ka demanded impatiently, finally growing tired of Cuh-trük's reasoning and advice.

Cuh-trük was slow to respond, affronted by the short tone the commander had taken with her. "Commander?" she said as T'Cuh-ka stared at the Royal Emperors in silence.

"Bring me two squads. I'm going down there," he said after thinking over his options. He did have a few choices: turn and flee, stand and fight, or see what the Royals were up to and hopefully negotiate a truce. Neither side seemed too keen to begin a fight.

"I don't think that would be wise, Commander. Please reconsider,"

Cuh-trük implored, knowing full well that once T'Cuh-ka had made a decision he would not waver. "Remember my advice you ignored at the Falklands."

The commander glowered at her. After the failed battle, Cuh-trük urged T'Cuh-ka not to separate from the PDA; he hadn't listened, which lead to disastrous results. A fact she never failed to bring up to him. "I no longer need your constant reminding of that," he said irritably. "This time, I truly believe you are wrong."

Cuh-trük sighed in resignation; if she persisted, it would only anger him further. Accompanied by a dozen Magellanic warriors, Commander T'Cuh-ka ambled his way down the slope. He projected confidence but was inwardly nervous as he approached Mearna. He didn't attend the Great Gathering and had never seen a Royal Emperor face-to-face, so he had to mask his surprise when the two Royals towered over him by more than three feet.

Masking his intimidation, the Magellanic commander stood before the Royal Emperors and announced himself. "I am T'Cuh-ka, Commander of the Magellanic forces of the Falkland Islands. You seem to have me at a disadvantage—you know me, but I do not know you."

Mearna put on her best diplomatic air. She offered a salute in deference to his rank. "I am Mearna, former aid to Overlord Antaean and Supreme Commander Liutites. This is my personal guard, Ceocilus," she indicated the other, who saluted as well. "We were on our way to meet our warriors, who will assist us in overthrowing Liutites when he ascends to Overlord."

From what he heard, the thought of Liutites becoming Overlord was even less appealing than the current ruler. "Antaean is dead, then?" T'Cuh-ka asked, not bothering to hide his surprise.

"No. Not yet. But the Supreme Commander will begin a coup very soon, and we intend for Liutites's reign to be a brief one," she answered. "I understood you had withdrawn from the PDA?" Mearna asked, changing the subject and putting T'Cuh-ka on the defensive.

"We had, but circumstances warranted otherwise," he answered cautiously as he surveyed the carnage around him in the dim light. "We are here to meet others who are hoping to achieve the same ends as you. They will be here shortly," he added, just in case Mearna had any ideas.

"Yes," she said with a knowing look. "I hope to see Commander Lavour as well."

Despite Mearna mentioning Lavour, T'Cuh-ka was still suspicious of her, if not more so. It would do her story well if she threw Lavour's name into the conversation. "This battle here," he said, looking up and into her eyes. "It appears as if Royal Emperors have killed Emperors." It was a statement, not a question.

"An example of the Supreme Commander's betrayal," she said without missing a beat.

"And you have a large group of warriors with you," he said on the edge of accusation. He had to be careful; if he pressed too hard, it could erupt into battle, but he had to get information.

"We must be cautious—the humans have fought us violently here. These warriors were loyal to the Overlord, and he can ill afford to be without them right now. We had nothing to do with this battle. We are only here to escort the warriors I spoke of."

T'Cuh-ka understood what she was saying without her saying it. By bringing these warriors out here, it weakened the Overlord, making it easier for Liutites to defeat him, which, in turn, would weaken Liutites. Even though it made sense, there was something he didn't trust about her. Then the cry of alarm came, and shortly after the alarm call ended, a Magellanic, sent from Cuh-trük, appeared alongside the commander.

The messenger began chittering feverishly in its native dialect, while Mearna and Ceocilus looked on in confusion.

At the end of the messenger's report, T'Cuh-ka looked at the two Royals. "A large group of Royal Emperors are approaching," he said without emotion, but his eyes belied his accusation.

"The warriors I spoke of, I assure you, Commander," Mearna told him calmly, trying to mollify the suspicious penguin. "They are vital to our plans."

T'Cuh-ka continued to study Mearna. There was *definitely* something he didn't trust about her. "They are still a good distance away. In the meantime," he said, looking to his messenger, "go and inform Cuh-trük to continue on defensive alert." He turned back to look at Mearna and Ceocilus and gauged their reaction. They had none. "If you will excuse me."

"It was a pleasure to meet you, Commander. Your skill and leadership will be a valuable asset to our cause."

T'Cuh-ka inclined his head and left without looking back.

"Bad timing," Ceocilus said after the commander had gone.

"No, Ceocilus," Mearna replied. "This is perfect timing."

"But if they feel threatened, they might attack."

"They won't and he won't. He doesn't feel threatened because he knows the AIC is on its way. And when Lavour arrives and sees the warriors under my command, he will be even more emboldened to attack Liutites. Our plans could not be going any better."

CHAPTER 42

Before the sun had risen, Supreme Commander Liutites was already stalking the halls of Pack Ice Command. Mearna should have been back, and he was beginning to think she had betrayed him as well. But after pondering over it further, he dismissed the idea. The timing was her idea. Mearna and her troops would arrive soon enough; he guessed they were just delayed by weather or something less sinister. *Unless*, Liutites thought, *they encountered humans.* He reprimanded himself for not keeping his mind on what he did know. What he did know was that today was the day he would finally rid himself of that corpulent waste of flesh, feather, and bone—Antaean. He would ascend to his rightful place on the dais of the Overlord. Then there would be no more deals with humans and suffering lesser penguins wanting to be treated as near equals. Regardless of their usefulness, the lesser clans would be servants to the Royals. Only then would there be order. Then they would find and conquer the North.

"But there are priorities right now. Captain," he said as he entered the quarters of his elite soldiers. The captain immediately snapped to attention. "The time has come—the Overlord plans to replace me. We will show him and those loyal to him the error of such thoughts."

On the captain's mark, five hundred elite Royal Emperor warrior penguins snapped their staffs at the ready.

∧∧∧

Overlord Antaean stood on his dais. His bulky but powerful frame was covered in layers of a cloak and thick sealskins to act as leather armor. "Issue a death decree on Mearna," he spat out to one of his attendees. "Her betrayal will not go unpunished." The attendee bowed and left the room at once. "Are my warriors ready yet?" Antaean called out, like a toddler having a tantrum, to his other attendee.

"Yes, my lord," the nervous, scrawny-framed attendee answered.

"Good. Kill all those who do not pledge their loyalty to me and me alone. And remember—see to it that Liutites finds his way through the mêlée to me. I shall enjoy killing him myself." The Overlord was eager to be done with Liutites. His son's desire for power had become tiresome and he grew bored with baiting the Supreme Commander with his insults. He showed no compunction about wanting to kill him, only a sense of excitement to move on to something else. "After Liutites is dead, we will immediately depart for the North. Make sure all of my warriors know this."

"Yes, my lord," the other said.

"We'll let Lavour and his band of pathetic sub-penguins have this place. They'll find PIC abandoned of all, except the corpses of Liutites and those fool enough to follow him. The humans will then rid me of that bothersome Chinstrap."

∧∧∧

Liutites stood behind the front phalanx of his loyal elite warriors as they entered the main hall. The great ice stalactite had just caught the first rays of sunlight. The room was empty, which was unusual, even given the circumstances. There should have been at least a few penguins inside when they entered. Right away, an alarm went off in Liutites's mind. "Sergeant, secure the entrances," he said while eyeing the room suspiciously.

As the sergeant went to do as ordered, Liutites stopped him. "Why would Antaean secede the main hall to me so easily?" He bounced the question off the sergeant.

"Maybe we caught them unaware, my lord," the sergeant suggested, already calling Liutites by his future designation.

Liutites liked it and decided this sergeant would go far under his regime. "Doubtful. I sense a trap." The same thought had occurred to Liutites, but he knew better. His father would be better prepared than that. He was up to something.

∧∧∧

"My lord," an elite warrior announced as he entered the Overlord's chamber from the rear entrance, "the Supreme Commander's forces have entered the main hall."

"Have all of his troops filled the room?" Antaean asked calmly.

"No, my lord, the Supreme Commander stopped them as they began to enter."

"He is smarter than I thought," he said almost proudly. "But not smart enough." The Overlord walked away from his dais, grabbed his spear, and jabbed the butt of it into an unseen hole in the floor. "If I cannot catch them all, I will separate them from their leader."

A low grinding noise filled throne room as Antaean re-ascended his dais.

∧∧∧

"Out! Now!" yelled Liutites at hearing the noise of the doors sliding shut, but it was too late; the doors closed quicker than normal. He tried to have them opened, but his warriors' spears no longer activated them. Liutites checked the other doors and found a warrior partially crushed underneath one.

"My lord, I saw the door closing and tried to get to you," the dying warrior told him.

"Let this be a lesson," Liutites said to his sergeant. "There will be no foolish acts of sacrifice or bravery." He looked at the struggling penguin, feeling repulsed by its weakness. "Sergeant," he said, turning away. "Put this warrior out of his misery."

^^^

"Send the main force through the anterior passage and kill them all, except for Liutites, and see to it that his other warriors find their way into the theater." Antaean barked out his commands and gripped his spear as tightly as he could, anticipating the fight.

^^^

Liutites and his remaining forces searched for ways out of the main hall. They called to those on the outside, urging them to find another way in. A hidden doorway opened to the left of the stalactite, and the Overlord's elite guards began to pour through the opening.

"Defensive phalanx," ordered Liutites. His remaining warriors made a wall of interlocking bodies with deadly spear tips thrusting forward.

Antaean's warriors rushed forward but came to a stop just out of reach of the opposing warriors' lances. For a few brief seconds all was still and none moved as the two sides gauged each other. Grossly outnumbered, Liutites prepared himself for a fight to the death. From the back of the room, the Overlord's commanding officer wailed the attack command and then hell broke loose.

Antaean's warriors rushed forward and Liutites's braced for the onslaught. Spears clashed against weapon and flesh as Antaean's warriors batted at the protruding tips of the phalanx, trying to make gaps in the formation. Facing superior numbers, the would-be Overlord's line began to crumble as their opponents found weak points in the defenses. Penguin after penguin fell, and the hall echoed with the calls of battle and death.

"Break ranks and thrust forward," Liutites called from behind the line. He smelled the blood of battle and was eager to take part.

Bathed in the prismatic light shining through the crystalline stalactite, Liutites surveyed the battle. It was a confusing blight of black and white, punctuated by smears of red.

One of Antaean's soldiers broke through the line and confronted Liutites. The warrior hesitated briefly and Liutites stabbed him through his neck. The Supreme Commander kept his beak buried in his kill until the last quiver of his opponent's death throe, then flung his victim to the ground. He looked at the fallen enemy's spear and longed for the grasping flippers of the warriors.

At the back of the hall, the door leading to Antaean's chambers opened and a dozen more combatants filed out.

"A fatal mistake, my father," Liutites said and began to make his way toward the open passage.

The Overlord's officer began to issue orders to the reinforcements as the newcomers joined the fray.

Liutites inched his way forward. A spear swung at him from his left, he lifted his flipper to block it, and it landed hard against his side. Liutites glared at his attacker and brought his flipper back down, pinning the pike against his own body. The surprised warrior tried to pull the weapon free, but Liutites quickly turned his body to his left, pulling the warrior forward and off balance. Liutites let go of the spear, causing the warrior to lose his balance further, spun back the opposite direction. He did a complete three-hundred-and-sixty-degree turn, ducked his head, and thrust his beak into his opponent's chest. Two more quick stabs and the warrior fell dead at his feet.

Liutites continued forward, dropping two more fighters with little effort. All that stood between him and the Overlord's chamber was Antaean's officer.

^^^

Liutites's warriors, who were stuck outside the main hall, traveled the length of the corridor to the entrance of the Grand Theater, knowing there was another entrance to the main hall inside. The leader thrust his spear into the keyhole. The door slid open and the four hundred or more warriors rushed into the dimly lit room. After entering, the large door behind them slid shut and several ice reflectors moved into position to harness more of what little light there was. The brightened room revealed more than a thousand of Antaean's elite. Liutites's soldiers almost collectively lowered their weapons, knowing they had been defeated.

"Brother warriors," a voice echoed from the stage, "it is the Overlord's desire that you lay down your weapons. If you do so peacefully, the Overlord will show you leniency and you will be allowed to return to your positions of honor under his command."

After a minute of murmuring amongst the trapped warriors, Major Hyodon stepped forward. "We acknowledge the offer and would accept it, but if the Supreme Commander succeeds in his bid to become Overlord, he will show us no such mercy after proving disloyal to him."

"If he does succeed, he will be our Overlord as well. As a pledge of a brother warrior, we assure you he will not know."

After a brief discussion, given the circumstances, the warriors laid down their weapons, leaving Liutites's bid for power solely on him.

ᴧᴧᴧ

The commanding officer squared off against Liutites. He had been given orders to let the Supreme Commander pass, but the dedicated warrior in him would not allow it. He would protect the Overlord at any cost, even if that meant disobeying an order. The officer was determined to save Antaean from his own poor decision.

Liutites looked back at the battle taking place behind him. It was difficult to tell who was winning. Liutites's warriors had fought well against enormous odds and appeared to have leveled the field. Six combatants from both sides continued to fight. He looked back at the officer, who had positioned his spear for attack. "Stand aside," Liutites demanded.

He did not want to waste any more energy nor time. He knew he had the fight of his life ahead of him and would need all of his strength. The next few moments could be pivotal. If either side lost one or more warriors, then the other side would lose. He wanted to be rid of Antaean before that happened. "This is between me and the Overlord. You are interfering in things you shouldn't."

The officer seemed to turn the thought over in his head but attacked in spite of it. Liutites reacted quickly and went low, diving at the oncoming officer's feet. The charging attacker's momentum carried him over Liutites's back and sent him sliding across the floor into the thick of the battle. Liutites quickly righted himself and looked back at his attacker, who struggled to get to his feet. One of Liutites's warriors saw an opportunity and drove his opponent backwards, causing him to fall over the downed officer. The warrior drove his spear into the back of the officer and then quickly dispatched the other fallen soldier. Liutites grunted in satisfaction at his warrior's work and waddled down the corridor to confront Antaean.

CHAPTER 43

The long night came without bloodshed, and Mearna greeted her newly arrived warriors. She did her best to assure the Magellanics of the newcomers' devotion to the cause. The two groups, though more at ease with each other, were anxious about Lavour still not arriving. For once, all was quiet, and the separate groups huddled amongst themselves in the cold. In the moonlit landscape, a large group of penguins were spotted coming from the west.

The reaction of both groups was immediate and nearly identical. The Magellanics formed into battle groups, as did the Royal Emperors. All of them stood tense and silent, and each party sent out a pair of scouts to investigate.

Mearna and T'Cuh-ka stood at the front of their respective commands and watched. Feeling the other's distant gaze, Mearna turned and met T'Cuh-ka's look. After a few moments, he turned away.

"He doesn't like you," Ceocilus said from her side.

"No, he doesn't. Whether he likes me or not is irrelevant—he is suspicious of my motives," she replied. "But it makes little difference. He is not necessary to our long-term goals." Mearna looked to the distance, not at the penguins, but at her future.

The two groups of scouts returned simultaneously and went to their respective leaders.

"Sir," the Magellanic said to T'Cuh-ka, "it is Commander Kiley and his armies."

"Commander Kiley? The King penguin—is Lavour with them?" T'Cuh-ka questioned, looking at Cuh-trük.

"No, Lavour is not with them, sir," the scout said before being dismissed.

"What do you think?" the commander asked Cuh-trük.

"I don't trust the Kings either," she said. "Too many of them are power hungry, and remember, in spite of the slaughter, Kiley was opposed to retreating from the Falklands."

"I remember. I was there," he said with a haunted tone at the memory of the debacle.

Just then, another call came out from the eastern side, and a Magellanic scout hustled to the commander and came to an unceremonious stop on the ice. "Sir, Commander Lavour is approaching," he said when he stood back up.

"Good, now we can find out what is happening and get on with this," T'Cuh-ka said, looking at Mearna, who was apparently receiving the same information. She glanced toward him and then looked away.

"She knows you don't trust her," Cuh-trük said quietly, almost conspiratorially.

"Then she is quite astute. We'll see if that distrust is unfounded over the course of upcoming events."

^^^

"So I said, 'those weren't contrail bubbles, my friend.' That taught her to try to ride in my wake," Leepoh said, barking out his usual laugh.

"He doesn't stop, does he?" Keerka whispered to Nok. She sounded exhausted, if not from the journey, then from Leepoh's constant babbling.

"No, no he doesn't," Nok said, sounding defeated. "But at least it passes the time."

"Don't say that too loud," Meuseaux said from the other side of Keerka. "You'll just encourage him to go on talking."

"Trust me, he doesn't need encouragement to talk. He'll do it regardless," Natoo added, eager to join in the Leepoh bashing.

"Oh, come now. None of you have ever done that?" Leepoh asked, feigning indignation.

"Not intentionally," Mevoule answered, and the others shook their heads.

"How about you, Commander Lavour?" Leepoh asked, trying to get him involved in the conversation.

"Only when you swim behind me," Lavour answered straight, drawing laughter from the others.

As they ascended the top of a rocky hill, Lavour ordered a halt. "There they are," he said in relief.

Leepoh came to his side. "Yes, sir—it looks like it."

"There's another group to the west," Nok said.

"Hopefully it's Commander Kiley. Mevoule," Lavour said as he turned to the captain, "is that Mearna?"

"I believe it is. I don't know what other Royal Emperor would be out here without fighting the Magellanics."

"Maybe it's Liutites, come to surrender himself to our might," Leepoh piped in.

"What fun would that be? No lesson taught," Mevoule said, looking at Lavour.

"And no vengeance exacted," Meuseaux followed up, drawing looks from the others.

Lavour took a deep breath in. "Let's move out," he said, breaking the sudden silence.

CHAPTER 44

"Liutites," the Overlord boomed when the usurper entered the room. His voice resonated throughout the chamber.

"Antaean," Liutites replied, mocking the Overlord's tone. His newly tipped beak glinted through the blood of his victims. He showed no signs of fear or trepidation.

"How dare you soil my hall with your insolence," the Overlord said in a disgusted tone. "I'd sooner have that Chinstrap Lavour in here than look at you and remind myself of the embarrassment I spawned." Antaean knew all of Liutites's triggers and took pleasure in pulling them.

Liutites stared at the Overlord silently, his fury welling up inside of him.

"Nothing to say, my *son?*" said the Overlord in a pompous voice. He looked at Liutites and his eyes seemed to grow darker as he narrowed them threateningly. "If you have come here to claim something, then come for it."

Liutites took a step closer. "Today you die," he said evenly, belying the passionate hatred he felt inside for Antaean.

The two penguins stared at each other. Both were equally arrogant in their belief that they were the most powerful. Without warning, Liutites charged up to the dais and Antaean moved to meet him. Liutites lunged forward, his long beak aimed at Antaean's throat, and was met by a hard strike to the side of his head from Antaean's spear. He stumbled to his right but kept his footing. He shook away the stars in his head just in time to see Antaean follow the attack with a hard slap from his brawny flipper.

Liutites moved to his left to minimize the impact and countered with a flurry of vicious slaps of his own, forcing Antaean to cover. He stabbed at the Overlord's massive body, puncturing his armor and flesh but not enough to cause serious injury.

Antaean howled with rage. With his sealskin cape billowing behind him, he swung his large head down on Liutites. Antaean struck Liutites solidly on the side of his skull, which sent him sprawling to the floor. He brought his spear to bear and stabbed downward at the Supreme Commander, but Liutites had sensed the attack and pushed himself forward and just out of reach.

The missed strike caused the tip of Antaean's spear to break off. Antaean swung his broken staff madly at Liutites as he tried to clamber to his feet. He beat the rod over Liutites's back repeatedly. The Supreme Commander scrambled away to gain distance between himself and Antaean's weapon.

"You are a weak fool, Liutites," Antaean growled, sounding more and more maniacal. "Your followers are either trapped or dead. Did you really think this poor excuse for an insurrection would succeed?"

Liutites said nothing. He tried to keep the trickles of self-doubt from turning into a flood. His plans weren't going as expected, but he never seriously thought it would be easy. He had hoped it would, but he knew better. "You are the fool, Antaean," Liutites snapped back. "Soon you will be overrun and your precious chamber will become your tomb."

Antaean snorted a mocking laugh. "Maybe you think your precious Mearna will save you?"

Liutites stiffened at hearing her name.

"Who do you think warned me of this coup? Those elite warriors you're counting on are under my command, as is Mearna," he said as they circled each other. "She pitted you against me so that *she* could become Supreme Commander. This is all of my own design, and now you are defeated, alone, no allies and no hope."

Liutites tried to deny Mearna's betrayal, but he knew it was true. He simmered inside for being blinded by her and for even trusting another Royal Emperor. Of course she had betrayed him. It was in their nature. But be that as it may, he still had work to do, and it didn't diminish the hatred he felt for Antaean. "You are very wrong, my *lord*," Liutites said, mocking the title. "Mearna is irrelevant. You pitted us against each other when you forced me to kill Temalus. And when Mearna returns, her body will lie alongside yours." In a sudden burst, Liutites attacked.

The speed of the assault caught Antaean unprepared, and Liutites drove his beak into his gut. Antaean dropped his broken spear, and Liutites drove his beak in again and again. The Overlord yelled out in pain. Antaean battered his attacker with his wings relentlessly. It gave him just enough space to stab his metal-tipped beak into Liutites's shoulder.

Liutites reared back in agony and Antaean smacked him hard across the face, knocking his head sideways. Antaean stabbed downward once again, but Liutites managed to duck out of the path of the sharp beak. It only grazed the back of his head, but it was enough to cause a gash. Liutites ignored the pain of the slash and let his rage take over. He stabbed upward and narrowly missed Antaean's vulnerable throat, but he still managed to cut him just below the eye.

Antaean growled and beat down on Liutites once again. The Overlord became frustrated at not having enough distance to stab at the Supreme Commander effectively. Liutites pulled back to stab at his throat again and got his beak caught in the Overlord's necklace. For a brief moment, Liutites was hung up in the strand, unable to move, which was all Antaean needed. The Overlord began to pound him once more. Liutites pulled his head back in frustration and broke the sinewy strand holding him to Antaean's side. They both watched as the collection of trophy teeth spilled to the ground.

Antaean glowered at Liutites. It was time to stop toying with Liutites and put him down once and for all. The Overlord gave in to his anger and began using his superior size and weight to shove Liutites backward, intending to crush him against the wall. Liutites's claws left furrows in the ice as they dug into the ground to try to keep from being moved. With the Overlord's massive bulk pressed against him, Liutites was no longer able to attack. He clawed at the ground desperately. He knew if he were to be pinned, then Antaean would most likely smother the life out of him.

Sensing victory, Antaean pressed against Liutites with even more ferocity, driving him back foot by foot.

Two meters away from the wall, Liutites stopped resisting. "Goodbye, Father," Liutites said in a barely audible hiss. The words goaded Antaean into pushing harder, thinking his fledgling had accepted his inevitable demise. It was then that Liutites simply let his feet go out from under him, and twisted his body as he fell. Antaean's sheer mass and momentum carried him over the prone Liutites.

The Overlord crashed to the ground face first and slid into the wall. Liutites quickly braced his beak against the floor and got back to his feet. Antaean was stunned by the impact of the fall. He attempted to get his corpulent frame upright, but his sealskin wrap caught underneath him and hindered his progress. Liutites took three deliberate steps toward his downed father, looked in disgust at the prostrate penguin, and attacked. He savagely stabbed at the back of Antaean's neck with his metal-tipped beak.

Antaean screamed out in equal parts pain and impotent rage as Liutites dug his beak in deeper.

Liutites withdrew for another strike and Antaean, hoping to catch his opponent off guard, rolled onto his back to bring his flipper around and strike Liutites with a decisive blow. But as he spun around, his flipper wouldn't move. His sealskin cloak had twisted under his body, and as he had rolled, it pinned his flipper to his side.

Liutites's eyes smiled with satisfaction at seeing Antaean lying on the ground, helpless. For the briefest of moments, the two combatants locked eyes, both knowing what the outcome of this battle would be.

Antaean drew his beak down to his chest to protect his most vulnerable area. Liutites struck hard and found his mark. Antaean let out a gurgled scream as Liutites found his mark again and again. Liutites was pleased at seeing Antaean's horrified and disbelieving eyes and struck again. He attacked madly, repeatedly, biting and tearing at Antaean's flesh until his work was done. As he stood upright from the macabre scene, Overlord Liutites took satisfaction in what he had accomplished.

CHAPTER 45

"At last we meet," Mearna said when Commander Lavour approached her.

"Yes, at last," Lavour said cautiously.

"Yes, well . . ." Mearna said and looked at Ceocilus. "Captain Mevoule speaks very highly of you," she said, looking at the captain, who straightened at hearing his name.

Lavour looked at Mevoule and then to Leepoh, Nok, Meuseaux, and the others who, for once, were acting very stoic. This did nothing to help put him at ease. He didn't trust the Royal Emperors, and he thought that once he met Mearna, his opinion would be different of her. But it wasn't; he still didn't trust her. The silent tension was palpable until Commander Kiley joined them. "Commander Kiley, this is Mearna of the Resistance Council," Lavour introduced the two. "She has brought us allies in the fight against the Overlord."

Kiley bowed his head in deference.

"You will have to inform me of your travels when we have time," Lavour told him. There was something in Kiley's demeanor since he had returned that caused Lavour concern.

"It was . . . productive," Kiley answered, looking at Mearna. "We garnered new allies to the north."

"The Humboldts?" Mearna asked, a little too enthusiastic for Lavour's taste.

"Yes, as a matter of fact. They were heavily persecuted by the humans and we relieved them of that particular distress."

"Excellent," Mearna said with far more satisfaction than what seemed necessary.

Lavour looked at the two of them and then to Nok and Leepoh, who shared his concern."Back to more pressing matters," Lavour said, interrupting the two.

"Of course," Mearna said, inclining her head slightly.

"You'll have to forgive me, Mearna, but I have to be blunt," Lavour said hesitantly.

Mearna exchanged cautious looks with Ceocilus. "Go on."

"In light of recent events, I have developed a certain . . . distrust of Royal Emperors. How can I be assured you are not leading me, or us, into a trap?" There, he had said it. Sometimes if you want an answer all you have to do is ask.

Mearna nodded her head in understanding. "There is no need for apology, Lavour. I understand the suffering you endured with the loss of your colony and the suffering all of the others have had to bear under the rule of Overlord Antaean and Supreme Commander Liutites. But I assure you there is no treachery on my part. Right now, Liutites is attempting to depose the Overlord." She paused to let the news sink in, and there was a rustle among all of those within earshot. "Whoever the victor is, the other shall be weakened. They are reliant on each other. Liutites can no more govern the masses than Antaean can lead them into battle."

"Is there a successor to Liutites?" asked Commander T'Cuh-ka.

"Not by Liutites's or Antaean's standards," Mearna said. "With Diutes already dead, I was in line—by default. But by now, I am sure they both know of my betrayal."

"And the Resistance aside, what betrayal was there?" Leepoh asked in his usual unabashed way.

For a touch of drama, Mearna waited a long moment before answering. "It was I who set up the coup. But I told the Overlord about Liutites's intentions so both of their forces would be heavily taxed. Whoever wins, I will have a death edict on me. Since these troops were destined to be his elite, Liutites will want to *personally* kill me." It wasn't a lie, but it wasn't the truth in its entirety. She failed to mention these warriors were loyal to her regardless.

The AIC commanders looked at one another and Mearna took notice. "I assure you they are now loyal to me. And in the end, this is all I can offer you—my assurance and my word that we all have a common goal: to stop this madness before it is too late for us all."

"I fear that it may already be too late. The humans have been relentless since this war has started," T'Cuh-ka said with heaviness in his voice.

"That's true," Kiley added.

Lavour nodded in agreement. "But there may still be a few humans who will listen to reason if we attempt a dialogue," he said, looking at Meuseaux.

"A few," Meuseaux answered and looked at Lavour. "Though to be honest, I fear they are like drops of rain in the sea. Too few will see reason."

The entire group stood in silence. Each of them contemplated the future which loomed before them all.

"Then we should delay no longer." Lavour finally spoke up. "If this truly is an uprising, then we should strike now, while they are at their weakest," he said with as much authority as, if not more than, he had ever before used.

"I agree," Commander Kiley said, always eager for a fight.

"We agree as well," Leepoh said for the others.

"What is the status of the Forward Commands?" Lavour asked, taking charge of the situation.

"They have all been abandoned under the onslaught of the human forces," Mearna informed him.

"There is a defensive picket surrounding PIC at a five-kilometer radius," the Adélie, Sergeant Kima of the Resistance Council, who stood nearby, informed him. "Sir," she added belatedly.

"Consisting of?" Nok asked.

"Mainly Adélie who will turncoat to our side when we arrive, but there is an interior perimeter of Royal Emperors," Kima answered.

"Do we have numbers?" T'Cuh-ka asked, looking from the Adélie to Mearna.

"The Royal Emperors should have fallen back to Pack Ice Command once they received word of the coup. There were only around five to six thousand warriors," Ceocilus informed them.

"I thought there were more Royals than that," Lavour said to Mearna.

"There are. However, many are out to sea until they reach full maturity," Mearna told him and immediately wished she hadn't.

"How many?" asked Leepoh suspiciously, speaking Lavour's thoughts.

"Thousands," Mearna answered plainly, stealing a quick glance at Kiley.

"Convenient," Leepoh chided.

"How so?" asked Kiley. He again sounded as irritated with the Gentoo as he had been on RHC 23.

"Don't you see? The Overlord began this war with the greater part of his forces away from danger. We do the hard work and pay with our lives. Then the Royals return to an empire devoid of any real competition from other clans."

"Seems a little extreme, even for Antaean," Kiley remarked but not convincingly. He sounded as if he knew it was the truth but didn't want to prove the Gentoo correct.

"Bah!" Leepoh grumbled. "You believe what you want to believe and I'll know what I know."

Lavour had been studying Mearna throughout the conversation as she stood silent, not refuting anything which had been said. "Is this true?" he asked her.

Mearna froze for a moment, regretting her earlier slip-up, even though it hadn't been detrimental; it could prove costly if she didn't handle it correctly. "Of course it is," she said. This caused a general rustling of feathers until she continued. "The Overlord's plan *was* to have your numbers *culled*, so to speak."

"Culled?" Leepoh asked, affronted by the notion.

"Reduced to a more manageable number," she clarified.

"Then we would be the servants to the master clan," Nok said, disgusted.

"Unfortunately, yes," Mearna confirmed and lowered her head as if she were ashamed.

"So what do you have to gain from this rebellion?" T'Cuh-ka asked, never being one to be subtle.

"What do you mean?" she asked, stalling to prepare an answer and shifting her weight as if preparing to be attacked.

With Lavour watching the Magellanic commander, T'Cuh-ka expounded. "It seems you had a lot to lose by doing this—you being the heir to throne and all."

Mearna glared at T'Cuh-ka. For a moment she seemed as if she were going to strike at him. But she relaxed, if only slightly. "I have *my* freedom to gain, Commander. Perhaps if you had to endure the advances of both Antaean and Liutites, you would understand."

After a tense silence, T'Cuh-ka remitted an apology. "You will forgive me, milady. I had to be sure of your loyalty. My clan has suffered greatly under the Overlord's reign."

Mearna finally seemed to relax. "There is no need for apologies, Commander T'Cuh-ka. You are a great leader and you do what is necessary to ensure your clan's safety."

The two penguins then raised their beaks respectfully to one another.

"Well, if you two are done preening each other's tail feathers, we have work that needs doing," Leepoh said, interrupting the moment.

Lavour sighed at Leepoh's lack of tact. "However inappropriately said, the general is correct," Lavour said, looking at Leepoh, who averted his eyes from him. "No more delays." Lavour looked around at all of those who were waiting on him expectantly and for once didn't feel awkward under their stares. "Are the Adélie forces loyal to our cause?" Lavour asked Kima.

"To the end, sir," the Adélie answered proudly.

"Hopefully the end will only be the beginning. Deliver a message to the Adélie commander on the defensive circle. Tell them to be expecting us very soon."

As Kima rushed off with three others, General Nok turned to Commander Lavour. "So, what's the plan?"

CHAPTER 46

"Get up," Colonel Maycotte said while kicking the chair Vance Lyons was slouched in.

"Why?" Vance asked without bothering to look up at the colonel.

"You're coming with us."

Vance sat up a little straighter at hearing this news. "Where?" he asked cautiously.

"We need you to verify the coordinates you gave us."

"Send a scout team or whatever it is you do. My part is done. You have the coordinates; go do your thing," Vance said while waving his hand at him as if he were shooing away a child.

"We need visual verification by someone who has actually been there," Maycotte told him, barely masking the contempt he felt for the man. "This isn't a request."

Vance looked at him, said nothing, and slid back down in the chair.

"It's just a flyby. We're not going to ground," Maycotte told him, restraining himself from lashing out at the man.

Vance looked at him suspiciously. "I don't think so," he said in his most arrogant child-of-privilege voice.

Colonel Maycotte raised his hands, and two heavily armed soldiers dressed in white fatigues came forward. "See to it that this man is in the chopper at eleven hundred hours," he said and then walked away.

"Hey! Wait a minute. If you remember, I have rights," Vance protested. "I'm a prisoner, not one of your army lackeys who you can just order around."

Maycotte stopped at the doorway. "You may be a prisoner, Mister Lyons, but until this is over, you are an asset. And as such, you will be used accordingly. I would advise you *not* to do anything to change that prematurely."

Vance looked up at his guards after the thinly veiled threat.

"You heard the colonel. Get up and gear up," one of them told him.

Vance weighed his options and, right then, he appeared to have none. *That's all right,* he told himself. *When I get back home, I have enough on these people to bring them crashing down from the bottom up.* A smug smile crossed his face and he got up a little more willingly.

CHAPTER 47

Liutites took his spot on the dais as the new Overlord while the attendees dragged away the body of Antaean. He was the Overlord, and *now* things would be different. He would lead his soldiers into battle and destroy the insurgency, and then he would hunt down Mearna and make her pay for her deceit.

"Guards!" Overlord Liutites bellowed. Two guards not assisting in disposing of Antaean snapped to attention. "Open the doors."

The elite guards dutifully opened the doors to the Overlord's chamber where the few surviving combatants were waiting in the main hall. They remained outside, unsure and wary of what was to come. The guards went out and opened the remaining doors, allowing those in the grand theater to enter.

"Enter," Liutites boomed.

Led by their surviving officers, squads of Royal Emperor warriors entered the chamber. They came to a stop when they spotted Liutites on the dais, his white chest now completely stained red. He was weakened by the multitude of injuries he had suffered during the punishing fight, but he refused to let it show as he strode forward to face his devotees.

"Behold," an attendee announced, "your new Overlord!"

The warriors snapped to attention as Liutites slowly moved forward. "I am your Overlord," he reaffirmed. "You will pledge your loyalty to me," he said, coming to stop next to a once empty pedestal. "Antaean is dead. I am the victor," he boasted, indicating the pedestal. On top rested the head of Antaean, sitting in a frozen puddle of blood, its eyes and metal-tipped beak forward, facing the crowd. It was presented in a fashion as to erase any doubt as to who was in command now.

A loud baying noise filled the chamber as the warriors called out in unison, hailing their new leader. In the midst of raucous crowd, a trooper moved forward and said something quietly to the Overlord. Liutites acknowledged the trooper and then turned back to the crowd. "Silence," he called out, and the chamber became still. "I received word that the insurrectionists have gathered en masse and that their attack is eminent."

The highly disciplined warriors remained stoic on hearing the report. "We knew they were coming, and it appears today is the day we will meet them on the ice and destroy them," Liutites said, looking each of his officers in the eyes. "Captain Caseocles, move all troops out the main entrance and form a defensive wedge. They may outnumber us, but they lack our strength."

After the chamber emptied, Liutites went back to his dais and became lost in thought. He thought about the events of the day and what was yet to come. His thoughts were disrupted by one of the chamber's attendees. "Yes?" he asked with the utmost patience.

"A gift for you, my lord," the attendee said. The attendees were rarely seen. They were tall and lean to the point of being nearly skeletal, gray feathered with large eyes, and short beaked.

"A gift?" he asked, a bit confused. *Barely on the throne for a couple of hours and already the sycophants have arrived.*

"For your protection in battle," the attendee said and unfurled a long sealskin cloak, not unlike his father's. He fastened it around Liutites's neck and stood back. "The previous Overlord left instructions that it was to be presented to his successor," the attendee explained and left the new Overlord to his thoughts.

The cold skins quickly absorbed his body heat and soothed his injuries. "So," Liutites said in a whisper, "the old fool knew his time was coming to an end and could do nothing to prevent it—I will not be so weak," he said a little louder as he marched out of the chamber.

^^^

With Pack Ice Command not far away, Lavour stood in front of the crowd and laid out his plans. "I will take the armies I have, along with Commander T'Cuh-ka—" he paused and looked at the commander who nodded his approval "—and lead a direct assault at the front of PIC. Commander Kiley and Mearna will take their forces in a wide, sweeping approach from our right, to cut off any escape through the nearby pass."

"If I may, Commander, I would have preferred to be in the frontline assault," Kiley told Lavour.

"I need the strength of your forces to cut off their retreat and also to drive them to us. Mearna requested it and she will need your support."

"What about the rear of PIC?" General Natoo asked.

"The rear of PIC only leads further inland. Theoretically they could escape that way, but they would have to traverse the mountains or go further inland. They would face starvation before they reached the sea," Lavour explained. He hoped that wouldn't be the case. He also knew there were probably other escape routes that only the Royal Emperors knew of, but Mearna hadn't been forthcoming if there was.

All the while, Nok was acting giddy. He eagerly anticipated confronting the Royals who had attacked his colony. "I like it," he finally burst out, feeling a bit foolish.

Lavour suppressed a laugh. "The plan is simple. It is our superior numbers versus their superior physical strength."

"And we have the greater desire for victory," Meuseaux amended.

"If there is nothing else . . ." Lavour paused. There wasn't, and he went before his soldiers. "This is for those who have been lost and for those who will be. May the spirits of all noble penguins be at our sides."

The great multitude of penguins cheered together and began their final trek to end the war.

CHAPTER 48

After landing at the American settlement McMurdo Station, which had been recaptured from the penguins weeks earlier, Colonel Maycotte escorted Vance Lyons from one landing pad to another.

"I thought you said we were taking a plane?" Vance asked after seeing the smaller helicopter on the landing pad.

"Change of plans," Maycotte said, walking with his eyes straight ahead.

"Your pack," a soldier standing next to the chopper said, handing a small backpack to Vance.

"What's this for? I'm not getting off of the helicopter 'til we're back," Vance said sharply.

"New regulations. Nobody leaves the base without it," the soldier said firmly.

Vance looked at two soldiers who had already boarded, then at Colonel Maycotte. All were wearing theirs, but he still refrained from putting his on.

"It's for survival, in the event of equipment malfunction," Maycotte said irritably. "Just put the damn thing on so we can go."

Vance did as he was told with the assistance of the soldier. The soldier gave Maycotte a subtle nod when Vance had turned his back.

"All set," the colonel said, looking him over. "Now get on."

The remaining passengers climbed in behind the cockpit. Vance sat next to the sliding door with his back against the rear wall and faced Colonel Maycotte. As the rotors began to whine, the colonel sat and stared at Vance stone faced. Vance got a sinking feeling in his gut as the helicopter lifted off and he rustled in his seat, nervously checking his restraints.

"Once we verify the information you gave us is indeed accurate, you'll be free. Well, after your trial, that is," Maycotte said with a slight smirk.

The colonel's expression made Vance feel more uneasy, but he couldn't pinpoint why.

"I'm sure they'll go easy on you—if these coordinates pan out, that is."

"I thought that was a given. Like I said, this goes much higher than me," Vance snapped at him. "I have names, I know things."

Maycotte looked at Vance blankly. "We know," he said. His voice, like his expression, lacked emotion.

Vance squirmed uncomfortably in his seat and broke Maycotte's icy stare by looking out the window. He wanted nothing more than to get off this ride, but with three armed men around him and the fact that he was over two hundred feet in the air, there was nothing he could do. So he sat back and looked out at the ice below him reflecting the rising dawn.

As the first crepuscular rays of the late winter sun crept across the landscape, Vance spotted something which caught his attention. He couldn't tell if it was several rocky outcroppings or something else entirely. At the same time, the pilot noticed the same thing. "Sir," the pilot said through the headset. "You need to take a look out your starboard window."

Maycotte sat up and leaned over to look out. "Hmm, looks like the photographer was right," he said without elaboration, referring to Randy's assertion that the penguins would work it out for themselves. "But it's too late to worry about that."

Vance took a closer look and, at first, he thought his eyes were playing tricks on him. Below were hundreds of thousands of penguins, if not millions, all headed inland. The sight was both breathtaking and horrifying.

Vance looked at the colonel. He had heard Randy speak of a penguin uprising against Antaean. "That's that, then. It's over—we don't have to worry about it anymore," He said, fumbling with the headset.

Maycotte gave Vance a wry look. "Are you kidding me? This is an unexpected boon. Once we know where their stronghold is, we can take them all out in one strike." Maycotte turned to his pilot. "Once we get a fix on that command center, we'll need to get to a safe distance for observation. This ends today."

Vance avoided further eye contact with the colonel. Instead, he found something very interesting on the floorboard and kept his eyes down. Everything had gone according to plan in the end. If the Overlord hadn't become so overly ambitious and not struck outside of the mainland, things would have been better. The military would extinguish the penguins and establish a presence here, which will break all of the treaties and protocols. His company was going to get the drilling and mining rights in return for their part, and all parties were going to be wealthier than they could possibly imagine. So why did he feel singled out?

Lost in his thoughts and half asleep, Vance didn't feel the helicopter descending. "So what am I missing?" he muttered as he fell into a deeper sleep. He thought he heard voices say something about this being the spot, but he paid it no mind. Instead, he let himself drift further away.

"Hey, Lyons, wake up," Maycotte said harshly.

Vance lifted his head in time to see the butt of a rifle coming toward his face. He felt the aching blow and felt ringing in his ears as he fought to stay conscious. He felt someone jostle him around and undo his seat harness. Vance could do nothing about it; all he could do was struggle to stay awake.

"Like you said—" he heard Maycotte's voice as if it were coming from the far end of a tunnel "—you have names and you know things."

Vance felt the icy blast of cold air as the side door slid open. The freezing air awakened him just slightly. It was enough for him to feel the trickle of blood running down his face and hear Maycotte saying something to him again. "Nothing personal," he heard Maycotte say through his fog. "Actually, it is. I *really* don't like you."

Vance felt the colonel's boot against his side and then felt the brief sensation of weightlessness as he fell through the air. A bone-crunching impact followed as he hit the frozen ground. His breath taken from him, Vance rolled onto his back, gasping for air through his broken body. He saw the helicopter hovering above him, growing smaller as it rose away, and then an enormous dark shadow blocked his blurry vision. With his mind slowed from the beating and impact of the fall, it took a few moments before Vance realized a Royal Emperor penguin stood over him.

"My father's ally," Vance heard the dark form snort derisively. He heard his own muffled screams before he heard no more.

As the helicopter lifted ever higher, Maycotte watched the carnage befalling Vance. "Is the transponder working?" he asked over the radio.

"That's an affirmative. We have a signal lock," a voice said in return.

"That's a relief," Maycotte said to his pilot. "I was afraid the fall might have broken it."

"Don't worry, sir," a soldier said. "I made sure it was secure in his pack."

CHAPTER 49

With the notable exception of seeing one human flying machination pass over them, the forces of the AIC's journey was uneventful. They had passed through the Adélie's picket and added them to their impressive numbers. And it was as Ceocilus had predicted; the Royal Emperors had retreated to PIC after hearing of the coup attempt. They traveled over the last few icy crags, and Pack Ice Command came into view. The sun was rising toward its zenith and only a few wisps of clouds were in the sky.

PIC was perfectly hidden among the ice monoliths, where the floes met terra firma. Even had they not already known where the entrance to PIC was, it was now obvious to all, by the mass of Royal Emperors protecting its entrance. On the gradual slope leading up to PIC stood the Royal Emperor army. Although they numbered only in the thousands, the Overlord had placed them in a defensive wedge. The base of the wedge was braced against the exterior of the PIC. The tip of the wedge consisted of five warriors, each individual backed up by two and so on. Each line was bolstered by the strength of those behind it, and each warrior carried a deadly spear.

Lavour looked to his friends and at the faces of those who had followed him and knew that many of them would not be here the following day. While the thought weighed heavily on his mind, he no longer harbored any doubts; he knew this was the right course of action. They had traveled so far and had endured so much, and now it was time to end this. Leepoh, Nok, Keerka, Mevoule, Meuseaux, Pín, T'Cuh-ka, and Natoo stood at his side. They gave him an affirmative nod as he looked to them. He raised his flipper and gave the signal to move forward.

When the AIC forces got to within fifty meters of the Royal Emperors, Commander Lavour called a halt to the lines. All was silent except for the howling of the wind as it blew through the nearby crevasses. The Royal Emperor warriors parted ways, and Overlord Liutites stepped forward. His sealskin cloak billowed in the wind as he strode around the body of a brutally killed human. With just twenty meters separating them, the two leaders faced each other.

"Penguins of the Penguin Defense Alliance, Antaean is dead—I am your Overlord now. There is no need for further bloodshed," he said, trying to sound sympathetic but failing miserably. "Rejoin me and there will be *no* repercussions. You do not need to suffer the same fate as your misguided leader."

None of the penguins stirred at Liutites's offer.

"Liutites," Captain Mevoule said as he approached. He threw Lavour a reassuring, but forlorn look. "It is you who is misguided. We are the penguins of the Alliance of Independent Colonies, and we serve no master but that of freedom. You and your predecessor, Antaean, have blasphemed the spirits of the Ancients, and you have sentenced all of us to an uncertain future, if not complete extinction," he said as he boldly moved closer to Liutites. "*You* have betrayed us all. *You* have destroyed our nesting grounds, and *you* have destroyed our loved ones. Your fate is upon you and you shall meet it." Mevoule finished with only two meters separating him from the new Overlord.

"Mevoule, what are you doing?" Lavour whispered to himself. Seeing Liutites's body tense, he started forward.

Captain Mevoule stood defiantly in front of Liutites, puffing his chest angrily.

Liutites struck. Lunging with his unexpected speed and agility, the Overlord pierced Mevoule's chest before he could react. With his beak still buried in the wide-eyed Chinstrap, Liutites lifted his head high and with a mighty heft, flung Mevoule's body into the air. The Chinstrap's body landed in a lifeless heap in front of Lavour. Liutites shook the blood and ichor from his beak and stared at Lavour with a glint of satisfaction in his eyes.

Lavour looked away and then back at his lifelong friend lying dead before him. He stared at Liutites, his eyes burning with hatred and sorrow. All that mattered now was killing this monster. Trembling with anger, he let out a loud, shrill call and charged forward. At Lavour's first move, Nok, Leepoh, and the entire alliance rushed to follow their leader. In a massive wave, the penguins of the AIC attacked.

Liutites saw that he was exposed to the overwhelming force and quickly ran and ducked behind the cover of his warriors. He kept running until he reached the entrance of Pack Ice Command.

Lavour paused briefly to see if there was life left in his friend and, finding none, he pressed on. He was engulfed by throngs of penguins when he reached the Royal Emperors. He ducked under the thrust of spears as the penguins behind him fell against them.

Lavour stabbed wildly at the stomachs of the Royals, doing little damage. He heard a screaming Rockhopper above him, looked up, and saw a Rockhopper impaled on the tip of a spear. With its weapon occupied, Lavour, along with another Rockhopper, a Magellanic, and an Adélie brought down the Royal. But as soon as it was down, it was replaced by another.

"Lavour, down!" he heard someone call. Lavour stooped low as a spear lashed out at where his head had just been. He looked up to see General Nok springboard off the back of a fellow Rockhopper and launch himself, claws forward, into the face of Lavour's assailant. The Royal was knocked off balance, and Lavour joined in the attack as Nok viciously slashed with claw and beak at the elite warrior. Finished with that one, they turned their attention to the next.

The crushing press of the AIC assault became so overwhelming that the Royals could no longer effectively use their spears, and it became a battle of claw and beak. Lavour spotted Leepoh and Meuseaux working in tandem, savagely tearing at a downed warrior.

"Over the top!" Lavour yelled above the din of battle.

Immediately the penguins of the AIC climbed the backs of those in front of them and began pecking at the faces of the defenders. With their attention turned upward, those on the ground began to work on the exposed and vulnerable underbellies.

Several of the AIC penguins made it over the top of the frontline and created gaps in the line of the defenders. From his position in the back of the wedge, Liutites saw this and began belting out commands. "Spears up, push forward,"

The sudden thrust forward from the rear line of the Royals pinned those on the frontline against one another. This wasn't much of a problem for the larger Royals, but for the smaller penguins, like Lavour, it was a big one. He was being crushed between the opposing forces. Lavour looked to Leepoh with panic in his eyes as he felt the air leave his lungs. Leepoh had found a gap in the mass of bodies but still wasn't able to help his friend. Lavour's vision started to become cloudy. He looked up and saw nothing but penguin feet as the penguins clambered over one another.

Lavour started to slip to unconsciousness when he heard over the clamor the familiar battle cry of General Nok. The Royal Emperor pressing against him began to thrash wildly, which was the break he needed to squeeze free and fill his lungs with air. Lavour stabbed his beak up into the flailing Royal's abdomen, and the warrior fell sideways. Nok still hung tight with his claws and continued the brutal attack. Leepoh squeezed through and got a few pecks in before the warrior was dispatched. The soldier immediately behind the fallen fell as well, and Lavour took his turn to finish one off.

Leepoh climbed on top of the bodies to get a better vantage point as the Royal push subsided. He had to duck his head sideways to avoid being impaled by a spear. He quickly took the weapon in his beak and jerked, pulling it free from the surprised warrior's grasp. Several Adélies and Macaroni took advantage of the weaponless elite and brought it down.

All around them, the dead were beginning to pile up with the bodies of Royals and Alliance alike. There was no longer white to be seen on the ice or on the combatants. All had been replaced by the crimson stain of blood. The sky could barely be seen through the maelstrom of feathers pushed aloft from the struggle below.

"This isn't working," Natoo said as he pushed his way to Lavour's side.

"Tell me something I could use, General," Lavour snapped before he plunged his beak into another fallen Royal.

"Any ideas?" asked Leepoh as he tried to get away from the front to take a breather from the heavy fighting.

"Leepoh, Nok, Meuseaux, Natoo, follow me," Lavour said, and they began to squeeze their way back to the rear of the battle. Once they reached the open ground, they found Commander T'Cuh-ka, who had been directing the battle from the rear.

"Commander Lavour," T'Cuh-ka said when he approached. "How is the front? It is difficult to tell from my vantage point."

"We're rapidly fighting to a stalemate. For every one they lose, we lose five or more," Lavour said, sounding somewhat despondent.

"But we are gaining ground," Nok chimed in. "They will fall eventually." General Nok was a gruesome sight. His yellow-crested feathers were pinned against his head from the blood of those he had felled.

"Are you injured?" T'Cuh-ka asked at seeing his appearance.

"He's not injured. He just enjoys his work," Leepoh answered before Nok could.

The Magellanic looked at Leepoh appraisingly, who was nearly as covered as Nok. "As do you, by appearances," he said.

"Indeed," Leepoh said with disturbing joviality.

"We need Mearna's troops—their strength should give us the boost we need to finish this," Lavour said.

"That appears to be a problem," T'Cuh-ka told Lavour. "There has been no sign of her or Kiley."

"They couldn't have gotten lost. Are there humans near?" Lavour asked with concern.

Nok and Leepoh were noisily describing their kills to each other, and Lavour slapped at them to be quiet.

"None that we know of," T'Cuh-ka said, looking at Cuh-trük.

"We have been betrayed," Cuh-trük told them with certainty.

"What makes you say that?" Lavour asked, though in his gut, he already knew. He hadn't trusted Mearna. He had dismissed it as his general distrust toward all Royal Emperors. Mevoule had trusted her, and he felt pangs of sorrow for his friend, knowing that his trust was misspent.

"Her intuition has been proven correct before," T'Cuh-ka said of Cuh-trük. "And you know Kiley is far too ambitious to let you take command without some resentment."

"I sensed that about Kiley—I was just unable to pinpoint it," Lavour admitted.

"I have already sent scouts to search for them. They are nowhere within sight, and very soon, darkness will be falling."

Commander Lavour weighed what few options he had. "We could pull back and regroup, but that would allow Liutites to do the same."

"I say we press on," Nok said.

The thought of continuing to send penguins to their death weighed heavily on Lavour. But he knew that, at this point, it was the only way. "We press on," he finally said. "Commander T'Cuh-ka, continue to direct the forces from here. Are you still with me?" he asked Leepoh and Nok.

"Until the end," they said.

"Natoo, Keerka, Pín," Lavour said to the three. "Stay and assist Commander T'Cuh-ka."

The trio of exhausted penguins didn't protest.

CHAPTER 50

"We certainly are taking the long way to PIC," Commander Kiley said from Mearna's side. Their trip so far had been arduous to say the least. They had to travel over dangerous crags and juts, and were currently circumnavigating a large rift in the ice that hadn't been there the year before. Kiley stopped walking and turned to Mearna.

Mearna looked at Kiley and then to Ceocilus. "So tell me about your new allies, the Humboldts," she said to the King penguin, ignoring his comment.

"Not many remain. However, I believe they could prove useful in the future, along with the Galapagos clan," he said, eyeing Mearna with a wary look.

They resumed their walk and, after a few minutes of silence, Mearna spoke. "You are a good commander—perhaps you should've led the assault."

"Perhaps," Kiley said evenly, not belying his true feelings. "But Lavour is more identifiable with the masses."

"Sometimes the masses need strength more than likeability to lead them."

"Sometimes," Kiley agreed, not revealing too much. He knew who and what Mearna was and had dealt with her in the past. He also knew she had shared his ideas, at one time at least, of authoritarian rule.

"I have allies as well, you know," Mearna said cautiously.

"Of that I have no doubt. But where are those allies now?"

Mearna looked at Ceocilus, who said nothing and kept his eyes forward. "They are the crested clans—the Royal Crested, the Snares, Fiordland, and others."

"And why aren't they here?" Kiley asked. His curiosity was more than piqued.

"They are not stupid," she said with a hint of nastiness. "They know that no matter who won, Antaean or Liutites, or if the AIC wins or the Royals win, that this place is not worth the fight. The humans won't stop coming and now they won't stop hunting us. Our best chance at survival is to leave this place and fight the humans where they least expect it, and for us to find a new home."

Kiley stopped and faced Mearna again. "You're speaking of the Northern Paradise."

"Of course I am," she said, meeting his eyes.

"The Great Auks did not fare so well there."

"They were too trusting of the humans—as were we in the early days. But *now* . . . now we know how to fight," Mearna said with a sudden passion filling her voice.

Kiley said nothing as he thought about what she was saying and where this was leading.

"The humans will keep coming," Mearna continued. "Antaean knew this. They won't stop, especially now. They won't stop until we, too, have gone the way of the Great Auks."

"I seem to remember the Overlord saying something similar," Kiley reminded her.

"The Overlord was not a stupid penguin. He was too caught up in his own visions of glory and conquest to see clearly." Mearna pressed her point. "All that awaits us here is death, and there is no glory in a futile death."

Commander Kiley knew where she was going with the conversation, and he wanted the same thing—to attack the humans on his terms, as he had in Cabo Redondo, and to find the northern ice pack. Deep down inside, he resented the fact that Lavour, a mere Chinstrap, had gained so much authority while he was made to feel like a subordinate. "What do you propose?" he asked with a new sense of determination.

"Leave them to their fate." She paused to let her words sink in. "Let them have their battle and we'll make our way to the Northern Paradise. We'll gather our allies and make the humans pay along the journey. We will establish a new Penguin Empire."

"With you as Empress, no doubt," Kiley said, speaking the unspoken implications of this.

"And with you as Supreme Commander."

Kiley stared toward the faltering sunlight. He would never attain such authority here. Even if Lavour somehow survived and became Overlord, he would undoubtedly put the Rockhopper, or worse, that Gentoo, in place as Supreme Commander. He looked back at Mearna. "To the north it is . . ."

Mearna only nodded. She said nothing as she turned and stole a glance at Ceocilus, who returned a furtive look. Kiley was a necessary ally, but he was too ambitious, and Mearna knew, in time, he would have to meet an unfortunate end. But now her designs and schemes were coming to fruition; now was not the time. Now they turned away and left Lavour and Antarctica behind.

CHAPTER 51

Colonel Maycotte had the pilot set the helicopter down on a large ice buttress north of the penguin battlefield. Through a spotter's scope, he was able to make out the dark mass of the penguin civil war taking place. "Command One, this is Outpost One," he said into a radio. "You have the location and the transponder is relaying—forward observation is in place, fire when ready."

"Copy that, Outpost One. Enjoy the show," the anonymous voice said from the other end.

"Prepare to witness extinction," the colonel said without a tinge of regret. Within minutes he heard the roar of the first cruise missile coming inbound toward its target. His thoughts perked up. He had done all that was asked; he had erased all of Lyon's bumbling, with the exception of Randy and Gina. For reasons unbeknownst to him, Maycotte was ordered to let them live. They had no proof of anything, no backing whatsoever, and no credibility. No one would believe the two even if they did talk. They weren't stupid; they had a good idea of the consequences of any indiscretion. Plus they may prove useful in the future. Colonel Maycotte sat back, knowing he was going to be very, very rich.

The first missile struck the penguin compound, exploded into a cloud of smoke and vaporized ice, and the colonel sighed with satisfaction. "That's a direct hit," Maycotte said into his mouthpiece. "Continue with the show."

"Copy that, Colonel," a different voice from before said in reply. "GT is clear."

"What was that? I didn't copy," Maycotte said, confused by the response.

"Command One out," was the reply.

Maycotte froze as realization dawned on him. "Pilot, get this chopper up now," he yelled in a panic, throwing off his pack.

"Sir, we can't take off during an air—" the pilot began to say.

"Just do it!" he screamed.

Colonel Maycotte heard, more than felt, the impact of the missile and seconds later, heard nothing else. Colonel Maycotte, like Vance Lyons before him, knew things.

CHAPTER 52

As Lavour headed back into battle, he caught a fleeting glimpse of something flying through the sky. Then all hell broke loose. He felt himself being pushed through the air, spinning, not knowing up from down, and then landing hard on the ice. He lay on his back as chunks of ice and debris rained down. He was able to hear his own breath and nothing else.

Lavour struggled to his feet and tried to survey his surroundings, but the air was thick with the superheated mist which, in the freezing air, was re-falling as snow. As the wind began to clear the air, he flinched when he heard a second explosion far off in the distance.

"Lavour," he heard a faint voice call out. He looked around and saw Leepoh and Nok stumbling toward him. He breathed a modest sigh of relief and then saw the devastation. Where there were once thousands of penguins locked in combat, there was now nothing. The bodies were everywhere. Some were struggling through their final breaths and others struggled to their feet just to walk about aimlessly.

The missile had impacted just to the left of the entrance of Pack Ice Command, and a large portion of the edifice was a crumpled heap of ruin. The penguins who had fought there simply didn't exist any longer.

"Where's Meuseaux?" Lavour asked as his friends arrived.

"He's all right, he's coming," Leepoh answered, in the same state of shock as Lavour.

"Keerka?" Lavour asked Nok.

"She's fine, she's safe," Nok said, not sounding too convinced about the safe part.

A badly wounded Adélie bumped into Lavour as it passed by in a daze. Lavour met his eyes but found no spark of recognition. "T'Cuh-ka," Lavour called out.

"Here," T'Cuh-ka returned the call as he, too, stumbled forward. Cuh-trük was by his side.

"Round up the survivors and head to sea. The humans *will* strike again," Lavour told him.

"I agree," T'Cuh-ka rasped, still trying to catch his breath. "This is the Falklands all over again."

"It's worse," Cuh-trük added.

"What about you?" T'Cuh-ka asked before going.

"I'll be along. I have to make sure Liutites is dead," Lavour said with determination.

"It no longer matters, Lavour," the Magellanic told him. "His army is gone. Even if he somehow survived this, he is defeated."

"I have to make sure. If he is alive, he is still a threat. Take the forces to the sea—you are in command now. I will meet you on Isla Fortuna," Lavour said and started to walk away.

"No, Lavour, you won't," T'Cuh-ka said. "I will lead them to safety, but after that I am truly done with this fight."

Lavour looked at him in understanding. "Then go in peace, my friend, and I will see you again when we are with the Ancients."

T'Cuh-ka bowed his head in respect to Lavour and departed.

Lavour began to walk toward Pack Ice Command and Leepoh, Nok, and Meuseaux joined him. "You don't have to come," he told them.

"Yes we do," Meuseaux spoke up. "Until the end, remember?"

Lavour nodded. "What about General Natoo?" he asked, looking around.

Nok shook his head and Lavour knew what was meant.

"Are you sure Keerka is safe, General Nok?" Lavour asked, concerned for Nok's impending family.

"Yes, she will wait for me by the sea."

They walked in silence through the grim sights that surrounded them. "We'll find his remains then go," Lavour told them.

"Where to?" Leepoh asked very solemnly, all of his humor taken from him by the sights of devastation.

"We'll find that paradise I've been hearing about. Together—you and me, Meuseaux, Nok, and Keerka, even Pín, if he wants to. We'll go somewhere far from war and destruction," Lavour told them.

"Sounds sound," Leepoh said.

CHAPTER 53

The closer Lavour and the others got to the entrance of PIC, the more difficult their task became. The destruction was unimaginable, and the approaching night made it hard to know if they had checked every body for signs of life. The ground was thick with the dead and, eventually, they had to give up trying to find survivors and go around the bodies, or simply walk over them.

The four companions spread out in their vain search for Liutites's remains. "Any sign of him?" Lavour asked as he watched the sky warily.

"Nothing," Meuseaux said. "If he is dead, judging by the look of things, I don't think there would be enough left of him to identify."

A flash of movement ahead caught Nok's eye. "There!" he shouted.

Near the shattered entrance to PIC, thirty meters away, they spotted Liutites struggling to his feet. He leaned against the broken doorway, turned, and spotted them. He let out a threatening hiss, spun around quickly, and with his tattered cloak flowing behind him, ducked inside the vast compound.

The four penguins came together and looked at the entrance. Lavour shook his head in disbelief that they were going to have to track him down inside of PIC. "Let's get this over with," he told them, and they followed Liutites into the relative darkness.

The main corridor had remained largely intact, but the interior was darkened. The reflective ice used for lighting had either been shattered or misaligned by the blast. Odd beams of light shone in random directions through a haze of floating powdery ice. When they reached the main hall, they found the once magnificent ice crystal stalactite lying in ruins. While the main passages were still largely intact, those going to the left of them didn't fare as well. The corridor leading to the grand theater and various penguin quarters were collapsed or blocked by huge chunks of ice. Several passages to the right were still open.

"I guess we don't have to check the theater," Leepoh remarked.

"Without a doubt," Nok said, looking at the damage with awe.

"It must've been some coup," Meuseaux said, referring the bodies of the dead Royal Emperors who had died hours before.

"That much less for us to deal with," Lavour said distractedly. "The Overlord's chamber is still open."

"Seems a bit obvious, don't you think? Even for a penguin as dimwitted as Liutites," Leepoh said.

"We have to be sure. Nok, come with me. You two stand guard," Lavour ordered.

Nobody spoke a word as Lavour and Nok started down the corridor to the chamber. The once pale violet light had changed to dark blue. The bas-reliefs had fractured but remained mostly intact. As they entered the chamber, Nok looked at the script etched into the cracked archway. "I never learned to read. What does that say?" he asked.

Lavour looked at the etchings and then back to Nok. "I guess now you can call it a prophecy. It says 'Behold and Beware'." Lavour looked at Nok and snorted with contempt at the words.

The rear of the Overlord's chamber had sustained a surprising amount of damage compared to the rest of the chamber. The secret passages had collapsed and the attendees had been crushed below the chunks of ice. The pair passed by the fallen pedestals which had showcased the Overlord's morbid trophies.

"Look," Nok said as he bounded over a small pile of debris.

Lavour came to his side and found the head of Antaean staring back at him with lifeless eyes.

"At least Liutites took care of some of our work," Nok commented.

Lavour cringed at the sight. He knew Liutites was responsible for the decapitation and began to second-guess his decision to go after him. "We must be careful. Liutites is even more dangerous than I imagined."

"Anything?" Meuseaux asked as Lavour and Nok exited the chamber.

"We found what was left of the Overlord," Nok told them.

"Which was?" Leepoh asked, looking at Lavour.

"Not much," Lavour answered without going into detail.

The quartet looked at the remaining passageways. There were five in total, but those branched off into other passages and rooms. Some went up and some went down. The task seemed too daunting to be considered. "This could take forever," Lavour said impatiently. "We could search this place for days and still not find him."

"Maybe we should split up," Nok suggested.

"No. You saw the condition of Antaean. I don't think it would be wise for any of us to face Liutites alone," Lavour reminded him.

"Then which way?" Meuseaux asked.

As they pondered which path to take, they heard a loud noise come from a passage that led upward. The group exchanged looks. "Up it is, then," Leepoh said, and they began their ascent.

The noise drew closer to them and they recognized it as the sound of panicking penguins.

"Those are Royal Imp calls," Meuseaux said with alarm.

"Quick, everyone hide. Get behind the rubble," Lavour instructed.

The group ducked for cover. The sound of the calls became deafening, and they braced for this oncoming new threat. The first of the Royal Emperors came sliding into view, followed by multitudes of others. When the belly-sliding birds got to their feet and started to scramble over the debris, Lavour cautiously peered from his hiding place.

"Females," he whispered to Meuseaux, who was hiding beside him.

"Of course—the rookeries," Meuseaux told him.

Lavour stood fully upright and the others followed his lead. The female Royal Emperors were, for the most part, not warriors; under the rule of Antaean, they were breeders only. Finally freed from their subservient role, they were making their escape. As the stampede of females made their way out of PIC, a large group of fledglings created their own noise as they attempted to keep up with the mothers who had abandoned them. These were not the cute, fuzzy gray-and-white chicks of the free Emperors. The Royal Emperor chicks were black-and-gray-feathered and, even at a young age, the glimmer of malice could be seen in their eyes. They were their father's chicks through and through.

After the last one passed, Lavour shuddered at the thought of what might have been.

"I think we can safely assume he's up there somewhere," Leepoh quipped as they climbed over the mess.

While climbing over chunks of ice to resume their journey, they heard the familiar scream of a supersonic engine.

"Brace yourselves!" one of them shouted as the missile impacted directly in front of PIC, instantly snuffing out the fleeing brood.

Their world turned upside down once again as the quartet was tossed against the walls of the corridor and slammed to the ground. Chunks of the ice ceiling and walls poured down on them and all they could do was tuck their beaks and cover. The ice shook for what felt like an eternity. Once the shaking subsided, the penguins struggled to free themselves from the fallen debris.

First to free himself was Leepoh who, in turn, helped Nok. Both assisted Lavour by knocking chunks of ice off of him with their beaks. The three looked around and saw no sign of Meuseaux.

"Meuseaux," Lavour called out.

All they heard in return was the snapping and cracking of ice as new fissures opened up. In the far distance they heard something large collapse, and the passage grew darker.

"Meuseaux," Lavour called out again. His heart pounded nervously at the thought of losing yet another friend. He was about to call again when he heard a faint call.

"Here," Meuseaux called out from somewhere out of sight.

The entire left wall of the upward passage had collapsed, leaving the lower passage and part of the main hall visible below. The three crept to the edge and carefully peaked over and spotted Meuseaux standing on a large section of the collapsed wall, less than two meters down. The piece he stood on was balanced precariously on top of a five-meter-high pile below it.

"What are you doing down there?" Leepoh asked in mock exasperation.

Meuseaux just glared at the Gentoo. He moved forward to try to find a way up, and his perch wobbled and shifted slightly. He stood perfectly still, not wanting to cause any further disturbance.

"Meuseaux, you're going to have to leap for it," Lavour told him after assessing the situation.

Meuseaux only nodded, afraid to speak. There was a ridge less than a meter above him, but it was still taller than he was. Meuseaux knew if he could make it to the perch, it would be a relatively easy scramble the rest of the way up.

"It's just like climbing an iceberg when we come from the sea. Jump, dig in your claws and beak, and climb," Lavour said to try to encourage his friend.

Meuseaux braced himself to prepare for the leap. The foundation rocked again; it was now or never.

"Hurry," Nok urged him from above.

Meuseaux leapt. As he pushed off, the chunk of ice he stood on crumbled and crashed to the pile below. He hit the face of his target feet first and clung tightly as he dug his beak into the ice like an ice climber's pick. He hung there for half a second and then pushed upward with his claws just enough to throw his beak over the edge.

"You got it. Just a little more—one more push," Leepoh said, encouraging him onward. The three penguins had no way to help him physically, except to verbally push him.

Meuseaux thrust upward one more time and managed to get the weight of his body over the top.

"That's it, you did it," Nok said excitedly.

Meuseaux lay on his belly for a moment to catch his breath, with his feet still hanging over the edge. It took an extraordinary amount of exertion for a Chinstrap to accomplish such a feat, and Meuseaux felt exhausted.

"Back up—give him room," Lavour told the others so that Meuseaux could shimmy forward and finish his ascent. Lavour let out a sigh of relief, and then another missile struck.

The walls and walkway shook and trembled violently once again. Large chunks of the cavernous structure tumbled and fell, and the penguins were battered once again by a barrage of falling debris.

Lavour and the others got to their feet as soon as the trembling subsided. They looked to where Meuseaux had been before the blast. The ledge was gone, as was Meuseaux. "No," Lavour said as he crept to the edge once again. "Meuseaux," he called out and received no response.

Leepoh and Nok went to the edge and did the same. As the clouds of ice-dust began to settle, all they could see were piles of the broken structure heaped below. They continued to call with no response. The cavern grew eerily silent except for the ominous sounds of cracking ice.

Lavour stood at the edge and knew no one could have survived the collapse a second time. "Come on," he said quietly. "We have to get out of here."

Nok looked at him. "What about Liutites?"

Lavour lowered his head, feeling defeated. "It doesn't matter—not anymore. We have to get out of here before we all die. Let Liutites rot in this hell." His thirst for revenge had led them there. Lavour realized he didn't just want to make sure that Liutites was dead; he wanted to kill him, to make him suffer and make him pay for all that he and his kind had done. But now he felt he was no different from his enemy; he was driven by a bloodlust of hatred against the Royals. Lavour had become what he despised, and he would not sacrifice anyone else for vengeance's sake.

Leepoh and Nok didn't argue the point. They surveyed their surroundings and saw the way they came had been destroyed.

"It appears that we can only go up," Leepoh said. "Let's get moving before we're hit again."

Leepoh led the way and Nok followed behind him. Lavour stopped and looked over again.

"Come on, my friend," Leepoh told him solemnly.

Lavour stood there for a moment longer. "Goodbye, Meuseaux," he whispered and joined the others.

CHAPTER 54

The three remaining penguins walked up the winding passageway leading to the rookeries. Most of the interior of Pack Ice Command had collapsed on itself, but a good portion of the eastern side had remained intact. The left and right walls of the passage were missing in spots. Several antechambers were, surprisingly, still undamaged, and they did a quick survey of each when they passed to make sure there were no surprises inside. In some instances, they had to press their backs to the wall and inch along the edge, as most of the walkway had disappeared into the ever-deepening chasm.

When they finally reached the end, they found the door to the rookeries ajar. "Do you think he's in there?" Nok asked, feeling a bit apprehensive about entering the darker room. Nobody answered his question, so he hopped through the entryway without waiting.

Leepoh and Lavour followed. Once inside, they were immediately buffeted by a strong wind blowing through the shattered ice windows in the ceiling. Downy feathers, remnants of the room's youthful occupants, illuminated by the moonlight, swirled and danced on the wind. If it were a different time and place, the scene would have been captivating. The floor was littered with breakage from the ceiling and walls, and the one-time noisy roost was eerily desolate.

They gave their surroundings more scrutiny, not wanting to enter an unseen trap, and walked cautiously ahead. Nok came to a halt. Hiding in the shadows, not twenty meters away, stood the former Supreme Commander of the Penguin Defense Alliance, and now Overlord of nothing, Liutites. He stood staring down into the abyssal gulf of what was once the stately interior of Pack Ice Command. His ruined cloak slapped at the wind, and from their vantage point, he looked defeated and despondent. The trio briefly entertained the notion that he would leap to his death and end his own life on the sharp and jagged ice below. But they hoped for too much. Liutites slowly turned to face them.

Liutites just stared at Lavour and no one else. The air between them became thick with tension until he spoke. "Your persistence surprises me, Chinstrap," Liutites said in his usual condescending tone. "I didn't think such a lesser species could be so capable."

Before his more brazen companions could say anything, Lavour stepped forward. "This is over, Liutites. The humans have won. You, me, all of us—because of you and your father's folly—we have been defeated. I am leaving this place and I will leave you to your perdition."

Liutites stared daggers at him. "How dare you. *I* am the Overlord. I command you and all that I behold. You will pay for your impudence! You and your insolent friends have invoked my wrath."

Leepoh leaned into Nok. "He sure likes using 'I' words. Impudence, insolent, invoke. I have a couple for him—how about idiot, insane, imbecile."

Nok looked at Leepoh as if he were all of those things.

"We better get out of here," Lavour said, sensing Liutites's mental instability. "That way," he said, spotting a gap in the outer wall, where the moon could be seen shining through.

Liutites started toward them. "You're not going anywhere. Your only escape is death," he yelled. The trio ignored him and made their way to escape.

"Move—faster," Lavour urged the others as Liutites rushed at them.

Nok hopped up on a chunk of ruined wall. Leepoh was close behind. "Up and out," Leepoh said, looking back at the insane penguin headed toward them.

Another missile struck.

The missile detonated near the center of the compound. Pack Ice Command shook at its foundation. The three companions tumbled wildly, back the way they came, as the floor buckled. Large pieces of the roof crashed down, narrowly missing the disoriented birds. Lavour slid down the now sloping floor and came to a stop precariously close to the edge of the chasm.

Lavour lay in a daze near the precipice until he gathered the strength to stand. He scrambled back up the slope and back onto somewhat level ground. With his head down, he started to walk until he bumped into something which made him stop. He looked up to find Overlord Liutites standing before him, blocking his path. He looked for an escape route, but there was nowhere to go.

"It seems fortune has brought you back to me, Chinstrap," Liutites hissed.

Lavour barely had time to react as Liutites swung down at him with his powerful flipper. He tilted his head just enough to avoid the full brunt of the attack. The slap was enough to knock him to his right. He stumbled, but he somehow managed to stay on his feet. He was not so lucky on the next strike, as Liutites followed up with a hard smack from his opposite flipper.

Lavour hit the ground hard. He shook the stars from his eyes and tried to slip away as Liutites lunged downward at him with his fearsome beak. The Royal Emperor managed to land a glancing strike to Lavour's side, and the Chinstrap scrambled further out of range. Although his injury was slight, he felt the searing pain as he got to his feet. He turned to look back at the now completely mad Liutites, who struggled to stand back up. Lavour almost turned to run, but as the Overlord's cloak fell aside, he spotted something on his shoulder which caught his interest: a blood-stained injury from his earlier battle with Antaean.

Liutites was injured and struggled to rise. Lavour knew he would never get another chance; the ember of hate that had engulfed him was fanned as he watched Liutites, and it became too much to resist. Without thinking, Lavour dashed forward and plunged his beak into Liutites's open wound.

Liutites roared in pain and blind fury as Lavour struck again. He thrashed wildly and caught the Chinstrap with a chance swing of his flipper and sent Lavour off his feet once more. Fueled by the adrenaline of his rage, Liutites got to his feet quickly and advanced on Lavour.

Lavour landed on his back and would not be able to right himself before Liutites reached him. This time he knew there was nothing he could do. Liutites was just too big and too powerful for a Chinstrap to deal with. He cursed himself for going on this fool's errand to begin with.

Liutites loomed over Lavour, his eyes showing the madness within. Lavour knew it was his time. "Now, I finish this," Liutites growled.

As Lavour helplessly watched his impending death bear down on him, he glimpsed the swift form of Nok leaping through the air, his claws forward. He looked like a bird of prey about to snatch its prize. Nok landed full force on Liutites's side, sunk his claws in, and immediately began to peck at him with intense ferocity.

Surprised by the assault, Liutites was knocked slightly off balance, but it was enough to give Lavour a reprieve. The new Overlord swatted the Rockhopper off with a simple lift of his flipper. But Nok landed on his feet and prepared to launch himself at the despot again when Leepoh entered the fray.

Distracted by the new attack, Liutites turned on Leepoh, but not before the Gentoo landed a solid stab in his soft underbelly. Nok took advantage of the diversion and leapt at the Royal Emperor again, repeating his first attack. Lavour, who had only moments before resigned himself to death, charged forward, stabbing violently at Liutites, hoping to finally end this madness.

Liutites swung wildly at his assailants with his beak. The close proximity of the attackers, and their diminutive stature, rendered him unable to land a solid stab. Liutites continued to flail his flippers at the trio, who, driven by their desire to protect one another, ignored the punishment being dealt. The outraged Overlord finally caught Leepoh under his beak with an upward strike, which sent him spinning away.

Momentarily free of one of his tormentors, Liutites brought his flipper down hard on the top of Lavour's head. The force of the blow caused Lavour to desist, but Nok clung tightly. The Rockhopper bit at the same spot repeatedly, causing blood to flow openly from the Overlord.

Liutites howled insanely and twirled his body until Nok finally lost his grip. In a lucky strike, Liutites caught Nok mid fall with his flipper and sent him crashing into the rock hard ice. Nok whimpered and fell unconscious.

Lavour and Leepoh saw their friend go down and rushed to attack again. Liutites was ready for them this time. He lowered his head, extended his beak, and lunged . . .

Time seemed to slow down for Lavour. He saw what happened, but it didn't seem real. How could it be? He kept his eyes on Leepoh.

Leepoh's eyes widened in disbelief and horror as he looked down and saw that Liutites had impaled him through his midsection.

Liutites thrust his deadly, sharp beak in deeper and then pulled it out. He looked at Leepoh with satisfaction at ridding himself of the insolent Gentoo. The evil Royal Emperor spun his head toward Lavour, sending droplets of blood coursing through the air.

Leepoh looked at Lavour, then down at his chest, and crumpled to the ground.

Lavour's gaze locked on Liutites, who narrowed his eyes menacingly. Lavour was certain he detected a hint of glee in the deep blackness of his eyes. Lavour had had enough. He was going to kill Liutites now or die with his friends. He started forward, and the world shook once more. He wasn't sure if it was from another explosion or the overwhelming hatred he was feeling.

Debris rained down all around, him but Lavour heard none of it. His mind was focused on what had to be done. He watched Liutites struggle to maintain his footing as the ground shook, but remained unaware of the shaking himself. He stole a glance at Nok lying unconscious and was thankful he did not have to witness the attack on Leepoh. He turned his head to Leepoh, who was still watching him.

Lying on his back behind Liutites and struggling to stay conscious, Leepoh made a motion with his head to Lavour. At first, Lavour didn't understand what he wanted. Leepoh made the motion a second time and Lavour finally figured it out. Leepoh had looked at Liutites and then made a motion with his head to bring him his way. Lavour felt a surprising surge of peace and felt the hatred melt away. He knew it would be over soon, he knew what Leepoh intended, and he knew what to do.

Lavour braced himself to attack and saw Liutites look past him. Lavour felt another presence join him and, at his side, Meuseaux appeared. He wasn't sure if he was seeing things or if it was an apparition until Meuseaux spoke.

"*Now* we finish this," Meuseaux said.

If Lavour had any doubts about being able to defeat Liutites, they were all extinguished by the return of Meuseaux.

All sound and time returned for Lavour. The two Chinstraps looked at Leepoh, who had laid his head back and closed his eyes. Liutites must have sensed what was to come; he opened his beak and let out an unearthly call as the pair charged toward him. Liutites took a few steps back to brace for the charge, and his foot found the body of Leepoh. He stumbled backwards just as Lavour and Meuseaux rammed their beaks into his torso.

Liutites fell over the prone Gentoo and slammed hard onto the ground. He slid on his back on the angled and broken floor until he came to stop with his head and top half of his body hanging over the edge of the rift.

Liutites balanced precariously over the dark chasm below and looked side to side. He desperately searched for a way out of his predicament. He dug his claws into the ice to keep himself from slipping further.

Lavour and Meuseaux sidestepped Leepoh, carefully crept down the incline, and stood at Liutites's feet. Liutites eyed the Chinstraps with complete malevolent hatred. He clicked and growled evilly. The two Chinstraps plucked his claws from their grip, gave him a nudge, and sent him over the edge. They watched as Liutites slid into the blackness and listened as he screamed in futile rage until his scream abruptly ended, along with his life.

Lavour stood, panting, and looked at Meuseaux. "Saying I'm glad to see you would be a tremendous understatement."

Meuseaux only nodded; he could think of nothing to say at that point. All he could think of was that he had done it; he said he would kill Liutites and he did. "I have to make sure," he said, surprising even himself by his own indifference toward death. Meuseaux inched close to the edge, being extra careful—he'd had enough falls to last a lifetime—and cautiously peered over. In what remained of PIC's lighting system, he was able to faintly see the crumpled form of Liutites. Satisfied with what he saw, he turned away.

"Well?" Lavour asked.

"It's done," Meuseaux answered. "Really done."

Nok began to rustle from unconsciousness and the Chinstraps went to him. "Can you get up?" Lavour asked him as he rose. "We have to get out of here."

Nok blinked his eyes open and jerked, startled, as he remembered where he was. "Where's Liutites?"

"Dead," Meuseaux said with relief.

Nok looked around and spotted Leepoh lying on the ground. "No," he whispered.

"Nok . . ." Lavour said as the Rockhopper bounded to Leepoh's side.

"Leepoh . . . Leepoh," he cried as he tried to urge his friend awake.

Leepoh fluttered his eyelids. His eyes were open, but they no longer saw. "Nok?" he rasped in a quiet whisper.

"It's me," Nok answered between sobs.

"This is some good time you showed me," Leepoh coughed out, trying to laugh.

"Let's go. We have to get out of this place," Nok said, not wanting to face the reality of the situation.

"Bah," Leepoh muttered. "Too late . . . for that."

"No," Nok said, feeling his strength begin to ebb.

"Take care of that family. Time to go, my friend—for us both." Leepoh's eyes closed as he exhaled softly.

Nok sat back and looked at his friend. *Not again, not again,* he thought. Everyone he cared for left him. He wondered if the same would be true of Keerka. The thought of Keerka touched Nok, and he stood upright. The hope of his unhatched egg gave him strength. He would mourn Leepoh always, but in Leepoh's last breath, he had told him it was time to go. Another explosion near PIC went off, which motivated him to move.

"Come on, Nok," Lavour said with the caring of a friend.

The room swayed as the floor buckled, cracked, and began to crumble. More chunks of ice from the ceiling began to fall, and the last light finally went out. The three penguins scrambled over heaps of the broken structure and dodged the falling pieces until they reached the gap in the outer wall. The edifice swayed violently. Meuseaux was the first to climb outside, followed by Lavour. Nok hopped onto the threshold, stopped, and turned back to look at where Leepoh was lying. He could no longer see him. He told him goodbye in his heart one last time and hopped though the breach.

Pack Ice Command began to implode behind the penguins as they slid and tumbled down the outer face of PIC. A succession of missile strikes hit the compound. What remained of the once mighty fortress exploded into near nothingness. The shock wave of the blasts catapulted the penguins further away until they finally came to a rest on relatively flat ground. They sprung to their feet and ran as fast as their exhausted legs could carry them.

Once they got a safe distance away, they stopped and turned to watch the spectacle as missile after missile struck where PIC once was.

"Wow, I guess they really wanted us dead," Lavour said.

All of them seemed to be at a loss for words. They guessed this really wasn't the end of their tribulations; they had simply exchanged one enemy for another. But Lavour hoped that if the penguins went back to their unassuming ways, the humans would stop their persecution. He hoped . . .

Nok was silent for other reasons. He stared at the spot where PIC had been, lost in thought about his friendship with Leepoh. Although it seemed like a lifetime ago since he had first met the *flippy* Gentoo, his friendship had come and gone in the span of a few months—too brief for a bond he would feel for a lifetime.

Meuseaux was silent. He didn't know what was to come or what was in store for him. The past couple months of his life had been about survival and retribution, but now that all had been accomplished, he no longer had direction. All he knew was that he couldn't stay there. He wondered about his human friends and whether they were safe. Beyond that, all he really wanted to do was leave this place.

Lavour looked at Nok, feeling the loss of Leepoh as well. "Come on, Nok. Keerka's waiting for you."

Nok seemed to perk up slightly at hearing his mate's name and, while remaining silent, the three penguins turned and started for the coast.

CHAPTER 55

The trio of penguins arrived on the ocean's edge at dawn the following day. Other than seeing several human flying machinations pass overhead, the journey there was silent and uneventful. A lone penguin anxiously awaited them—Keerka. She spotted their dark forms in the distance but kept her excitement at bay until she knew it was him. Once she had confirmation, all of her anxiety dissipated and she rushed to join him. They greeted one another warmly by rubbing their beaks together, accompanied by soft noises.

Keerka pulled away to inspect Nok's bloodstained feathers. "Are you hurt?" she asked worriedly.

"No," was all Nok could say. He was overtaken by emotion as he looked at her.

Keerka looked at Lavour and Meuseaux, who were trying to avoid looking at the pair. "Leepoh?" she asked quietly, already knowing the answer.

Nok couldn't muster the words to tell her that Leepoh was gone. He just shook his head and lowered his beak.

"I am so very sorry," she said while nuzzling him softly.

The scene reminded Lavour of the last time he was with Lannera, when he still had hope for a future with his loved ones. It was too much to bear at that moment. He turned away from the pair and walked to the edge of the ice. The sound of water lapped against the ice, meters below. Lavour gazed over the sea of floating bergs and to the horizon. He contemplated his future. As far as he was concerned, his days as commander were over. He knew this place was no longer home. He had no idea where to go. Only that he had to go.

Meuseaux, followed by Nok and Keerka, joined Lavour. "Where are the others?" Meuseaux asked.

"They're trying their luck on Isla Fortuna. Pín went home," Keerka answered.

"And where are you going?" Lavour asked Nok. "Are you going to Isla Fortuna?"

"No, we're going back home," Nok answered, looking at Keerka for confirmation, who gave an indifferent shrug. "Well—for as long as it's safe," he added. Nok knew what they might face, but with a chick on the way, he wanted to nest where he was familiar. "What about you?" Nok asked Lavour.

Lavour returned his gaze to the horizon. "I've been told of a place far to the north," he said. "Maybe I'll go and see it for myself."

"If you don't mind some company, I'd like to join you," Meuseaux informed him.

Lavour studied Meuseaux; he had intended just to go away, to finish his days swimming the extent of the seas. But Meuseaux, with his one simple request, reminded him that with a friend at your side, you shouldn't just exist. You should live as well. "Yes, Meuseaux," he finally said. "I would like that very much."

"It has been an honor serving under you, Commander Lavour," Nok told him proudly, giving him a high beak salute.

"It's just Lavour now, General," he replied. "Just Lavour."

"Goodbye, my friends—be safe," Nok said with a touch of sadness at seeing another penguin he cared for leave him.

"You as well, my friends," Lavour told him. "And take care of that family." He braced himself and looked at Meuseaux. "Let's see what's out there," he said, and the two Chinstraps dove into the sea.

Nok and Keerka watched the Chinstraps until they disappeared from view. "May our paths cross again one day," Nok said quietly, turning for one last look in the direction his friends went.

"Perhaps they will, Nok. Perhaps they will," Keerka told him as she leaned in close to him. "Now let's go home."

Epilogue
Seven months later-

LATE MARCH, AVILA BEACH, CALIFORNIA: A small town nestled between the Pacific Coast Range and the Pacific Ocean. It was the first decently warm day of spring after what had been a particularly harsh winter, by California standards. Beachgoers crowded a boardwalk, which was teeming with vendors, restaurants, and struggling artists selling their wares. Undaunted by the still-chill water of the quiet bay, people of all ages and sizes splashed in the surf. The festive atmosphere felt as if the people were celebrating and rejoicing at the sun's reappearance, which had brought them from a winter slumber.

Randy Lee stood near the end of a long pier, which jutted out from the center of the small sandy beach. He leaned on the worn wooden rails and watched the waves roll in as he waited for Gina. In the months since they had escaped the icy hell of Antarctica, Gina had left her home in Southern California and moved in with Randy in his apartment in the nearby town of San Luis Obispo.

Things had not worked out for the pair financially. After arriving at GT's corporate headquarters in Santa Monica, not only did they find that there was no check waiting for them as Vance had promised, but also that everybody working there seemed to have no recollection of any one from their expedition ever working for them, Vance Lyons included. It was as if the past year and a half of Gina and Randy's life had never happened.

After they inquired with the military about Colonel Maycotte, they met with the same story: *Colonel who?* They gave up on researching anything further after they received an anonymous note, which simply read, *Consider yourselves lucky.*

Both Randy and Gina, not being able to verify employment or that they had even existed for the past year and half, were having trouble finding work. Randy had been able to sell some of his photos of the penguins to a couple of supermarket tabloids, with one in particular being especially persistent in wanting the story, but beyond that not much work came his way.

"Hey, daydreamer," Gina said, coming up behind Randy and startling him from his thoughts. She grabbed him around the waist in an affectionate embrace.

"Hey," he said, spinning around to return the hug. "How'd it go?" he asked, referring to the job interview she had just returned from. The look in her eyes told him all he needed to know. "Same thing, huh?"

"No verifiable recent work history, you're over qualified, blah, blah, blah," Gina said in a deep mocking tone. "I guess the degree doesn't matter."

"Don't worry about it—you'll find something. They can't keep us down forever. And there's always that offer" he said. The two had derived a theory that this was some sort retribution against Randy for him selling his photos. It probably wasn't, but they needed something to blame for their streak of bad luck.

"I just wish GT would've at least followed through with the bribe to keep us quiet, instead of this," Gina said, still feeling a bit defeated despite Randy's optimism.

"That was dirty money anyway," he reminded her. "And it was the other *instead of* that I was worried about. Colonel Maycotte was none too vague when he told us to consider ourselves lucky. And if that wasn't enough—the note was a strong reminder."

"Yeah I know," she said and took a deep breath as she leaned against the rails. "And like you said, I have that offer still."

The two leaned against the railing and watched people play in the distant surf until Randy spoke. "Things are going to change soon," he said.

"And exactly how are they going to do that, mister optimism?" Gina said as she rested her chin on his shoulder.

"I decided to take that studio photographer job."

Gina pulled away slightly and looked at him. It had been a bit of a contentious issue between them, with her wanting him to stay true to his ideals. Randy reminded her of the same on their way to Santa Monica when Gina decided to take the money Vance had offered. "So you're going to take pictures of people's screaming babies all day?"

"They're portraits, not pictures, and it won't be all day, because it's only part time," he said with a smile. "It's not forever."

They stood in silence for a while longer and then Randy decided to change the subject. "Did you hear they found another fishing boat with its crew either dead or missing?"

"How did you find *this* out?" Gina asked skeptically.

"I listen to AM radio."

She shook her head in mock amusement. "Where'd it happen?"

"Down around Catalina," Randy said distractedly as he looked at several people who began to gather around the end of the pier.

"*Pirates* again?" she asked mockingly, making quotations in the air with her fingers. "They said everything had been taken care of after we left. Except for the New Zealand debacle, that is."

Randy didn't hear what she said. His attention was on a commotion at the end of the pier. "Let's see what's going on," he said, taking Gina's hand.

As they drew nearer to the end of the pier, they heard somebody mutter something about a tsunami, and a few of the people started walking hurriedly back toward the shore.

"I doubt it's a tsunami; with the warning systems in place now, we'd know," Gina said, more to ease her own mind.

"Well, I don't know what it could be, then," said a man who overheard her as he looked through a whale-watching telescope.

"Do you mind if I take a look?" Gina asked the man, who looked her up and down as if he were affronted by the very idea.

"She's a climatologist," Randy told the man.

Gina's title didn't necessarily mean that she was any more qualified than the next person was to judge oceanic phenomena from the vantage point of a pier, but upon hearing *–ologist,* he surrendered the scope without further objection.

Gina peered through the scope and was jolted at the sight. "Oh my God," she said with a rush of fear. "Randy . . . look. Tell me if it's what I think it is."

"What?" Randy and the other man asked simultaneously. Randy grabbed the scope and quickly pressed his eye against the viewfinder. After no more than a few seconds, Randy pulled away. "No," he said, horrorstricken. "This can't be. What are the odds? No, no, no, no."

What Randy saw wasn't a tsunami or any naturally occurring wave. It was penguins, and they were close. From a distance they did indeed look like a wave. Thousands upon thousands were headed straight for the little town.

Randy's body tensed as he stood there with the full realization of what was to come. "God no," he said and then looked at Gina. "Run!"

Gina knew at once that this was really about to happen. "Everybody get out of here," she yelled. "Get to your cars and go—now!" She took Randy's hand, and they began to run toward the boardwalk over a quarter of a mile away at the other end of the pier.

The crowd of surprised people saw that the pair was serious and decided it wouldn't hurt to follow suit.

"How long do we have?" Gina asked between breaths as she ran.

"Five minutes," Randy answered in kind. He stole a glance at the sea and spotted the first wave of attackers porpoising through surf. "Maybe less," he amended.

The crowd of fleeing people grew in size as more sightseers along the pier joined in the exodus.

Randy and Gina reached the boardwalk in less than three minutes and stopped briefly to catch their breath.

"Where'd you park?" asked Randy.

"In the lot on 1ˢᵗ street," Gina told him, referring to the public parking lot.

"That's too crowded; we'll never get out. I parked on San Rafael, up on the hill. Let's go. I think we can make it."

"What's going on?" the man who gave up the telescope asked them before they left.

"Just get out of here if you want to live," Gina told him abruptly.

"But my wife, she's on the beach," the panic-stricken man said.

"Get her and go," Randy told him, and they started to run again.

As they ran, Gina looked out at the beach and the hundreds of people on it. "Wait," she told Randy. She stood at the seawall at the rear of the beach and shouted as loud as she could. "Get off the beach now! Everybody go and get to your cars!" She looked at Randy and nodded her head. "It's all we can do. Let's get out of here." They knew what was about to happen, and they knew that there was nothing more they could do to help. It was unfortunate and it was tragic, but soon there would be no escape. They had to go.

ᴧᴧᴧ

The few beachgoers who either could hear Gina or had paid her any mind looked back in confusion. Some even looked back in anger for having their pleasant day disrupted by a screaming lunatic. Some, however, seeing the people running from the pier, became concerned themselves and began to gather their belongings. But, to their detriment, they moved without urgency.

The first wave of penguins struck. People began to scream when they saw those who were playing in the surf fall victim. The penguins exploded from the sea. They immediately began to attack any and every person in sight. The humans tried to flee but were blocked one way by a rocky cliff wall and the other by the San Luis Obispo creek. The only way to go was up the stairs at the seawall. People bottlenecked as they all tried to escape at once, and the penguins took advantage.

Severely winded by the run and fear, Randy and Gina looked over a railing at the top of the hill near where Randy had parked. The sight was horrifying. Those who were able fought against their attackers. But in the end, it only delayed the inevitable. Wave after wave of penguins came ashore and overwhelmed the defenders and escapees.

Gina grabbed her cell phone to call for help but stopped at hearing the sirens of the county sheriff's cruisers arriving at the scene. The pair watched in disbelief at the unbelievable bedlam taking place. It soon became too much to bear. "We'd better go," Gina said, and the two got in the car.

Cars crowded Avila Beach road, the only feasible way for most to get in or out of the town. A collision blocked the flow of traffic. The penguins crowded the streets and attacked the cars stuck in the jam with their reinforced beaks. Gunshots began to ring out as the cops started to fight back.

Randy and Gina made their escape from the penguins once again and, as they left the scene, they could not escape the new, unimaginable reality . . . The penguins were here.

More from Rockhopper Books

Rise of the Penguins Saga

Rise of the Penguins
Book 1

The Warlord, The
Warrior, The War
Book 2

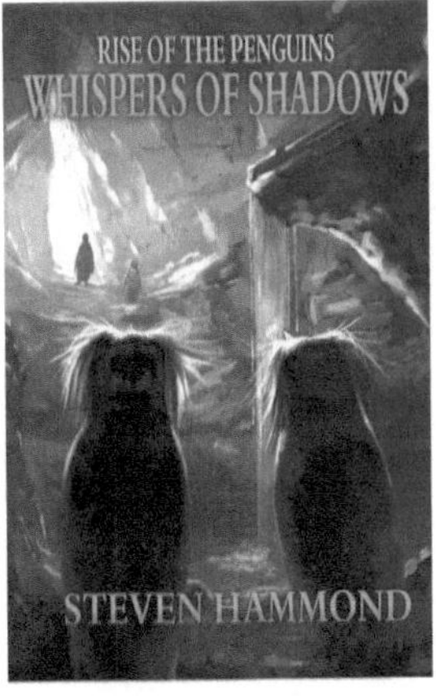

Whispers of Shadows
Book 4

The Royal Creed
Book 5

Order of Kings
Book 6

The Great Auk War
Book 7
(coming soon)